Praise for Cl~~~~~~ ~~~~~~~~

Rest Home Runaways

"A search for one last shot at freedom leads four elderly runaways on an adventure that at once touches the heart and leaves readers rooting for the 'escapees.' This is a beautiful, heartfelt story." —Randy Peyser, author of *Crappy to Happy* as seen in the movie *Eat Pray Love*

"Geriatric anarchy breaks out in this poignant and funny new novel by Clifford Henderson, who writes with verve and compassion about the loss of self-determination that comes to the elderly and the difficulties that descend on their children. Underlying this fast-paced story is one clear message to our older selves: Do what you need to do. Give them hell."—Elizabeth McKenzie, author of *Stop That Girl*

"As much as anything this is about exploration, finding out who we are and who we are capable of being. Life can put us in boxes to do with our age that we aren't ready for. In this charming story we watch as each group fights against those restraints and chooses who they want to be—old and consigned to the scrap heap, or living life as an adventure to be taken. This isn't a romance, but it is full of romance nonetheless."—*Curve Magazine*

Maye's Request

"Henderson has a way with oddball families…The novel's serious subject matter—shattered families, religious fundamentalism, emotional instability—is balanced nicely by Henderson's flair for lighthearted prose that carries the narrative without undercutting the serious issues she explores."—Richard Labonté, *Book Marks*

"Clifford Henderson takes the reader on a frightening journey of physical, emotional, and spiritual illness to a place of love, enlightenment, healing, and forgiveness. There are times in this story that will be difficult to read, but you will feel no choice but to continue because the writing gently nudges you forward to come out the other side, hopefully unscathed. *Maye's Request* is Clifford Henderson's third novel, and like the others before, she continues to excite, enthrall, and entice."—*Out in Jersey*

"I truly laughed out loud at some passages and cried at others. A beautifully written and touching story of love, healing, family, and truth. Ms. Henderson has made me an instant fan!" —*Bibliophilic Book Blog*

The Middle of Somewhere

"The characters in this book are easy to relate to, I found myself caring about their struggles, and celebrating their triumphs... Clifford Henderson writes with depth and ease. Her writing gives you the sense that her muse was not only visiting, but had moved in."—*Out in Jersey*

"Henderson grabs her readers in a firm grip and never lets go. *The Middle of Somewhere* is a wonderful laugh-out-loud read filled with pathos, hope, and new beginnings."—*Just About Write*

"I loved this book. I was laughing from the first paragraph all the way to the end, and in the meantime fell in love with all the characters. Although this is Henderson's first published novel, her writing is replete with complex characters and a full-bodied plot, sort of like a well-rounded Merlot. I can't help but give this book a hearty two thumbs up review and hope that you'll read it. I know you'll enjoy it just as much as I did."—*Kissed by Venus*

Spanking New

"Clifford Henderson has written a masterpiece in *Spanking New*... Henderson's clever exploration of her protagonists' feelings leads the reader into a world where gender and identity are fluid. *Spanking New* should be a required reading for all gender and queer study courses. While the author addresses serious issues, her book is fun, fun, fun! The playfulness, curiosity, and fresh naivety as portrayed through the eyes of the storyteller is refreshing and often humorous. It is pure genius on Henderson's part to write from this perspective. The protagonists are endearing and very human as you follow their struggles to navigate through life. The reader is able to sympathize with the antagonist's feelings as well in this richly developed exploration of human beings' struggles to make sense of their worlds."—Anita Kelly, LGBT Coordinator, Muhlenberg College

"*Spanking New* is a book that brings the fantasy of what happened before I was born, to life. If you have ever wondered what you were, or where you came from, Clifford Henderson gives you an interesting, oft times hilarious answer. The gender benders in this book are lovable characters, the most memorable being 'Spanky' the 'floating soul' that is looking to attach to his parents. When Spanky finally does manage to finagle a meeting of his soon-to-be parents Nina and Rick, the sparks fly, and all seems right with the world that he is about to enter, until Spanky finds out he is a girl! Other than being hilarious, this a poignant point of view, and makes for a fun and interesting read."—*Out In Jersey*

"Clifford Henderson took a warm look at people in her first novel, *The Middle of Somewhere*. She continues her warm looks in *Spanking New*. *Spanking New* is a book I found myself talking about with others, and one which I won't soon forget. This is a wise and funny book."—*Just About Write*

By the Author

The Middle of Somewhere

Spanking New

Maye's Request

Rest Home Runaways

Perfect Little Worlds

Visit us at www.boldstrokesbooks.com

PERFECT LITTLE WORLDS

by

Clifford Mae Henderson

2018

PERFECT LITTLE WORLDS

ISBN 13: 978-1-63555-164-8

THIS TRADE PAPERBACK ORIGINAL IS PUBLISHED BY
BOLD STROKES BOOKS, INC.
P.O. BOX 249
VALLEY FALLS, NY 12185

FIRST EDITION: JUNE 2018

CREDITS
EDITOR: CINDY CRESAP
PRODUCTION DESIGN: STACIA SEAMAN
COVER ART BY DUKE HOUSTON
COVER DESIGN BY MELODY POND

Acknowledgments

This novel had a long gestation, and consequently many people helped along the way.

In order of appearance:

Ross Gibson for sharing with me the history of the underground tunnels of Santa Cruz. Thank you.

Stephany Buswell, who baked alongside me at Plaza Bakery before the earthquake and was a great resource in recalling the details. (I also stole her last name for one of my characters.) Thank you.

My many beta readers who gave me feedback: Martha Allison, Anne Laughlin, Susan McCloskey, Elizabeth McKenzie, Paola Bruni, Jory Post, and Abby Reifsnyder. Thank you.

The folks in my writing salons (you know who you are) who at different times heard pieces of the novel and gave feedback. Thank you.

Dixie Cox, who has heard every version of this novel multiple times, given great feedback, and still loves me. Thank you.

Duke Houston, who created this fabulous book cover that I love, and my beautiful website. Thank you.

Eileen Burke-Woodward, who helps me maintain my website. Thank you.

The highly capable folks at Bold Strokes Books: Len Barot, Sandra Lowe, Ruth Sternglantz, Stacia Seaman, my wonderful editor, Cindy Cresap, and the rest of the gang who keep the ship afloat. Thank you.

And of course, you, reader, for making me a part of your life. Thank you. Thank you.

Together twenty-seven years, married one, this is for you, my sweet Dixie. Thanks for always believing in me.

A s a child I had this terror of the night. It would kick in after Alice nodded off. I'd lie in bed and listen for the moment her breathing changed from the quick, light breath of her wakefulness to the long, peaceful sucking and blowing of her sleep. Next, I'd listen for my dad wearily plodding in from the garage, my mom putting up the last of the dishes, straining my ears for the click of the lights being switched off as they trundled to bed, imagining the house growing darker with each click. Kitchen. *Click.* Outside porch light. *Click.* Living room. *Click.* Hallway. *Click.* The small standing lamp at the end of the hallway. *Click.* Water would run. The toilet would flush. Depending on the house and on how much they'd been drinking, I would hear my parents' muffled conversation or argument or the soft thump-thumps of their carnal roughhousing, my father's rhythmic grunting, my mother's, *Oh...yes... oh...oh...ohhhhh!* A door might slam. A peal of laughter might ring out.

Under no circumstances were Alice and I allowed to disturb them once their bedroom door was closed. My mother's rule. "It could scar you for life, trust me," she'd say. I didn't trust her, but knew better than to go against her. So I'd lie there imagining the terrifying hush of the darkness wrapping itself around the throw pillows on the couch, around the ankles of our kitchen table, creeping its way up the stairs to where I lay, wide-awake, frightened out of my mind. I'd feel as though I were the only person alive.

Old enough to understand the difference between sleep and death, I was still unable to calm my racing heart, and would tune my ears to the outside world, seeking comfort in the random stoppings and startings of the traffic outside, the slam of a car door, an eighteen-wheeler on a distant freeway, a neighbor's dog barking—anything to assure me that, somewhere, life continued, that I wasn't really alone. Blankets pulled up to my nose, my feather pillow pulled down over my eyes, I'd focus on the *suck-blow suck-blow* of Alice's breath. Try to match it.

Some nights I was so scared I had to wake her. I hated doing it. She was my little sister and should have been the one scared and waking me. But, unlike me, Alice took refuge in the night, when the complicated social demands of the day were finally finished.

"Alice! Alice! You awake?" I'd whisper, then listen for her to blindly reach past the little Scottie dog lamp standing sentinel on the nightstand separating us, past the meticulously placed ChapStick Alice always kept on her side of the nightstand so she could coat her lips before going to sleep—God forbid I should ever touch it!—finally landing on her thick black glasses with the rubber headband. What purpose she supposed those glasses served her in the dark, I cannot tell you. Understanding the reasoning behind Alice's decisions was like trying to understand an appliance manual printed in a foreign language. The one thing you *could* be sure of, whatever choice she made was thought out, in triplicate.

I'd roll onto my side, prop myself up on my elbow, hoping to give the impression of the untroubled, slightly annoying big sister I so wanted to be, my eyes dissecting the shadows until I could make out her knees tenting the blankets of her bed, her elbows poking out as she adjusted the elastic strap of her glasses.

"What?" she'd grumble.

"I just wanted to see if you were sleeping."

"Obviously, I was. What do you want?"

"I heard Mrs. Kearin say that they're closing down the school library next week for renovations."

This might or might not have been true. The point was to get Alice talking, and if there was one place Alice loved, it was the school library. Anytime she wasn't required to be in class, you could be sure to find her at the library, even during recess. Whatever new school we were thrust into—and we were thrust into a great many, we moved a lot—she'd immediately stalk the librarian until the poor woman had no choice but to befriend her, which would activate the second step of Alice's campaign: to gain early morning and recess access. I suspect this was to bypass the cruel teasing she invariably endured in each new schoolyard, but as I said, one never really knew with Alice.

Alarmed, and shifting around in her bed, she'd respond to the news of the library closure just as I'd hoped, with a good dose of wide-awake adrenaline. "What?! Why didn't she tell me?"

"I dunno. Guess she forgot."

"She wouldn't forget to tell me that," she'd say. Or something along those lines. "Mrs. Kearin doesn't forget things like that. Then again…she's been busy. A whole bunch of science books got donated; need to be catalogued, they do. Or maybe it's because her dog's been sick. She told me about it Wednesday when I was helping her restock books…"

If I chose my topic wisely, Alice might go on for some time, weighing out the possibilities and consequences of this new bit of information. I'd pretend to listen, yawn a few concerned *huhs* and *ohs*, her muttered gripings lulling me to sleep.

Now she is gone.

Seventy-seven years old and she just had to climb that ladder to clean our leaf-filled gutters. From the look of it, the earth was at fault, not Alice. No surprise there. It gave way under a leg of the six-foot aluminum ladder, sending her toppling into the stucco garage where she slammed her head against its sharp corner. Probably due to a collapsed gopher tunnel. Alice hated gophers. I'm horrified to admit that last week, when she was setting a trap, I called out to her, "These gophers are going to be the death of you!" I was annoyed with her at the time. I can't remember why.

I'm the one who found her, sprawled out on the cement path between our small yard and the garage, her head resting in a halo of congealed blood. I'd just come back from my daily beach stroll—the only thing that keeps my bad hip from seizing up. I didn't find her right away. Went first to replace my sneakers with house slippers, as I always do, then wandered out to the yard to ask if she wanted lunch. A pointless question: we always lunched after my walks.

For all I know, this dramatic death was part of her plan. In the past months, the ever-practical Alice seemed to be intentionally putting herself in harm's way—no doubt to avoid the nuisance of a slow, excessively needy death. She straddled the pitched roof to replace some rotted-out shingles; did some rewiring of the garage; rescued the neighbor's mewling kitten from our old, non-bearing, avocado tree; each task seemingly begging karma to drop that final calling card.

I confess, karma is my thought, not Alice's. Alice did not—would not—buy into the concept of karma. Cause and effect, sure. Cosmic scorekeeping? Way too hocus-pocus for Alice.

I had misgivings about moving in with Alice. She is—*was*—not the easiest of people. Nor was she wild about me moving in, but

I expected that. She never welcomed change. It wasn't programmed into her DNA, which is what I'd counted on four years ago when I lost Kim, the love of my life, to pancreatic cancer: a healthy dose of Alice's rigidity to anchor me back to life. I reminded her that the house where she was living, once our parents' house, officially belonged to both of us. Promised not to mess with her studio in the garage. Promised not to leave dishes in the sink. Promised not to rearrange things without her approval. Promised not to make her try new foods. She relented, at last, and we made it work, she and I, and in the end, I think she was happy to have me.

Now she too is dead and I have officially outlived everyone who cares about me. My childhood nightmare, in earnest.

My name is Lucy Louise Mustin. I am seventy-nine years old and occupy the last branch of our family tree. It's October 23, 2015, 1:59 a.m., in Santa Cruz, California. Exhausted as I am, I can't sleep. The day was unseasonably warm and breezy. We're four years into a terrible drought. Fires rage in the hills up north—at least one of them believed to be the work of an arsonist. When the wind is up, the foul odor of smoke blows through my open window. I am settled into my favorite Morris chair with a cup of chamomile tea on the small cherry table next me; on my knees, my favorite of Kim's crocheted blankets; on my heart, a secret that's been harbored there too long.

Alice killed our mother.

Or maybe we both did.

This unresolved distinction has been rattling around in me for twenty-six years.

Actually, that's not quite true. There have been periods of time when I put the whole horrible episode to rest; however erroneously, I convinced myself that I'd come to terms with what happened that night. But tonight, left with only my nit-picking inner critic, whose sole goal seems to be to make sure I meet my maker with an uneasy conscience, I am experiencing a troubled wakefulness, much like that of my childhood.

If you are reading this, I ask that you refrain from judging me, or Alice, too harshly. Then again, for all I know, no one will ever read this. But that's of no consequence to my purpose. I need to tell the truth of what happened that night.

Outside, the barking of restless sea lions reminds me that life does, indeed, go on.

WHEN ALL WE HAD WERE LAND LINES

October 9, 1989, Portland, Oregon. I was sitting in my small kitchen with my best friend, Toi. My second-story flat sat right under where the aerial tram is now. Like many photographers, Toi made a good portion of her living shooting weddings. I baked custom cakes. We were both single lesbians and, ironically, got much of our business from Dune, a wedding planner, also gay. He was every bride's dream: a screaming queen who could talk tulle and shrimp canapés until even the most eager of brides howled uncle. Called his business Fabulous Weddings. I'm not kidding. We were quite the outfit: middle-aged, single homosexuals preying on the happily-ever-after dreams of young, starry-eyed heterosexuals, at a time when we couldn't legally marry.

"I'm dreading Sunday," Toi said, topping off her glass of Cabernet. Toi loved her Cabernet. Tall and muscular, she cut a striking presence. Her skin, a gorgeous olivey cocoa, had an amazing sheen, and she moved like a professional athlete, hopping over chairs, slaloming through tipsy guests and tables covered in fancy finger foods to get the perfect shot. "The bride's mother has called me a gazillion times," she continued. "She's an amateur photographer and worried about the light. Thinks we should move the gazebo. I keep telling her I know the park. I've shot weddings there before."

I pulled a tray of chocolate chip cookies from the oven. "Pass her off on Dune. That's what he gets the big bucks for."

I was a few years into being single, and its perks were starting to wear thin. As for Toi, she was in one of her I'll-never-date-again phases, which is to say we were both more or less happy hanging out in our sweats on a Monday night, drinking Cab and feasting on homemade chocolate chip cookies.

Toi peeled a molten cookie off the pan. She had asbestos fingers, that one. "Think I should get my hair cut?"

"Why?"

She carried her cookie over to the small round mirror above my kitchen light switch. I had little mirrors positioned all over my second-floor flat, an attempt to feng shui myself into abundance and well-being, and while I hadn't noticed a dramatic change in either category, I hadn't given up hope.

Toi fussed with her shoulder-length dreadlocks. "I've been thinking of shaving my head. Just to shake things up."

"Shaving your head at our age smacks of midlife crisis." I cranked open the window to fend off an oncoming hot flash. "That, or people will think you have cancer."

"I told you about that dyke zygote that called me a Whoopi Goldberg wannabe."

I'll admit, I'm embroidering the scene a little. While it's true Toi was always calling young people zygotes or embryos or guppies, I have no idea if she'd just done so when the phone rang. I'm just giving you a taste of the carefree life I was living at the time. I'm sure I waited for the answering machine to pick up. I wouldn't have picked up with the cookies just out of the oven. (Since my home phone also served as my business phone I had to draw the line somewhere.) I'm equally sure, when I heard who it was, I picked up immediately.

"Emma, I'm here. Is everything okay?"

Emma Buswell lived across the street from my mom and Alice in Santa Cruz. She was a nosypants, but I appreciated her immensely. She called when the ambulance hauled off my dad. Called when my mom tripped on the curb and sprained her wrist. Called when Alice was using a leaf blower at 6:00 a.m. on a Sunday morning. Okay, so I didn't appreciate *that* call so much. But in general, I welcomed her communications. A middle-aged, self-proclaimed Earth Mama, she wore scads of jewelry: rings couched in the fatty pillows of her blunt fingers, an army of silver bangles that jangled at her frequent gesticulations. I could hear the bracelets over the phone. *Clinkity. Clink. Clink.* "You need to come."

"Why? What happened?"

"I haven't seen your mother *or* Alice outside for weeks. Not since the middle of September when Alice hauled a bunch of furniture out on the street and stuck 'Free' signs on it."

"Wait. What? She gave away Mom's furniture?" I glanced at Toi. She knew Alice, knew how uncomfortable I felt leaving her and Mom living alone together.

"Not all of it. But a stack. You know that nice couch? That walnut roll top desk?"

"Mom's leather couch?"

Toi shook her head and chuckled. "Hoo boy."

"I'm going to give Alice a call," I said, by way of closing out the conversation. "Thank you for calling." The woman would talk your ear off if you let her.

Toi topped off my wine glass. "Trouble in Surf City?"

"Do you mind if I...?"

"Of course not. Go at it. But no guarantees there'll be any cookies left by the time you get off the phone. And say hello to that nutty sister of yours."

I took the phone into the small alcove off the kitchen, and gazed down onto the mossy, postage-stamp yard where my downstairs neighbor was trying, unsuccessfully, to grow pot. What had I been thinking leaving Alice and Mom alone in the house after Dad's heart attack? I'd known Mom was starting to lose it, even then. The truth was, I'd let Alice convince me that everything would be fine. "We've lived cheek by jowl this long, sis. I'm sure we'll do okeydoke."

She picked up on the second ring. "Mustin residence. How may I help you?"

I pictured her in the cramped hallway between the bathroom and her bedroom using the mustard-colored phone with the long cord. It was the only phone she'd use, despite my having bought her and Mom a new cordless one. She saw no point in it. Why would she want to walk while talking on the phone? I pictured her wearing one of her kilts and a light sweater or T-shirt, knee socks, and a clunky pair of shoes or boots. I pictured her gray hair pulled back in a ponytail, her thick Clark Kent glasses pushed up high on the bridge of her nose. She had a wide selection of kilts, collected them from all over the place; it's all she ever wore.

"Alice, what's going on? Emma says you haven't been out in months."

"Pretty much housebound these days, sis. Mom's short-term memory is pushing up daisies. She's packed her bags and returned to years gone by. Got her a walker, I did, but she refuses to use it. Thinks I'm Aunt Evockia half the time. Getting her out of the house is more trouble than it's worth, it is. Can't leave her alone, I can't. No. No. No. Unless we want all hell to break loose."

I tried not to panic. With Alice, "all hell breaking loose" could mean anything from a light left on to a four-alarm fire. She was born with Asperger's disorder. Or that's what I believe. She might have just had a monster case of OCD, or some other syndrome they have yet to classify—the *Alice Syndrome*—but she was never diagnosed as a child, and refused to be as an adult. Unless you counted one of the many diagnoses my mother gave her over the years: inhuman, devil child, stupid little goat…Or the one the small town doc gave her, which was actually a diagnosis of Mom. He called her a "refrigerator mother," said Alice's behavior was a result of her "lack of maternal warmth." While it's true that Euvonda Mae Mustin was not the nurturing type—if you came in crying from a busted open knee, she'd point toward the bathroom and say, "Don't go bleeding on my good carpet!" followed by, "I swear! Somewhere, in a Louisiana swamp, there's a tree stump with a higher IQ than you!"—it stands to reason her lack of maternal warmth would have similarly affected me. It is also true that other mothers might have shown a bit more patience with Alice.

"If you can't leave the house, how are you grocery shopping?" I asked.

"Found a grocer that'll deliver, sisteroo. Everything is fine. Shipshape. Aye aye, Captain."

I ignored Alice's attempt at humor. "Could you put Mom on?"

"Put her on what?"

Thanks to what I like to call Mom's *Hollywood Therapy*, which basically consisted of forcing Alice to watch hours of TV and movies in the hope that she'd learn to at least give the impression of being normal, listening to Alice was much like listening to a bad actor recite lines. She'd emphasize the wrong words, would go up in pitch when the sentence wanted to go down.

"Alice, I'm serious."

"Okay. Let's do it. Get on with it. Make it happen." There was a pause on her end. "Be right back." Another pause. "A slight caveat, sisteroo: since her bladder infection, she hasn't been the Mom we all know and love."

"Bladder infection? When did that happen? Why didn't you call?"

There was no response. Apparently, Alice had already gone to get Mom.

I scrolled through my mental calendar. How long had it been since I'd visited? Five months? Six? I tried to get down as often as I could. Dad's death had accelerated Mom's mental decline and I didn't think it fair for Alice to have to go it alone. I'd stay a couple of nights, do some cooking. I worried that taking care of Mom was too much for Alice. Mom's dementia made her even more impatient than usual, but Alice always assured me she had things "under control." I can't tell you how many times I cooked up something special only to have both of them dislike it. I think they were relieved each time I left. So was I. My relationship with my mother was strained long before she started losing her mind.

Gripping the phone, staring down at my neighbor's sickly pot plant, I could feel my comfortable life in Portland shifting beneath my feet. I returned to the kitchen for my wine.

Toi shook her head. "That bad, huh?"

I didn't know how to answer. Just tossed back what was left of my wine, poured myself another glass, grabbed a cookie, and headed back to the alcove.

I was two bites into the cookie when Mom came on the line. "Hello?" She sounded like she was holding the receiver to her neck. I could hear Alice instructing her to put it to her mouth. "Hello?" she said again, her voice all warbly.

"Mom. It's me. Lucy. How are you doing?"

"We had breakfast for dinner. Used up all the eggs."

"Two weeks ago," Alice interjected. "That's when." I got the feeling she was holding the phone for Mom.

"I told you I wanted soup!"

"O-*kay*," I said. "Besides that, are you feeling all right?"

There was some shuffling on the other end.

"Mom?"

"She left," Alice said. "Got distracted, she did."

"Alice, what's going on?"

"Told you. Since her bladder infection, she's been more confused than usual."

"Has she been to a doctor?"

"Yes, indeedydoo. Didn't offer too many helpful hints, if you know what I mean. Antibiotics. All that. Infection's gone. But she's still confused."

"Well, what did they say? Tell me exactly, Alice."

"Hardening of the arteries. It's natural. She's old."

I walked past Toi to the calendar in my closet-slash-office where I had a desk wedged in next to my sweaters. I was supposed to deliver thirty-six birthday cupcakes to Johnny Slattum's third grade class on Wednesday. My thought was to drive down after dropping them off at the school, stay for a couple of days, see what was what, then tank up on caffeine and make the eleven-hour drive back for Sunday's wedding cake—two cakes, actually, a lemon poppy seed cake with butter cream frosting and a bizarre groom's cake too (his mother's recipe). It would be exhausting, but I could do it. During wedding season I'd been known to pump out up to three cakes a day, but in the fall the jobs were few and far between. I really needed the money. "Okay, look. I've got a few things I need to take care of, but then I can come down for a couple of days. Can you get the spare room ready?"

"Will do, sisteroo."

I didn't wind up leaving until Thursday.

CUPCAKES

My reluctance to see my mother was fueled, in part, by the horrible argument we'd had the day of my father's funeral. Mom didn't want me bringing my girlfriend, Blue. Mom had met Blue, even liked Blue, called her "an awful lot of fun," but she hadn't told any of her friends about Blue, and while I could pass for straight, Blue never could, never would. She was a New Mexico cowgirl with multiple ear piercings, a Georgia O'Keeffe flower tattooed on her wrist (bold, back then), and wore her hair in a faux hawk. I thought I loved her. She thought she loved me. It was one of those relationships that mistook intensity for love. No matter. She should have been with me at my dad's funeral, but Mom said if she came it would make the whole day about me instead of Dad, which was ridiculous, of course, so I brought her. Sprung for a motel. After Blue and I checked in at the Drift Inn, I went to check on Mom, leaving Blue in the room watching TV. That's when I found out about the open casket.

"The family viewing is from five to six," Mom said, handing me a program with the mortuary's insignia of two crossed lilies right beneath my father's name. "Still, you should look nice. Some of our close friends are invited for that time too."

I was floored. Dad had had an unnatural fear of worms. He wanted to be cremated. I knew it. Mom knew it.

"You're kidding!" I said.

She took a final drag on her Winston. "Don't give me that look." She stubbed the smoke out in a potted orchid, then discreetly tucked the butt beneath the accompanying condolence card. "I am a woman in mourning."

She was wearing a stylish black silk dress with a row of tiny rhinestones around the neckline, clearly purchased for the occasion. Had had her hair and nails done too.

"Blue's at the motel room," I said coolly.

"Don't you dare bring her to the funeral," she said. "You'll turn the whole thing into a circus." There was alcohol on her breath.

I didn't respond. Just stormed back to the motel without even saying hello to Alice and dumped onto Blue all that Mom had dumped onto to me, upsetting Blue, naturally.

"Fuck it! I'm not going," she said.

"You have to!" I said.

But there was no talking Blue into anything.

I wound up boycotting the family viewing. I didn't want to see my dad dead in a casket. Then, at the service, I couldn't stand the thought of other people having seen him while I hadn't, so I looked. I immediately regretted it. Mom had him duded out in a snappy Western shirt and bolo tie she'd given him for some birthday, an outfit he thought looked "hick" and had never worn. Alice told me the shirt didn't even fit anymore, that it had to be slit up the back. At the reception at the house, Mom had Alice filling everyone's champagne glasses and taking their covered dishes when they arrived, while she, the newly widowed, in her new black dress and new, pretty hair, held court among the mourners. I made myself stay, made myself smile when Mom introduced me to her friends, did my best to help Alice keep the potluck table looking fresh, drank my share of champagne, stuck around for cleanup, all the while keeping my emotions in check. When the last of the guests finally said their good-byes, I couldn't get out of there fast enough.

That is, until Mom intercepted me at the door.

"Where are you going?"

"In case you've forgotten, you asked me to leave my girlfriend at the motel."

"You're just going to leave?"

"What do you want me to do? Sit around drinking spiked hot chocolate with you while Blue sits by herself at the motel? Is that what you had in mind?"

We were both on the wrong side of intoxicated, both speaking without thinking, which is why, no doubt, she let this slip out: "You being gay always ruins everything!"

Her words couldn't have hit me harder than if she'd delivered them with a slap. "How?" I said. "How does my being gay ruin things?"

She knew she'd gone too far, but she wasn't going to back down. She wanted the whole world to hurt as badly as she did; she was a wrecking ball gone rogue. "Has it never occurred to you," she slurred,

"I might have liked to have *one* normal daughter? One whose wedding I could plan? Who would provide me with a handsome son-in-law to bring me flowers and tell me how young I look, even when we both know he's lying? You don't think *that* would have been nice? And how about your father? You don't think it broke his heart that he never got to walk one of you girls down the aisle? Huh? You don't think that might be part of what killed him?"

I think her spew stunned even her, because we both just stood there for a second listening to Alice emptying trash into the bin out back, our eyes filling with tears. Then I walked out the door. A week later, when I talked to her on the phone, she acted like everything was fine between us. It's possible she didn't remember the fight; forgetfulness was certainly becoming an issue with her. But I don't think so. The silence smoldering under the small talk was deafening. Then, over time, she really didn't remember. Couldn't.

I did, though, and still hadn't found a way to forgive her.

Don't get the wrong impression about Mom. People loved her. It was hard not to. The mother of my youth had a style all her own: martini glass cupped in the palm of one hand, cigarette snugged between two slender fingers of the other, the next witticism teasing the corner of her crimson lips. She had impeccable timing, waiting for the perfect moment when a conversation lulled to deliver her bon mots with panache: "That dress on Darla Jenkins spreads her out like a cold supper!"

But one too many cocktails turned Mama Jekyll into Mama Hyde.

Growing up, Alice and I would watch warily as she fried up our fish sticks and tater tots, cocktail in one hand, grabbers in the other, happily singing show tunes. We knew that one more drink and she'd be slamming Alice's and my plates down on the table, blaming us for Dad coming home late. "Lucy, would it *kill* you to try and look nice for a change? And, Alice, quit playing with your food and eat like a *normal* person!" Still gripping her cocktail, she'd pace the kitchen, chain-smoking and berating us while we sat there, trapped, until we cleared our plates of the burned fish sticks and tater tots. "If I had known how *hard* it was to have children, if anyone had had the *decency* to clue me in, I woulda thought twice, that's for damn sure. I swear, raising you two is like being slowly pecked to death by a chicken! Honestly, coming home to you two! Who'd want to?"

She expected a lot from life. At eighteen had been crowned East Texas Yam Queen. Then, having reached the pinnacle of what small town life had to offer, she'd gone off and eloped with a traveling salesman—I'm not kidding. Dad was a Fuller Brush man at the time—and together they headed off for a bigger, bolder life.

I adored my dad. There was nothing I loved more than watching him wow the crowds on league nights at the bowling alley. Cigarette dangling, monogrammed bowling shirt hanging off his wiry frame, hair slicked back with pomade, he'd put a spin on that ball that would smack of a shooting star.

At home, though, when Mom wasn't demanding his attention, which she was most of the time, it went to Alice. He'd step in when Mom lost patience. Would come up with things for him and Alice to do together: building a radio in the basement, helping him change the oil in his car. It made me insanely jealous. I wanted to be the one handing him screwdrivers and wrenches. Instead, I'd get stuck fending off Mom's attempts to make me appreciate the joys of nice china, a well-cut dress, the wonders of womanhood. Mostly, though, Mom kept Dad to herself. She liked to point out that they were both left-handed, while Alice and I were both right-handed, as though this set us in different camps.

But there was one area where I was Dad's number one: when he began dreaming of a new business venture. I was so desperate for his attention, I'd agree with whatever scheme he came up with. Once he got me on board, he'd approach Mom and Alice. "Lucy and I have been talking…haven't we, kiddo?" I'd nod enthusiastically, and for a little while, *I'd* be his special girl. His ruffling of my hair, his cigarette dropping ashes on my head, and his words: "As long as I've got you riding in my sidecar, we got nothing but green lights all the way, kiddo!" was worth suffering through Mom's whining about the inconvenience of a move, worth the fights I'd have with Alice about her wanting to arrange our new room exactly like the old one, her going so far as to rearrange it while I was gone, even if it meant blocking our window with a bookshelf to get it *exactly* like the last room. In those instances, I'd go straight to Dad, expecting him to take up for me. I'd wait until he was having his drink in the living room, his socked feet resting on the footrest of his La-Z-Boy. "Give it a rest," he'd say, barely looking up from his newspaper, "or I'll never hear the end of it from your sister."

"But, Dad—"

"Please, kiddo? Do it for me?"

Of course I would. I would do anything for him.

But this story isn't about him.

Or maybe it is.

Maybe it's about the shattered family he left behind after his heart attack.

He was lifting a fifty-pound bag of flour at what would be his last business venture, the Plaza Bakery. He dropped to his knees in front of a class of third graders, the visiting children being one of his many schemes to pump up sales.

Had he outlived my mother, none of what I'm about to tell you would have happened.

Of that one thing, I am certain.

On Tuesday, I baked Johnnie Slattum's cupcakes. Then I took my old Volvo in for a tune-up while the cupcakes cooled; wrote the copy for a Lucy's Custom Cakes ad to be placed in a local weekly's food issue; cut the neck and sleeves out of a sweatshirt, decided it looked stupid, and turned the whole thing into rags; picked up my Volvo and was told I was in dire need of new tires; went into debt on the tires. On Wednesday, I iced and delivered the thirty-six lemon poppy seed cupcakes to Woodland Elementary, mentally patted myself on the back for not having had children, then made the decision *not* to drive down after delivering the cupcakes, as I'd indicated I would, rationalizing that I didn't want to do that much night driving. Instead, I got wretchedly drunk with Dune and Toi and we laughed ourselves silly over a potted plant that looked like a vagina. Once they'd left, I threw some clothes in a suitcase, set my alarm for 5:00 a.m., and tried to sleep. My mind, though, wouldn't quit chewing on itself. Had Mom really been holding the phone to her neck, did she really not remember how it worked? Mom, who spent so much time gabbing with her friends on the phone that she'd yellowed the mouthpiece with nicotine stains?

L est you think I am sitting here typing all this out on my laptop, let me relieve you of this misconception. Some months back, Alice got sick of me asking for help with my computer and installed an app that lets me speak my commands. It also, I have learned, converts my spoken word into text on the screen, which has been immensely useful as I am a terrible typist. It was a bit odd to use at first as the words on the screen lag behind, and I'm clearly going to have to proofread after each session (it autocorrected vagina to fajita), but it will allow me to get the story out. I'm due at the funeral parlor at ten this morning, which gives me time to put down a few more thoughts.

I miss Alice. The vision of her sprawled out there…How long did she suffer? The paramedics told me it would have been instantaneous, but I imagine they say that to everyone. No one wants to think of their loved one lying there suffering. To add insult to injury, I spotted that damn gopher out there this morning when I went to take out the trash. He was peeking his beastly little head out of a fresh mound, not a care in the world. The sight of him got me crying all over again.

Cleaning up the blood was awful. I used Alice's towel (it seemed appropriate) and lots of bleach. The cement is still slightly stained, but I did what I could. Alice would have had a method to get it all up, I'm sure. She had a concoction for everything. I don't mind the stain so much. It seems right that she should leave her mark, that any of us should. We will, each of us, be forgotten soon enough. I've just now spotted, through the sliding glass door, an aluminum water bottle on the back deck. One of the paramedics must have left it. Or maybe one of the neighbors. So many people trooped through here yesterday, so many wanting to help. The regulars: Emma Buswell and the nice young Realtor across the street…No doubt, he's wondering what's going to happen to the house when I die. They probably all are. Real estate has gone nuts around here.

One particular neighbor surprised me with her sincerity: a lovely, androgynous thing whose name I've forgotten. She asked if there was any blood, and did I need help cleaning it up. I thought her macabre at first. Turns out her dad has a hazmat business of some sort, which put my mind at ease. I think she's a student at the university. Has a million tattoos and those ear things that aren't quite earrings, more like placeholders for where the lobe used to be. They remind me of those little white donut-shaped stickers we used to paste on our three-ring notebook paper to keep the holes from ripping. She has some spunk, though, I'll give her that. Rides around on a skateboard, jumping curbs, taking the corners sharp. It surprised me that she would offer to help. Most of the university students look right through me as if I'm a specter. Still, I refused her. To be quite frank, I didn't want anyone touching Alice's blood. She was my sister; her blood, my blood. It was nice of the girl to offer though. I hope I didn't come off too rude. I just feel so raw.

How I will do without Alice is a worry. We've gotten on quite well these past few years, like two old pennies in a purse, not much use to anybody but ourselves. Now it'll just be me rattling around here making a mess of things. I had to make my own coffee this morning. Honestly, I had no idea how much coffee to scoop into the pot, but I managed. Just as I did without Kim. Somehow, we do. And Alice has all her affairs in order. As do I. After our mother's death, and the house going into probate due to her lack of a will, you can be sure we had our wills drawn up. Alice left everything to me and I to her. It was like a game of Russian roulette, which one of us would go first, but I always thought it would be me. It's just the house really, and whatever happens to be in the bank account when the time comes. We both are to be cremated. Alice asked the very practical question of what the survivor is supposed to do with the other one's ashes. Her point was a good one. At the time of our father's death, Mom bought a double plot for him and her, leaving us to fend for ourselves. Not that either of us felt the need for a headstone, but something had to be done with the ashes, so we decided the survivor would cast them out to the bay. Alice wasn't too keen on the idea. "You'll be sad," I said. "You'll need to do something."

She took me at my word. It never occurred to me I'd be the one left with the ashes.

I'm going to have to rethink my will. Going to have to rethink a lot of things. But there will be time for this. Or maybe there won't. Who knows, really? Today, though, is not the day. Today is the day to begin the process of putting Alice to rest. I've gone through it with my father, my mother, Kim, and now Alice. You could say I'm getting good at it. Not something I'm proud of, just something that's true. I don't feel much urgency in regard to the legal end of things. A few bills taken out of her name, the house put into mine, all the death certificates gotten so that this can be accomplished. First, though, I want to get on with my story, our story, because until it's told, Alice will not rest. I won't let her.

I still have to write her obituary, but I have time. I'll have the paper run it Sunday when there are the most readers. People knew Alice. Or knew of her. Hard to miss the old kilted woman who was always riding her bike through town. They deserve to know she died.

FORT MUSTIN

On next to no sleep, and several cups of high-octane French roast, I made the eleven-hour drive in one shot, leaving at 6:00 a.m. and stopping only for bathroom breaks, more coffee, and one very soggy tuna sandwich. I barely noticed what was usually breathtakingly beautiful scenery along the way: Ashland, Mount Shasta, Castle Crags State Park. The day I'd been dreading had finally come, the day we were going to have to figure out what to do with Mom, or so my gut was telling me—shouting at me! Meanwhile my poor little brain was running laps around my skull trying to figure out logistics. We didn't have the money to put her somewhere, or the money to hire someone to look after her, unless we sold the house. But where would Alice live? Would I have to move down to help with caretaking? How was *that* going to work? I got to Santa Cruz in what seemed like minutes.

The house was situated in the quirky West Side Circles. Not half a mile from the bay, the Circles are an eclectic jumble of family homes with landscaped yards featuring colorful play structures; trashed-out university student housing with overgrown lawns and too many parked cars; surfer crash pads with rusted-out cruiser bikes in the driveway and wetsuits draping the fence; and giant, zero-lot-line vacation dream homes that lord over the neighborhood like watchtowers. The lots are small and sprung up, revival style, in the late 1890s orbiting around a church. You can thank Alice for this bit of trivia. Part of her adapting-to-a-new-home strategy was to learn the history of each place.

Once Dad died, Alice and Mom stayed put in the Circles and lived off the paltry retirement money he'd managed to save and the income from the Plaza Bakery, which, thanks to the veteran staff, more or less ran itself. Or so I thought...

I made the turn onto Mom and Alice's street. I was a bundle

of stressed-out fatigue. My lower back ached. My eyes stung. I had a sour stomach. Pulling up to the house didn't help. What were once tasteful clumps of bamboo dotting the perimeters of the yard had turned into an impenetrable hedge. I couldn't even see the one-story stucco bungalow from the street, just the garage, where Mom's dust-and-bird-shit-covered Acura was parked in the driveway. Cobwebs were knitted around the side mirrors. Had the bamboo been that tall when I'd last visited, or had it just grown really fast?

My chest grew tight. I was having trouble breathing. I considered not stopping, maybe taking the block, or two, to center myself. But I flicked off the air conditioner and slipped the keys out of the ignition. Outside was hot. Unseasonably hot. And I'm not just saying that because I was a Portlander, and menopausal. Santa Cruz was in a full-on Indian summer, and I was dressed in jeans, a long-sleeved jersey, wool socks, and sneaks. It was October, for God's sake!

I hoisted myself out of the car and took in the surrounding street. It was a little after 5:00. The sun was still shining; a gaggle of kids was playing kickball; a group of young men clutched beers and stood around a car with the hood up, their radio blaring Mexican music; someone had a barbecue going. Just a regular neighborhood with one huge clump of bamboo stuck in the middle. Definitely the Boo Radley house.

I decided to leave my baggage in the car—and by that I mean my small suitcase and pillow; my psychological baggage was not as easily abandoned. I took another deep breath and prepared to breach the fortress. The waist-high gate had been replaced by a six-foot-tall one. That was new. There was a slot for the mail neatly cut dead center. I recognized it right away as Alice's work. She was a self-taught carpenter, a good one too, and was big on home improvements.

I lifted the gate's heavy latch and stepped inside the yard, then sighed with relief. The small square of lawn was neatly mowed and edged. The walkway was swept. Things couldn't be that bad. I mounted the three steps onto the small porch, scanning for other clues of what I'd find inside: the windowsills and railing were wiped clean of any dust or grime, the rocking chair on the porch was free of cobwebs, as was the porch light, and the firewood was perfectly stacked. The obsessive tidiness probably meant Alice was doing all right. Then again, it could mean just the opposite.

I'll admit I felt like putting my ear to the door for a listen, but it felt too stalkerish. This was family! Why was I feeling so unnerved? I tried the knob, found it locked, and pushed the doorbell. Alice must have been standing right there because she opened the door immediately. "I thought you were going to be here at five."

I looked at my watch. "Alice, it's five fifteen."

She exhaled loudly and marched into the house, leaving me to shut the door behind me.

"Aren't you going to give me a hug?" I called after her.

She pivoted mid-step, returned to me, did her version of a hug, clasping my shoulders with her wrists and dipping in slightly, keeping her torso as far from mine as possible. Alice did not like touching. But since the rest of the world did, she had to make some concessions. Having completed her duty, she resumed her trajectory to the kitchen, tossing over her shoulder, "I'm making stir-fry!"

I followed. "Where's Mom? And what happened to all the living room furniture?" The place was gutted. All that was left was Mom's gold La-Z-Boy, a small table next to it which held the TV remote, the green wingback chair, which I assumed was for Alice, the old oak TV console, and another small table by the door for keys, mail, and such. Gone were the doilies, the china cabinet, the matching floral couch and love seat, the tacky landscapes.

Alice put her fingers to her lips then whispered, "In the bedroom napping. And we didn't need it."

"What if somebody visits?"

"They don't."

"Like, I don't count?"

"Not to worry, sisteroo, I have it all figured out. TV nights, you can use a chair from the kitchen." She switched to a slightly British accent. "What is the projected timeline of your visit, might I ask?" It was her attempt at humor.

"Um. Not really sure." I clutched the kitchen doorframe and leaned forward to stretch out my shoulders. I was already regretting not having picked up a bottle of wine on my way in. The kitchen looked fairly intact. "How come you left four chairs in here? Planning on throwing a little kitchen party?" Teasing Alice rarely produced the desired effect, but it never stopped me from doing it. I *was* her big sister.

She looked up from a bag of rice, stared just to the right of me through those Clark Kent glasses of hers. Clearly, she thought I was dense beyond words. "Couldn't break up a set now, could I? It would ruin the resale value."

I thought about the "Free" signs Emma Buswell had told me about; swallowed back the words: *Some resale value.* But there was no arguing with Alice. She would wear you down with her logic every time.

She clipped off the corner of the rice bag, measured one cup—to the grain—and poured it into the rice cooker. She gave the same exacting attention to the water. Then came the bouillon cube, which she shook from a jar, carefully unwrapped so as not to miss one crumb, and tossed into the mix. "Using low sodium these days I am. Mom's got high blood pressure. Shooting through the roof! You still allergic to green peppers, still breaking out in hives at the mere sight of them?"

"You should have told me you were giving everything away."

"No peppers it is. A pepper-free dinner for one and all."

I opened the cupboard to get a glass for some water. There were exactly four glasses, four plates, four mugs. I didn't ask. "Alice, I'm serious about the furniture."

She plunked a bottle of something called House Red Wine on the table. "Relax, sis. I've got it under control, wrapped around my little finger, got the cue ball all lined up. We eat at six."

The bottle of wine looked to be a small step up from cooking wine. I didn't care. Every nerve in my body was screaming for a drink. "Thanks, sis."

"No problemo." She handed me a corkscrew. "Had it delivered with this week's groceries, I did. Don't let Mom see it."

"Why? She's not drinking? How did *that* come about?"

"I stopped buying it."

"And she was okay with that?"

"Not at first, she wasn't. Then she forgot."

It was hard to imagine Mom forgetting about drinking, but easy to understand why Alice would want her to. Alice had difficulty navigating the stormy waters of Mama Hyde. She didn't get sarcasm, Mama Hyde's preferred mode of communication when she was drunk.

Alice set a sturdy white coffee mug on the table, the kind you used to see in coffee shops. "Use this. And hide the bottle."

As long as I wasn't the one being cut off, I was happy to oblige. I don't mind telling you, I drank a bit more than I should in those days. I wouldn't go so far as to call myself an alcoholic, but I would say my relationship to wine was one-sided; I loved it more than it loved me. Most mornings I woke feeling like I'd been left in the dryer too long. But a glass of wine signaled my nerves they were off duty for the day, no easy task when you're self-employed, and single. There's always more that can be done: advertising, bookkeeping, recipe-gathering, batters to be mixed. A glass of wine always did the trick. The glasses that followed, well, they followed.

I popped the cork and poured myself a mugful. "So, how is Mom?"

Alice looked up from cutting the tough outer skin off the broccoli stalk. "Gotta keep a close watch on her, keep my eyes peeled. Wanders off, she does."

"What do you mean 'wanders off'?"

"Takes off down the street for who knows where? The mall? The corner market? Kingdom come? Then can't find her way back, she can't. The gate, it keeps her in."

"When did this start?"

"Been going on a while, it has. And I did tell you."

"When?"

She continued stripping the broccoli. "Nothing you could do, sis. Not a bling-blang thing you could do. Not all the way up there in Portland. Whoo-wee, no. It was up to me to take care of, so take care of it I did."

Her use of the word "it" when talking about Mom was starting to worry me. I gulped down a swallow of House Red.

After Dad's funeral, it just made sense to leave the two of them living together; they'd always lived together. Who was I to barge in and make other arrangements? Besides, Alice was the most capable person I knew. But here's the thing: Dad buffered Mom and Alice's interactions. And I knew it. It's not that he understood Alice much better than Mom did, he was just more likely to take the path of least resistance. "For Christ's sake, Euvie! Let 'er have it her way," he'd say. "Would it kill us to have a coupla tomato beds in the front yard instead of those damn roses that always look half dead?" I could see the toll his absence had taken on Alice. Her face looked pinched; her choppy ponytail was showing a few streaks of white. "Hey," I said, "You doing okay? You still making your bottles?"

Her gaze shot up from the broccoli, as if she'd been short-circuited. "Indeed I am, dear sister of mine!" She set down the paring knife with a flourish. "I surely am! I've taken over the guest room. You can go look. See the latest, the greatest, and all the rest. It is the world of worlds. A place of mystery and magic."

I will admit my first thought was: *If you've taken over the guest room, where am I going to sleep?* But I didn't want to spoil this moment with her. She seemed so happy that I'd asked. Clutching my mug of House Red, I tiptoed down the hall so as not to wake Mom. I didn't want to relinquish my time with Alice, and Mom liked to be the center of attention. I'll leave it at that.

I was surprised to see Alice hadn't gotten rid of the happiest-ever family photos lining the hall: me and Alice on swings; me, Alice, Mom, and Dad sitting around a picnic table; me and Dad flying a kite; Alice on her first bike with Dad cheering her on; Alice and me looking miserable all gussied up like baby dolls, our naturally straight hair forced into Shirley Temple ringlets; an Olan Mills photo of Aunt Evockia and Uncle Frank; and, of course, in the center of all the photos, the most cherished of all, Mom in her gown posing as East Texas's Yam Queen. I wouldn't have blamed Alice for putting the lot of them out on the street with the rest. The photo ops were always horrible events with Mom prodding Alice to "Smile! Smile!"

I rounded the corner into the guest room and stopped abruptly in the doorway, stunned.

I'm sure you've seen ships in bottles, those tiny little frigates suspended in their glass tombs. Alice took this art to a new dimension, creating whole miniature worlds, each bottle unique, each with its own locality, its own genre. She used any number of materials, whatever the particular scene called for: wood (usually balsa), polymer clay, feathers, toothpicks, paperclips, cork, glitter, tiny googly eyes, found objects like charms and bobby pins, and, of course, the bottles themselves. Her tools were more run of the mill: oversized tweezers, glue, chisels, paint, twine.

She'd been making the bottles since she was in her early twenties and rarely gave them away. At the time, I was the proud owner of three: a scene featuring my first car, an old Pontiac sedan; a beach scene complete with dolphins arcing up out of the water; and one that actually had me in it, holding up an elaborately decorated cake. How she managed to fit these mini scenarios inside her bottles, I never had the patience to figure out, but I treasured the ones I owned. They made quite the conversation pieces, and gave me a perfect opening to talk about my nutty family.

That day, though, the sheer number of them was stunning—alarming, really. There were shelves of them, some two bottles deep, others three. It was overwhelming. Then, smack in the middle of the room, in the middle of those bottles, was a flimsy-looking foldout cot and a milk crate nightstand. There was also a small dresser inside the closet and a few empty hangers. That was it.

"What do you think, big sister of mine?" Alice whispered. I hadn't even heard her come up behind me. "Can you believe your eyes? Can it be real? This world of a million worlds?"

I negotiated my way around the bed so she could join me in the small room, stifling my urge to scream: *What the hell did you do with the Danish bedroom set?* I loved that set, had always privately hoped when Mom died Alice would give it to me. But I hadn't been there long enough to start in with Alice. Besides, she was exhibiting as close to excitement as she ever got, bustling around, dusting off the dustless bottles with her sleeve, so I did my best to view the gallery.

The bottles were much more complex than her earlier works. One bottle contained an exact replica of our old dining room. In it, the table was set, the little bowls filled with something like chili, a favorite of Alice's. Another featured the Plaza Bakery. Another, our childhood street. But the bottles weren't all autobiographical. There was a section dedicated to movies: *Casablanca*, *Star Wars*, *Harvey*; a section to fantasy: knights, sorcerers, sword fights; a section to crime: several murder scenes, a bank heist. It was too much to take in after the long drive. But I tried. "Wow, Alice. You've really been hard at work! These are wonderful!" If I'd looked more closely, I would have noticed that for each bottle filled with a happy scene, there were six or seven filled with disturbing ones. But all selfish me could think about was filling my now empty wineglass; that, and if it was too late to check into a cheap nearby motel.

A loud *crash! thunk!* coming from Mom's bedroom, followed by Mom's distressed, "Alice! Aaaaaa-lice!" robbed me even of that.

It's difficult to look back on my life without a degree of contempt. I was so negligent in regard to Alice and Mom's well-being! In my defense, it was a difficult time in my life. My last breakup had left me feeling as though I were incapable of a healthy relationship. And while Lucy's Cakes kept me afloat, it didn't do much more than that. And it was degrading making wedding cakes when I wasn't allowed to marry. As much as Toi, Dune, and I pretended to be above it, we weren't. Why else were we drinking ourselves stupid after each wedding?

One more clarification: For all the challenges I might have felt interacting with my mother, I loved her. When we were kids, she was by far the coolest mom, the one the other kids wished was theirs. She threw us the best birthday parties, made carpooling fun. Later, when Alice and I failed to marry and produce children (a great annoyance to her), she threw the wedding and baby showers for the daughters of her friends. And while she was hard on us in private, always pushing us to be what we weren't, in public, she had our backs. Always. I remember one time when some kids were bullying Alice after school, making fun of the way she spoke. I was standing off to the side. Stepping in to defend her was social suicide and ran the risk of flustering Alice further. Still, it was awful to watch. I hadn't even noticed Mom driving up or getting out of the car. But she walked right into the thick of those bullies, identified the leader of the pack, a handsome kid in high-dollar shoes, and took him on. "Look at you making fun of someone different than you. Does it make you feel like the big man? Is that it?" Then she turned to his followers. "You think hanging out with this loser makes you cool? You think he wouldn't turn on you if it made him look good?" Then she did the remarkable: She invited them all to join us down the block at the ice cream parlor and sprang for a cone for each of them. All but the one bully, that is. I won't say it made Alice and me instantly popular, but it did take him down in the eyes of the other kids, which was revenge enough. Of course, when we got home, it was a different story: How could I have not stepped in to defend my sister? Why did Alice have to act like such a numbskull? But that was Mom.

THE DELOREAN TIME MACHINE

The *crash* turned out to be a glass of water that had shattered to the floor; the *clunk*, an alarm clock, which apparently had taken a similar dive. Mom was sitting sideways on my parents' hideous, king-sized, white and gold rococo bed, Dad's side, her veiny legs bent at the knees and dangling, her hands folded in her lap, the knuckles the size of large ball bearings.

The sight of her there, dwarfed in that bed, without any makeup, her thin white hair a series of haphazard parts showing through to her pink skull; her light pink floral muumuu, stained and twisted around her middle like a straitjacket, might as well have shot an arrow through my blindsided heart. When had she gotten so old? So weak? Had she had a stroke? I was furious with Alice for not letting me know how bad she'd gotten, for letting her *get* so bad. Furious with myself for blaming Alice.

"Mom?" I said. I didn't mean it to come out as a question.

She briefly glanced at Alice then let her gaze rest on me, her once fierce blue eyes now milky with cataracts. She glanced at Alice again. Clearly, my presence was disturbing to her. She frowned, rubbed the swollen knuckles of her age-spotted hands, then said to Alice, "You got my shoes wrong! These are the wrong ones!"

I glanced at her feet. They were bare. Careful of the broken glass, I stepped in closer to make sure she saw me, then bent down so we were face-to-face. The years of beauty products promising everlasting youthfulness had failed her. Skin chalky and thin, her face and neck were a tapestry of hairline wrinkles. The corners of her eyes drooped. "What shoes are you talking about, Mom?" I spoke gently, kindly.

She made a point of not hearing me, averting her eyes as if caught in a lie.

I realized she had no idea who I was. It was surreal. Horrible. Hurtful. I too turned to Alice.

"Been a lot worse since the bladder infection, she has," Alice said to me quietly.

"What shoes is she talking about?" I whispered.

She shrugged. "Not a clue, Professor Plum, but they've been weighing heavy on her mind today." She spoke to Mom doing her Alice-best to sound bright and cheery. "Well now, that's a real conundrum, it is. A real hiccup in your day."

"I don't see why you can't get it right!" Mom spat, her face flushing with splotches. "I've told you a million times!"

It was unsettling to see her without her hair styled. Her weekly trips to the beauty salon had been one of the few constants of our lives. She slept on satin pillowcases in between visits to keep her "do" looking good. I reached out my hand to smooth a cowlick. She recoiled.

"Who *are* you?" She looked to Alice. "Who *is* this?"

"Who she says," Alice said. "Lucy. Your daughter. Remember? I told you she was coming."

Mom looked momentarily confused. "Who?"

"Lucy. Came all the way from the Portland, she did. To see the one and only you."

"Don't be a silly," Mom said. "Lucy's dead."

That threw me—big time. It was one thing not to be recognized, but to have been killed off!

Alice began picking up the larger pieces of glass from the floor.

"I broke Mama's lamp," Mom said.

I started to correct her. Alice shot a look to shut me up. "No problemo, Mamasan. It'll be taken care of in two shakes of a lamb's tail."

Mom squinted at me, then went back to her lamp. "We're going to get in trouble. Mama loves that lamp."

"Keep her on the bed," Alice said. "I'll get the broom." Then she scurried off down the hall.

From Mom's perspective, Alice had left her with a complete stranger, one she didn't like the looks of. "Now, *who* are you?"

"I've been gone a long time," I said. "But it's me, Lucy."

She leaned forward, looking me right in the eyes, and for a moment, I was sure she recognized me. Then she said, "Mr. Marshall says she's not right in the head." She gestured toward the hall where Alice had gone. "Told me she didn't belong in his school."

Mr. Marshall, I recalled, was the spit-and-polish principal of our first elementary school in Long Beach, and I'd no doubt he'd said that about Alice. He was always angling for reasons to expel her. It was hard to justify when her grades were so good.

I adjusted Mom's muumuu so it didn't hang off her shoulder. (In point of fact, it wasn't a muumuu; other women wore muumuus, she wore "floats." A difference in semantics, maybe, but it added a little flair to those lumpy dresses.) "Mom, it's me, Lucy, your oldest daughter. I've come to see you."

She could feel something was expected of her but wasn't quite sure what it was. She patted her thinning hair in an attempt to poof it up, the soft white skin hanging off her arm like pancake batter.

I spotted a plastic tortoiseshell comb on the dresser and snatched it up. "I came especially to see you, Mom."

Like a watchdog who lets the bad guys pass when offered a nice juicy steak, she let down her guard and allowed me to run the comb through her hair. Anyone willing to contribute to her beauty couldn't be *all* bad. "What time is it?" She brushed the front of her float free of invisible crumbs. "Aren't we supposed to be going?"

I was unsure how to respond. Did Alice have something planned?

Alice returned with the broom. "Cleanup on aisle five. Watch where you step. Slippery when wet." She swept as if her life depended on it, as if she were responsible for the broken glass. "It's just a little thing. Just glass. Nothing that can't be taken care of lickety-split." She spoke to herself more than to us, surrounding herself in a protective wall of words.

"Are we going somewhere?" I asked.

She glanced at Mom, then back at me. Shook her head slightly. "She's been having a bad day," she whispered. "A bad, bad, bad day." She swept the last of the glass and water into the dustpan. "Woke up all out of sorts, she did. Wrong side of the bed."

"Stop your mumbling," Mom said. "You're giving me a headache."

I picked up the alarm clock and placed it back on the nightstand, anger rising up my throat. Why in God's name hadn't Alice told me what was going on? Why hadn't she reached out for help? Because reaching out for help wouldn't have occurred to Alice. The same way it wouldn't occur to her to complain.

Complaining made no sense to Alice. Just a week or so ago, I was complaining about the lack of mobility in my hands and she said, in that stilted manner of hers, "I don't get it, old sport. Why are you talking about it if you can't change it?" I tried to explain to her that whining serves to communicate discomfort and gives other people a chance to pitch in and help. She didn't buy it.

"Does Mom have some slippers or something?" I said. "Just in case we've missed a sliver."

"Slippers are in the closet. Starboard side."

I had no idea which side starboard was, but was happy to have a reason to turn my back on the two of them. I needed a moment to calm myself. I found the slippers. They were stained but appeared recently washed. I handed them to Alice. It sounds selfish, I know, I could have put them on Mom's pale, little feet myself, but in my defense, Mom was looking at me as if I were some solicitor who had barged my way into her bedroom. She tugged on Alice's T-shirt then jerked her head toward me standing by the door. "Is she staying for dinner?"

"Yup," Alice said, "and then some. We're having stir-fry."

I watched as Alice helped her to her feet, watched as she set Mom up with a walker, watched as she began guiding Mom toward me. I stepped out of the way. "When did she get a walker?"

"After her last fall. But she forgets to use it, she does. Don't you, Mom?"

Mom didn't respond, just purposefully thunked that walker down the hallway, Alice in her wake.

I lingered in the bedroom for a moment. I was suffocating. Like the rest of the house, Mom's bedroom had been stripped to only essentials. Gone were her antique perfume bottles, her earring tree, her collection of lace hankies—none of which had ever been sullied by snot. All that remained were the frilly curtains and that damn rococo bed set she made us haul every time we moved, saying, "You'll be glad I did. It's going to be passed on to one of you girls someday." I'd respond silently: *Over my dead body.*

I was just about to leave the room when I spotted Dad's mahogany suit rack behind the open closet door. Dad called the rack Henry. Whenever the ice cream truck rolled past, or there was some needed trinket, Dad would say, "Go ask Henry," and we'd race to collect whatever change was in the little tray. Seeing Henry standing there, empty of one of Dad's fine suits, shot me back to him duded out in that casket, to Mom's and my screaming match. There would be no reconciliation now. There couldn't be. The mom that had had that fight with me was gone.

I blew my nose, wiped my eyes, and headed toward the kitchen, where Alice was frying up a wokful of broccoli and chicken, and Mom was emptying the fridge for reasons I couldn't fathom. I didn't bother asking. I had to get out of that house.

"I'm going to go—"

Before I could get out another word, Alice spun around and hollered a desperate, "No!"

Mom looked up from the jar of mayonnaise in her hand. "What?" She had a carton of orange juice in her other.

"I was just going to say 'go out to the car to get my bags.'"

Alice did her version of eye contact, staring just past my right shoulder. "I thought you were leaving." She nudged her glasses up her nose, tugged on her kilt. "Thought you were fleeing the coop, old sport."

Her obvious distress cured me of any wishful delusions that I *was* just popping down to Santa Cruz for a short visit. "No, I'll be right back. Wouldn't want to let that wine go to waste." I could barely look at Mom.

"Wine?" Mom said.

Alice glared at me.

Mom set the mayo and orange juice on the counter. "What wine?"

I shot Alice an apologetic look. She sighed dramatically. "It's not here yet, Mamasan, but it's on its way."

Mom stood for a couple more seconds, considering this new bit of information, then said, "Well, good! I could use a drink." Moments later, she was back to emptying the fridge, seemingly having forgotten all about the wine.

By now, my anxiety was blooming into a full-blown panic attack. The house felt riddled with land mines. "Be right back," I said, and made for the front door.

The fresh air helped immensely, but it was more than that: cars were parked in orderly fashion along the street; trees were growing upward toward the sun; the sidewalk was sectioned off in tidy squares; the whole world hadn't gone mad, just my family. But there was no time to tarry. Alice needed me. So did Mom, even if she didn't know it.

I returned with my bags and dropped them in my room, then started cranking open windows in the living room. The house was stifling. Mr.

Scratch, Alice's old, gray tabby, crouched in a nest of gray hair on the seat of the wingback chair. He looked miserable. I sat on the arm of the chair and scratched his neck. "How you doing?"

His purring sounded like it hurt.

"What's going on with Mr. Scratch?" I called into the kitchen.

"Tumor!" Alice called back.

I touched his nose. Warm and dry.

Alice stepped into the doorway, wiping her hands on a dishrag. "Vet came out. Said all I could do was make him comfortable. Made him a spot in my bedroom, but he likes that chair, that last bit of sun, he does." She walked over and patted the old guy on the head, three little taps. "Dontcha, Mister?"

Mr. Scratch didn't so much as look at her. He was in bad shape.

He was actually Mr. Scratch number four. Each time one of Alice's cats died, she got another just like the last: all gray tabbies, all male, all named Mr. Scratch. Now that I think of it, the very first one was named Mittens, at least initially. Then Mom started calling him Mr. Scratch to keep little Alice from getting hurt. (Alice liked to pull his tail.)

"Alice," I said. "I'm so sorry. I had no idea what all you were dealing with."

A smile teased the edges of her mouth. "Welcome to Mama Headquarters, where we do the best we can, but it's never enough, by golly."

"Is Mom…" I didn't have a clue how to phrase what I wanted to ask, wasn't even sure what it was.

Alice glanced over her shoulder then spoke in a whisper. "It's like riding in the DeLorean time machine in *Back to the Future*. Jumps back and forth in time, she does, willy-nilly. It's worse when we go out, so we stopped."

"Do I feel a draft?" Mom yelled from the kitchen.

Alice nodded toward the open windows. "She hates it when the windows are open."

"But it's boiling in here."

"I feel a draft!" Mom yelled.

"I'll get her a sweater," I said.

Alice lifted an eyebrow.

"What?"

Alice didn't respond, just returned to the kitchen.

"Sweater in July?" Mom said when I came back with it. "Ridiculous!" Never mind that it was October.

When we finally sat down to dinner, Mom wouldn't stay in her seat. Said she had to get ready for her "guests," which essentially meant pulling items from the fridge and arranging them on every available surface. I couldn't stand it; I had to stop her. "Mom," I said, getting up from the table. "Nobody's coming. Sit down and eat. Alice has made us this beautiful meal."

She reared back and glared at me. "You keep it up, young lady, and I'm going to jerk a knot in your tail. You bet I will." A thing I'd heard her say a million times as a kid.

"Don't worry about it, sisteroo," Alice said to me. "Empties the fridge all the time, she does. Makes her hap-hap-happy." Then to Mom, "Nothing like opening your home to friends, is there? Quite the thrill it is."

Mom pulled a jar of relish from the fridge and set it next to the milk.

Later, I sat and watched Mom eat her now cold dinner while Alice washed dishes.

In between bites, she said, "When it comes right down to it, family is what counts." I had no idea if she was talking about us now, us from the past, or some other family entirely, but I tried to take it as a good sign, even if she was holding her fork upside down. I turned it over so Alice's excellent stir-fry wouldn't keep falling off.

The young man at the funeral parlor is a good egg. I'm told I met him yesterday. Apparently, he came out to the house at my request. I remember calling, and I remember talking with someone, but I don't remember him. As I said, I met a lot of people yesterday. And I was a wreck. I'm still a wreck, but a bit more coherent of a wreck. At least I hope so.

I managed to drive to the funeral parlor without incident this morning. I never should have let myself get out of the driving habit, but there you have it. Use it or lose it, as they say. And I haven't lost it entirely, not at all. Perhaps I'll do something daring like drive up the coast later in the week. The farmers should have their pumpkins out.

The funeral parlor itself is tastefully furnished: comfortable chairs, muted mauves and grays, fresh flowers. They've done everything possible to avoid the morbid, black ostrich feather plumes of the Victorian era. We don't do death like that anymore. Don't wear black clothing for months on end, no black armbands or veils to give people a heads up that we're in mourning. Nowadays, it's chop-chop and back to work with you. Or, in my case, chop-chop and back to the lackluster routine I call life.

I've turned into a bit of a recluse, it's true. Kim's death knocked the joie de vivre out of me. That's how Alice put it shortly after I moved in with her. We were in the backyard. She was replacing a rotting board on the fence; I was out fussing with a few of Kim's succulent pots, those I'd taken with me. They were all shriveled, mourning her green thumb, I'm sure, wondering at their bad luck being stuck with me, a human so depressed she could barely lift a watering can. Alice abruptly stopped her hammering and faced me. "You okay, old sport? You seem kind of down in the dumps."

I said, "I'm fine. Really."

"I don't think so," she shot back. "No, I do not. I think Kim's death knocked the joie de vivre right out of you, I do."

Doubtless I'd been taking too many trips to the bathroom. I didn't like crying in front of Alice. It agitated her and she'd get overly helpful, trying to find ways to fix the situation: milkshakes, a game of gin. The bathroom was my refuge. I took long showers to cover my sobbing. But she was right, I wasn't finding ways to motivate myself, hadn't kept up with my friends, and now I've lost touch with them entirely, though I recently received an email from one letting me know that Dune's Prince Charming had passed.

Dune and I drifted from one another's lives long ago. The last time I saw him was at Toi's memorial where he had the decency to make a brief appearance. I barely got a chance to say two words to him. I shouldn't be so judgmental. He and Paul would have been together for at least twelve years now, but when Dune fell in love, he forgot all about me and Toi, jumping into his new life with Paul's friends. It hurt at the time, but then, so it goes. People change. In truth, I enjoy this quiet life I've made for myself, my beach walks, my trips to the market, and Alice is—*was!*—plenty of company.

Now a new chapter is beginning. Alice is gone. It's up to me to mow the lawn, pay the bills, check the expiration dates on the food in the fridge, and, of course, to take care of the details of her passing. It all seems insurmountable. The funeral home is being helpful, though. They filed and ordered the death certificates, set up the cremation (not cheap!), encouraged me to honor Alice's memory by purchasing a pricey urn, which of course I didn't do. I told him I would come up with something. Nor did I want to hold a service. (Which I could tell was a disappointment for the nice young man, Matt, I think his name is, or perhaps it's Michael. I should have written it down.) I'll have some of the neighbors around for a can of Alice's favorite Red Bull, let them each choose one of her bottles. For anyone else I run into, who knew her, I'll offer them a bottle too. I've no idea what I will do with the rest of them. There are 139 in total. The 140th is under way, an underwater scene, all kelp and pretty fishes. Ironic, or prophetic, seeing as Alice's favorite euphemism for death was "swimming with the fishies." The bottles are all stored in the garage, much like a wine cellar, each with a little card stating its title and date of completion.

She moved them out there when people started taking an interest in her work, turned the garage into a proper art studio.

And still, the dreaded obit waits to be written. I just can't bring myself to do it. Not yet. Not until I come clean about what we did.

VERONICA LAKE, THE ISLAND OF LILLIPUT,
AND THE BIG BAD SNEAKER WAVE

All I wanted was a little time alone with my new best friend, Table Red. That, and some peace and quiet to process what to do next. But Alice, feeling excited, or anxious, probably both, to see me, had rented *The Great Gatsby*—the 1974 version with Robert Redford and Mia Farrow—as our evening's entertainment. I got the feeling she and Mom watched movies every night, but not *The Great Gatsby*. That was special; that was Alice's favorite.

Having no intention of propping my exhausted self up in the rigid kitchen chair that Alice had set out for me, I pulled a couple of outdoor cushions off a backyard lounger and made myself a pallet on the dull hardwood floor. We watched a lot of movies growing up. A lot of TV too. It was all part of Mom's plan to make Alice normal. Who better to school her in the ways of human interaction than the people who did it for a living? At least, that was Mom's thinking. But for all Mom's "Do you think Veronica Lake would give one hoot if her schoolbook got a little scuffed?" and "I don't think Rita Hayworth is too proud to shake someone's hand," the only thing Alice ever picked up from Mom's Hollywood regimen was her love of movies and a collection of odd phrases and gestures that peppered her dialogue.

Alice glanced down at me sprawled on my makeshift divan. "Best part ever." Her hands were clasped tightly in her lap, her body rigid with excitement. I think she identified with the tortured Jay Gatsby, recognized in him a kindred spirit, a man who never truly fit in.

"Here he comes…Here he comes…" She was talking about the scene in which Daisy first sees Gatsby in the mirror and is overcome with astonishment. I can't imagine it was the romance of it that Alice loved. She was pretty much asexual. Well, there was a brief period in high school when she'd blush around boys, but it didn't last long.

Either something happened or she just decided it wasn't for her, which wouldn't surprise me. The complications of love would have been messy for Alice.

"Shall we have some tea?" Mom said along with Nick Buchanan. Then she farted.

"Mom!" I said.

"Does that all the time, she does," Alice said, not taking her eyes from the screen. "Don't you, Mom?"

"Maybe you shouldn't give her so much broccoli."

"Broccoli is very healthful," Mom said, "delicious too."

I heaved myself up from the floor. "I'm going to get more…" I stopped myself from saying *wine.* "Can I get anything else for anybody?"

"Not me," Alice said. "Right as rain, I am."

I took Mom's lack of response as a *no* and proceeded to the kitchen where I filled my mug of wine and drank it down. Then I filled it again to prepare myself for Jay Gatsby's being shot for something he didn't do.

❖

Sleep was impossible. The room was too stuffy, the bed too lumpy, as Goldilocks would say. I had the one window open but had to keep the door shut, so was unable to create any kind of cross draft. Mom may have had no idea what year it was or who she was talking to, but she knew, by God, if there was a window open anywhere in the house. I couldn't imagine how Alice stood it. And then there were the bottles.

At some point, I couldn't handle one more second of those tiny people waiting for me to nod off. I pictured them going back to their tiny lives the moment my breathing changed. I felt around on the crate nightstand for my watch. It was 12:30. I'd been lying there over two hours. I'd slunk off after helping Alice put Mom to bed. I say helped, but Mom wouldn't let me touch her, which in this case was a relief. The vision of the two of them standing by the toilet, Mom leaning into Alice so Alice could pat her privates with a wad of toilet paper had been swimming laps around my brain for the last hour.

I got up, flicked on the overhead light, and found myself staring at a miniature *Night of the Living Dead.* I reached under the bed for

my purse, pulled out a small notepad, and made a list of things rattling
around in my brain, hoping to put them temporarily to rest.

1. Broach the subject of adult diapers for Mom.
2. Talk to doctor about the handful of pills she's taking.
    What are they? And does she really need them all?
3. Talk to Alice about the bakery. How's it doing? Is it time
    to sell it?
4. Call vet about Mr. Scratch.
5. Buy Mom some new floats.
6. Call Toi and ask her to water plants.
7. Call Dune and ask him if June Fernberger has made up
    her mind about icing.
8. Bills?

I still couldn't sleep. So I rolled out of the squeaky bed, pulled on
my jeans and T-shirt, grabbed my flip-flops, and tiptoed barefoot out to
the backyard. It was wonderfully cool outside—too cool for the way
I was dressed, but I didn't want to risk waking Mom by going back
inside. I slipped on my flip-flops. A mockingbird was singing its little
heart out, trilling and scolding, rasping and clucking. It was nice to
know someone else was up.

I noticed a thread of light peeking out from under the garage
door, heard a soft shuffling coming from within. I sauntered over and
cracked open the door. Alice stood at the workbench wearing goggles
and holding a soldering iron, an amusing juxtaposition against her kilt
and knee socks. "Hey, old sport," she said. "Hope I didn't wake you."

"Naw. I couldn't sleep. What are you working on?"

She put down the soldering iron and the teeny tiny thing she'd
been soldering, then held up what initially looked like a long matchbook
with a string coming out its side. She pulled the string, and the
matchbook-looking thing rose up to the beginnings of what was clearly
a barbershop. Everything but the barber's chair. "*Sweeney Todd*," she
said. "I'm working on the chair. It's tricky. Have to place it into the
bottle after the shop. Still have to make the bakery and meat pies."

Her subject matter never failed to amaze. "Cool." I'm sure she
was hoping for a more enthusiastic response, but I was too wired and
tired to come up with one. "I'm going for a walk." I noticed a navy blue
hoodie hanging by the door. "Can I wear this?"

"Did you neglect to bring your own, sister of mine?"

"I have a sweater inside, but I don't want to wake Mom."

She considered this, then said, "Under the circumstances, I will allow you to wear my sweater, but please, in the future, wear your own."

I spotted her old, green three-speed cruiser leaning against the wall. I gestured to it. "Can I borrow this too?"

She pursed her lips. "It's night. I don't have a light." Which I doubted very much. Alice knew how to lie. I'm the one who taught her. As a kid, she'd blurt things out like: *That woman's fat! She needs to go on a diet!* Or, at the grocery: *Mom, you can't go in that line. You have eleven items! It says only ten.* Any deception would drive her crazy. So I worked with her. I figured I was doing her a favor, that it would help her make friends. Besides, I reasoned, any child of Hugh and Euvie Mustin needed to know how to lie. It was pure survival. That Alice got to be so good at it, well, that was all on her.

"Have you looked outside?" I said, my hand resting on the handlebar. "The moon is outrageous."

She tried to ignore me.

"Come on, Alice. Please?"

She released a heavy sigh. "O-*kay*."

I flipped the kickstand back. "Thanks, sis."

I hadn't been on a bike in years so was a little wobbly at first, but by the end of the block, I was cruising and reached the bay in no time. It was breezy on the cliff-side bike path. I welcomed the fresh air, the moonlight icing the waves and silver glazing the tall rocks. A wispy string of clouds passed in front of the almost-full moon and made for a dramatic show of shadow and light.

I rode out to the lighthouse—home to one of the best surfing spots in the country, Steamer's Lane. There, I got off the bike and climbed over the safety rail to the rock outcropping overlooking the bay. I didn't want anything between me and the pounding surf. The cold metal of the safety rail pressed into my spine as I settled onto the sandy outcropping, bent knees pulled to my chest. I felt like a speck in the universe. Smaller, even.

Grief, I knew from the death of my dad, showed up at the most unexpected times: when a guy in line at the bank smelled of Old Spice, or out shopping and finding a sale on argyle socks. Still, I wasn't prepared for a surge of grief before my mother was even dead. Sneaker waves, the Coast Guard call them. They come out of nowhere and snatch people up, the lone eight-footer rising from an otherwise glassy sea. Bam! And so the grief hit me. One minute I was feeling pretty good about my midnight ride, the next I was sobbing so hard I could barely breathe. Waves were crashing, sea lions barking, and all I could do was cry and cry. My mom was gone. Gone! And I didn't get a chance to say good-bye. The pain was excruciating and felt so different from losing my dad, who went from fully living to being fully dead, his heart simply saying "Enough!" that day at the bakery. This was different. Cruel. Mom was there, but not there. The anger I'd been holding on to since my dad's funeral had nowhere to land, so it turned on me instead. How could I have been so petty? So pigheaded?

Memories of Mom bombarded my brain: her painting our solid oak kitchen table red because she thought the kitchen needed "a little brightening," her kissing her hand and slapping the dashboard of our gray Comet before backing out of the driveway, her cinching in my bra with tape and staples so I'd show more cleavage in my prom dress, and that ability she had to turn a neighborhood squabble into an almost mythic tale of heartbreak and loss. She'd even end it with some thought-provoking ironic twist because she didn't believe in happily ever after, said if happiness were that easy to come by, she'd have found it by now.

I blotted my tears on the sleeve of Alice's hoodie, blew my nose into my hands, then wiped the snot onto a patch of scrappy grass growing out of the rocks. I needed to get back to the house; its undertow was tugging at me. Exhausted and shaky, I stood, dried my eyes one last time, then straddled the safety rail. That's when I spotted two wetsuited surfers sitting upright on their boards in a shimmering patch of ocean. They must have been there all along, surfing in and out of the shadows, I just hadn't seen them. A set of waves lifted and dropped them. Lifted and dropped. I got the feeling they weren't so much surfing as enjoying each other's company. I began to tremble.

To have someone to stand by me through life's many crests and dips, to hold me when it felt as though my soul were being cleft from my body, suddenly, I wanted that so badly I would have traded in all my earthly goods for just one taste of it, would have sold my soul. Not that I missed any of my old relationships. Even while I was in them they felt like placeholders for the real deal. But didn't there have to be someone, somewhere, who would make my life easier, not harder? Someone who would love me for who I was, not for who I *could* be? Of course, I reasoned, love like that was a two-way street. Maybe it wasn't so much that I was unlovable, as that I was incapable of loving. Tears once again blurring my vision, I turned my back on the surfers and continued over the fence to safety, dislodging an envelope from the pocket of Alice's hoodie. I snatched it up off the ground before the breeze whisked it out to sea.

It was something official, but the moon wasn't bright enough to make out exactly what. I strolled over to the streetlamp of the adjacent parking lot. I had to. The larger-than-life night made the ordinary falling of an envelope from a pocket seem like destiny.

Leaning against the lamppost, I stared at what was now clearly a bank statement for the bakery. On the surface such a commonplace thing. But for me it was so much more than that. The Plaza Bakery, my dad's last business venture, and not his most intelligent one.

He'd grown tired of his vending machine business. While lucrative, it didn't provide the sense of community he longed for in his old age. The machines had grown tired, too, and needed to be replaced. On top of that, someone had been robbing them. So on a whim, he sold the business and bought the Plaza Bakery, a mainstay at the time, at the top of the outdoor Garden Mall in Santa Cruz. He bought it from an old Italian who knew most of his customers by name. It was an old-fashioned bakery that sold cookies by the pound, tiny cookies scooped into pink boxes and tied up with string, cookies dusted in powdered sugar and, what would now be considered toxic, sprinkles. None of the specialty ones boasting "80% cacao!" and "gluten-free!" that are so popular now. What my dad had failed to recognize was that the majority of loyal clientele was well over eighty and dying off. And die they did in those first five years. Plus, my dad knew nothing about baking. The old Italian, a savvy businessman, had convinced him that if he kept the staff, the bakery could run itself. And maybe if my dad had been able to do this, to let the staff run the place, it might have done better. But my dad didn't buy the bakery to let it run itself, he bought the bakery to run it, because that's what my dad did, he bought businesses and then he ran them. Honestly, I think the timing was just bad. The eighties were a time of big hair, big boom boxes, and big cookies. The Pacific Cookie Company had just opened up and was serving plate-sized cookies with names like Dr. Midnight and Mint Condition. My dad never stood a chance, but he never stopped trying. He called me all the time asking about this recipe or that one. And, to his credit, he listened sometimes. But he was also listening to those eighty-somethings who, although few in number, were still ringing the cash register.

When he died, Mom talked about selling the bakery, then somehow never got around to it. She and Alice, who used to work the counter, replaced themselves, and took on more managerial duties. That was my understanding. It was also my understanding that the bakery was doing okay financially. That is until I looked at that bank statement. The place was barely breaking even.

I squinted up at that big moon and prayed I had the strength to do what was being asked of me. To untangle the mother of all knots: my family, or what was left of us. The sea lions barked hysterically.

THE ESCAPE HATCH

Day two of Santa Cruz, I woke obsessing over what to do about the bakery. Mom was so far gone she no longer knew how to wipe herself—and I was thinking about the bakery. Her dementia had turned Alice into a prisoner—and I was thinking about the bakery. I don't know what psychologists call this kind of reassignment of worries, where a person dumps worries about one situation onto another. Transference? Projection? Denial? But that is what I did, plain and simple. That's how freaked out I was, and how much I didn't want to move to Santa Cruz. Or move Mom to Portland. Or kick Alice out of her home. These were the three options when it came right down to it. Without selling the house, we didn't have the money for in-home care or to put her somewhere, and we couldn't—wouldn't!—put her in some government nursing home. I'd delivered a ninety-sixth birthday cake to one once, and it was the saddest place I'd ever seen. But if I could swing it to where the bakery would bring in a decent profit, we could hire a live-in caregiver, remodeling the garage into a studio apartment where she could stay.

Without changing out of my rumpled sweats and tee, I strolled into the living room where Mom was watching a movie. The sound was close to inaudible.

"Coffee?" Alice called from the kitchen.

"Yes, please."

Coffee was the only thing in those wine-drinking days that made getting out of bed seem like a good idea. Coffee and a good hour to myself. I shuffled into the kitchen, sloshed coffee into one of the thick white ceramic cups that looked like they'd been swiped from a diner, mumbled some kind of morning greeting to Alice, who was sitting at the table hunched over what looked like bills. She looked up. "Do you still have my sweatshirt?"

"Uh. Yeah. In my room. Do you want me to get it?"

"Not this second, but please return it to its hook at your first convenience."

"Will do. Did I park the bike right?" We were falling into one of our old patterns; Alice trying to rein in my carelessness; me, trying to get her to lighten up. "Was it facing the right way?"

She shrugged and returned to her paperwork, but it was obvious I hadn't put the bike back correctly.

I headed into the backyard, where I was assaulted by the sound of the neighbor's lawnmower and its cloud of dust. I made an about-face into the kitchen. So much for my hour to myself.

"Hungry?" Alice spoke without looking up. "There be bagels in the breadbox."

"Not yet, but thanks. I'm going to visit with Mom."

The gold brocade curtains in the living room were shut tightly, casting a depressing gloom on the emptied out room, the straight-back chair and lounger cushions from the night before returned, I assumed, to their "proper" places; it was just the two chairs now, and the TV, of course, always the TV. I walked over to open the curtains.

"Watch the draft!" Mom said before I'd even pulled the cord.

"Just letting in a little light."

"It'll let in the draft."

"We open them after lunch," Alice yelled from the kitchen. "That usually works."

Hearing the two voices confused Mom. She squinted at me, her eyes full of suspicion. "Who are you?"

"Lucy. Your daughter."

She looked at me as if I'd just spoken Chinese, then turned back to the TV.

I had no reason to be hurt. I knew that. Her brain was malfunctioning, not her heart. Still. I settled into Alice's green wingback and took a sip of coffee. It was good, a dark, oily brew I hoped wouldn't roil the acid in my stomach too much. "How's the movie?"

"Good," Mom said.

She was wearing the pink and green floral float I'd sent for Christmas. That was something. Her hair was combed but not styled, and her face lightly dusted with powder. Alice's work, I assumed. A pair of ivory colored leather slippers rested on the floor beneath the recliner's footstool where her bare feet were propped up. The length of her toenails was both amazing and horrifying. Ten little shovels. Someone was going to have to deal with them. The thought made me queasy. I took another sip of coffee. They'd have to wait. At least until the caffeine kicked in. Maybe even until after I'd gone by the bakery.

"So what's the movie?" I asked the side of my mother's head. I was trying to sneak up on her by sounding casual, like I was someone who was around all the time.

There was no telling from the generic car chase going on: a black panel van in hot pursuit of a red Camaro. Lots of sound effects, little or no dialogue. With the sound down so low, the smashes and crashes sounded like muffled little poofs and pops. But I could tell the good guy from the bad. Good Guy had a cool swoopy hairdo, perfect teeth, and a nice car, while the bad guy had greasy skin and blackened teeth, and was just plain ugly. I remember thinking it convenient that the good and bad were so clearly delineated: good=pretty teeth, bad=ugly teeth.

"What're we watching?" I asked again.

Her powdered brow furrowed as she tried to come up with something. "My show," she said at last, and seemed quite pleased with herself for this tricky maneuvering.

I took that as a win. She hadn't recoiled from me.

Good Guy pulled into oncoming traffic, his pursuers hot on his trail. Panicked drivers careened into a roadside ditch to keep from hitting them.

"Right," I said. "Your show. That sounds good."

She spoke without looking at me, the way TV-watching people do. "Evie should be dressed soon. Then we can go. Don't forget the deviled eggs." She laughed. "Oh, wouldn't that beat all. To forget the eggs after all that work."

I wanted to jump into her experience so badly, to see her and Aunt Evokia getting ready for wherever it was they were going. I missed Aunt Evokia acutely. No one helped me negotiate Mom the way she did. "Deviled eggs are ready to go. We're good on that."

Mass carnage broke out on the TV highway, cars slamming into one another right and left. But Good Guy and Bad Guy remained unscathed, uncaring, their mutual hatred binding them together like the two ends of a Slinky.

"Are you staying for lunch?" Mom asked.

"Today is Turkey and Cheese Wednesday!" Alice called from the kitchen.

"Yes, I'm staying." Then to Alice, "Yes! Thank you!"

The neckline of Mom's float was askew, accentuating her neck, the skin sinewy and pale.

"Turkey and Cheese Wednesday," I said. "Mmm."

Good Guy careened off a bridge and was trying madly to unhook his seat belt as water seeped into the cracks around the windows. After several tries, Good Guy got the seat belt unhooked and started fumbling to unroll the window. Water gushed into the Camaro.

I pinched the bridge of my nose to keep from crying. I didn't want to upset Mom. Surely a little food would help. Hadn't Alice said something about bagels? I got up, kissed Mom softly on the top of the head, and was grateful beyond words that she didn't recoil. Maybe we were making progress. On my way to the kitchen, I nearly tripped over Mr. Scratch crouched in a square of sun by the doorway. He was panting, his eyes gluey, his coat matted. Was there no corner in this house that wasn't filled with despair? I bent down and pinched his skin to see if he was dehydrated. "Any appetite?" I asked Alice.

"Mom or the cat?"

I'd meant the cat, but said, "Both, I guess."

"Mom, yes. Cat, no. You saw Mom eat last night, old sport."

"Seems dehydrated," I said.

"Mom or the cat?"

"Mr. Scratch." I was in no mood. "I saw Mom drink last night. Remember?"

Alice looked up from her bills, her Clark Kents pushed snugly up on the bridge of her nose. She blinked several times as if trying to bring something past my right shoulder into focus. Her eyelashes, long and lush, were accentuated by the thick lenses. "Mom's used to you being on the phone, old sport."

That stung, although I don't believe Alice meant it to. She was just speaking the truth.

"Is there an eyedropper in the house? I want to see if I can get Mr. Scratch to take some water."

She pointed to Mr. Scratch's bowl. Next to it was a green saucer with an eyedropper on it. "May the Force be with you."

I got up and stretched. My neck snap-crackle-popped, but the coffee was doing its job, prying fissures through the muddiness. I picked up Mr. Scratch. I might have had no idea what to do with my mother, but I sure as hell knew what to do with a dehydrated cat. Holding him under my arm, I snatched up the eyedropper and bowl. "What does the vet say?"

"I told you yesterday. To make him as comfortable as possible."

I took the chair across from Alice, clumps of gray hair coming off in my hands. "You're not a comfortable cat, are you, Mister?" I stroked him a bit, trying to relax him, then squeezed the sides of his jaw open and dribbled a dropperful of water into his mouth. It pooled there as if his throat were on strike, or plugged. He twisted in my lap, trying to get free, but the poor little guy didn't have the umph. I rubbed under his chin to encourage him to swallow. He turned his head from one side to the other. The water slid down his fur. I glanced at Alice. She was busily writing checks.

"Those for the bakery?"

She spoke without looking up. "Indeed they are. It's payroll time—everyone's favorite day of the month, young and old alike."

"You know, I was thinking about the bakery. If we could just—"

Alice abruptly scooting her chair out from beneath the table cut my sentence short. She didn't follow through and stand, just sat there in pause mode. Whatever she had to say, I was sure had to do with me. Excuses lined up in my head, little soldiers, each one ready to do battle on my behalf. She gripped the edge of the table. My excuses huddled together, forming a wall.

"Drew is the one who delivers the groceries," she finally blurted. She was talking to the salt and pepper shaker more than to me. "I pay extra. But not much. Very affordable when you think about it. Considering he's using his own car. It's his business. To take groceries to people. He works at a bar too. At night. He bartends. He doesn't drink himself. Or so he says."

Alice's rapid-fire patter could mean any number of things. That she was upset, excited, scared. It was exasperating to listen to, because she'd start miles away from her point, filling in details you in no way needed to know. But that morning all I could think was: *Thank God it's not about something else I've done wrong.*

"Is he a friend of yours?" I asked, trying to hone in on her target.

"Not a friend, no. Not really. He just delivers. But he came in the house one time. He needed to borrow the bathroom. I didn't want to let him. Mom was napping and I didn't want him to wake her. But he was feeling desperate. That's what he said. And I know what that's like. Indeed I do. I can't eat dried fruit anymore. Not if I plan to go out. No siree bob. Gives me the Hershey squirts, it does. But mostly we just talk in the yard. Sometimes I bring him a glass of water. Or juice. He likes juice. Especially Cranapple. But came in that one time, he did."

I began to have a bad feeling about where this was leading. "Did he hurt you, Alice?"

This stopped her dead. "Hurt me? No. Why would you say that? Drew is nice. He always offers to bring the groceries inside. But I don't let him. Mom doesn't like it. Gets confused, she does."

Mr. Scratch squirmed in my lap. I gave him a few more pats and placed him gently on the floor. My black sweats were covered in gray hair. He padded weakly back to his patch of sunlight. "So why are you telling me about Drew? Why is all this important for me to know?"

Alice scooted her chair back in under the table and returned to her pile of checks, stacking them neatly and stuffing them into a manila envelope. Whatever was going on had her very upset. "Saw my bottles, he did. Walked down the hall, he did. Couldn't very well help but notice, could he? Thought they were very good. Very creative. That's what he said. That I should bring a few down to the bar. That maybe the owner would like to have them there. For people to look at. While they're drinking. I could go this morning."

I cannot tell you the relief I felt. The whole song and dance had simply been Alice's attempt at bragging, a behavior that always made her uncomfortable. I got up to make another pot of coffee. "That's so cool. Do it this morning. I was going to head down to the bakery. If you want I'll deliver the pay—" My sentence could not be completed due to a head-on collision with reality.

Alice wasn't bragging, she was asking a favor—a behavior she hated even more than bragging. Mom could not be left alone. If I wanted to go to the bakery I would have to take her with me, which was unthinkable. To be dragged off by someone she didn't know, or didn't think she knew, in a strange car, to a strange place…well, it wasn't an option.

Alice gripped the envelope of checks, her gaze focused somewhere just beyond them. Likely, she'd been dying to take her bottles down to the bar for weeks, months, who knew how long, but had been unable. And now, here I was, her escape hatch.

"So, um…" I stuttered, and dumped the wet coffee grounds into the trash can. "You should do it, take them. I can, um, stay home and cut Mom's toenails."

Alice slapped the envelope of checks down on the table. "Aaaaand, ladies and gentlemen, we have a winner! Alice Mustin of Santa Cruz, California, gets to take her bottles to the Catalyst, a feat she's been trying to accomplish for weeks on end!"

"Okay, okay." I peeled a new coffee filter off the pack. "Enough with the histrionics."

She stood up. Then sat down. Then stood up again. "Where, oh where to begin? Check the air in my bike tires? Wrap the bottles? Put on a clean shirt?"

"Do you know which bottles you're taking?"

"Affirmative, Captain. Had those picked out Day One."

"Well then, get to it, girl! I'll just have myself another cup of coffee and a bagel and then *I'll* get to it!" It was hard not to get caught up in her enthusiasm. "I assume I'll find everything I need in the bathroom? Clippers? File?"

"Yes indeedy. I'll get them for you, I will." She sped out of the kitchen.

I felt good, useful, for the first time since arriving. I'd spend the morning with Mom, the two of us getting used to each other. Maybe I'd sing to her. See if I could get her to join in. She was always singing when we were kids: Hank Williams, Johnny Cash. I hummed the "Dog House Blues" as I scooped fresh coffee into the Mr. Coffee. "By the way," I called to Alice. "I can take the payroll checks in this afternoon when you get back. I want to go by the bakery to see how it's doing."

Alice appeared in the kitchen doorway, pale as milk and breathing heavily. "She's cut and run."

I took a step forward stubbing my toe on the chair. "Ouch! What?"

"You left the gate open when you came in last night. She's gone. So is her walker."

"Shit!" I charged out the back door, letting it slam behind me, unwilling to believe Alice's assessment, belatedly realizing I wasn't wearing shoes. Tiptoeing my tender Portland feet over the prickly drought-stricken, burr-covered lawn, I checked behind the shed and in the garage, circled the house, peered out the front gate, up and down the street. Alice was right, Mom was gone. Unless she was still in the house. I dashed back to the living room.

Alice was sitting cross-legged on the floor, wrapping several of her bottles in newspaper.

"Alice, wha—? We need to find Mom."

"You said I could take my bottles."

"Christ!" I stampeded through the house, took one last look, grabbing my flip-flops along the way. "You can take them later! We need to find Mom. We'll take my car."

How pathetic the next few hours were! Me, behind the wheel, turning this way and that; Alice navigating—reluctantly, very reluctantly. She was as mad as she got. It made no sense to her why I couldn't do this myself. She had. She would. And we'd made a deal. Deals were deals. I didn't have the energy to argue. I was just glad she was there.

"Turn here," she'd say. "She might be at the salon." Apparently, Mom did this enough that Alice knew her spots, or possible spots. It was more than I could fathom. "Or her friend Rosie's. If Rosie's not there she'll be on the back porch on the chair." Alice would wait in the car, leaving me to race into the various businesses, knock on the various doors. The night before I'd been sobbing my eyes out because I'd *felt* like I'd lost my mom; now I really *had* lost her, for there was no doubt in either Alice's or my mind that I was to blame for this torturous junket.

Ultimately, I found her at Safeway—a good three-quarters of a mile from the house—without her walker. We found that early on in our search, in somebody's driveway. (How Mom managed to get all that way without it remains a mystery.) She was standing in the health and beauty aisle—where else?—bracing herself on a shopping cart. It was filled with an array of beauty products, also a bunch of pasta, two eggplants, and six cans of tuna. I was so relieved to see her my knees started to buckle. She was chatting with the store manager, a kindly man with a thin mustache.

I rushed down the aisle toward them. "Mom!"

You could tell she had no idea who I was, but that she didn't want to seem rude. She patted at her limp hair, glanced coyly at the store manager, then back at me. Men always brought out the Yam Queen in her. "There you are," she said brightly, pretending she knew me. The leafy web in her hair, the streak of dirt on her arm, made her theatrics all the more tragic. "I was just telling…" She shot another look at the store manager, hoping he'd supply his name. Of course he did. Who could resist such old-fashioned Hollywood charm, even when it was coming from a doddering old woman in a stained housedress? "…Yes, Steve…" she went on, "…how I cannot get either of my girls interested in their hair. Both of them could have such beautiful hair if they just made the effort."

If a heart can break, mine surely did in that instant. Hair care had been a lifelong battle in our household. While I liked the slight wave in my hair, Mom was always trying to get me to accentuate it by sleeping in rollers or getting a perm. And Alice, well, you can imagine.

I reached out my hand to Steve, painfully aware that I'd rushed out of the house wearing tattered, cat-hair covered black sweatpants and without having brushed my teeth. "Hi. I'm Lucy. One of the daughters."

He had a flaccid yet friendly handshake. "You have a lovely mother."

"Thank you. I hope she hasn't—"

"No, no." He waved his palms like opposing windshield wipers. I wondered briefly if he was gay. "But she does seem a little confused. One of my employees brought her to my attention. I was just trying to figure out—"

Mom banged her shopping cart into a shelf of hairspray, dislodging several cans of Aqua Net. "Uh-oh. Look what I've done."

I took hold of the cart; he bent down to pick up the Aqua Net.

"Mom, where do you think you're going?" I said it teasingly, trying to put her at ease. My appearance rattled her. She seemed to know something wasn't right.

"I'm plumb tuckered out! I need to put my feet up."

I thought of her toenails digging into those leather slippers. At least she'd had the wherewithal to slide them on. "I'm sorry," I said to Steve the Safeway guy. "I should get her home. Is it too much of a bother if—" I gestured to the cart with its odd assortment of things.

"That's fine," he said. "I'll get one of the stock clerks to put things back. You just get her home."

It took some doing to get Mom to give up the cart. I had to convince her we were stepping outside for just a second and would be back for the cart momentarily. She gripped my arm as we walked through the swoosh of the sliding glass doors. Whether she recognized me or not, she put her trust in me, at least for those few moments.

"What were you thinking?" I teased her. "Walking all this way? I would have driven you to the market." I was so embarrassed for her, or for the mom she used to be who would have died to see herself like this.

"Oh! Would you look at that!" Mom pointed at a harried-looking mother and her child. "That negra's child is running around like a little pickaninny!"

Now I was embarrassed for me. I glanced around to make sure

no one had heard. Racist language had been part of her upbringing, but she'd always prided herself on "Rising above the ignorance of the South," as she put it.

"Mom, you sound like a bigot."

She slapped my arm. "Don't be silly."

We made our way back to the car without further incident, Alice less than helpful. The morning fog had burned off and the world was blindingly bright. Not for the first time since we'd taken off that morning, I wished I'd thought to grab my sunglasses.

Mom wanted nothing to do with my car. I convinced her it was fine, a friend's car, on loan. She bought the white lie but wanted to sit in the front—meaning Alice had to move, which Alice wasn't happy about. She slammed out of the front passenger door, slammed into the back. I tried to cajole her out of her mood. "Does Mom even like eggplant?"

"Unknown. To my knowledge she's never tried it. *Now* can I go do my bottles?"

"You don't even want to hear about it? About how I found her?"

"Why?" Alice said. "She's back."

Just returned from my walk. I made it all the way to the Lighthouse. The waves were tall, clean. Surfers were crawling all over them and the cliffs. Life goes on. Which brings me to Alice's obit. I'm still resisting writing it. I have to get it to the paper by Friday. It's Tuesday. There's time. But it weighs on me. How can I describe her in so few words? Alice would say: *Just tell them that I'm dead, old sport, so they don't expect me to show up somewhere.*

This afternoon, I stood in front of her closet of kilts, intending to empty it, and had a good cry instead. It felt odd to be in her room. I am so rarely. We were both very particular about our rooms. I didn't want her straightening mine up; she didn't want me so much as placing a letter on her dresser. No chance of that now. Sooner or later, I'm going to have to empty hers out, though.

But the day hasn't been a total waste. I wrote out a list of businesses that need to be contacted: gas and electric company, phone company, insurance…I need to get them out of her name and into mine. And I watered the succulent pots. (I've kept only those that refuse to die.) Once again, I am thrust into taking responsibility. It will be only one Social Security check now; that's going to be an issue. Property taxes are high: what was once a quirky college town has turned into the Silicon Coast; real estate is going through the roof. I could sell, but have no desire to move. Where would I go? I'm told I should consider a reverse mortgage. I'll have to look into that. Securing one might be a bit tricky. Alice stipulates in her will that, upon my death, or if I should sell the house, her half of the proceeds go to *Save the Frogs*. In the last few years, their plight gripped her. She managed to fit their possible extinction into any conversation. "Tadpoles help keep waterways clean," she'd say, greeting me first thing in the morning. "Eat algae, they do."

I wonder if the last frog alive will know that it is?

THE CANDY CLUB

Mom conked out in front of the TV as soon as we got back. Alice went back to bubble-wrapping bottles, like nothing had happened. Like we hadn't almost lost Mom. By contrast, I was shaking like a leaf! And starving. I made myself a sandwich. Offered to make Alice one too, but she wasn't interested. I had a strong urge to phone Toi or Dune—I needed a dose of sanity—but the phone was in the hall, meaning no privacy. Plus, I didn't want to wake Mom. So, sandwich in hand, I escaped to the back deck where Alice's bottle-wrapping operation was in full swing, where the *snuff puff snuff puff* of Mom's snoring wasn't quite so distracting.

"You sure you don't want to eat before you go? I'll make you a sandwich."

Alice didn't look up. "Sure as eggs is eggs. Gotta catch the daytime manager, the big man on campus. Doesn't stick around all day, he doesn't." She was sitting cross-legged on the back deck; she made it look effortless. Clearly, we hadn't inherited the same knees.

I wiped a few leaves from what I was beginning to think of as "my" lounger and settled onto it, placing my paper-towel-wrapped sandwich on my lap and my bottle of iced tea on the giant spool that served as a table. The Oregonian in me was grateful for the shade the house provided.

At some point, Alice had changed into a new, fancier ivory and maroon kilt and a button-down blouse. Each had the crisp folds of never having been worn. I peeled a clump of cat hair from my rumpled sweatpants. A neighbor revved up a Weedwacker. Alice's shoulders climbed up her neck. She was sensitive to sound.

I sank my teeth into the spongy white bread of my sandwich. It was like biting into a cloud. Once I'd swallowed, I said, "Remember when we used to make little balls from this kind of bread?"

"There's whole grain in the freezer."

"I wasn't criticizing."

She ripped a piece of bubble wrap from the roll. Clearly, she was upset with me.

"I don't know my way around Santa Cruz," I said defensively. "I needed your help. I'm sorry it got in the way of you bringing your bottles to the bar."

She ripped another piece, carefully laid it onto her pile, and began wrapping up a miniature *Psycho*—the shower scene.

"Cool. You're taking Hitchcock."

She wrapped the next five bottles acting like I hadn't said a word, like I wasn't sitting there, making me feel like a giant gnat. I thought again about calling Toi or Dune, pictured myself grabbing up my car keys and searching out a pay phone. But what could they say that would make me feel better? *Good luck? Hang in there? Come home soon?* I needed more than that. I needed someone who knew Mom, who knew she wasn't always a mixed-up old lady, who remembered how, when Mom didn't feel like cooking, she'd take us out for banana splits, saying, "Dairy and fruit, you could do a lot worse!" I needed my sister. I needed Alice.

"Could you at least talk to me?"

"About what?"

"I don't know. You? What you've been up to?"

Alice picked at a roll of packing tape that had stuck to itself. "The caretaking of an elderly parent often drains the caretaker of any of the leisure time to which he or she is accustomed."

"So you've been taking care of Mom. I haven't. But I'm here now."

She found the end of the tape and stretched it free of the roll. "Just speaking the facts, ma'am. I've had little time on my hands to pursue my heart's desire."

"What about the bakery? How's that going?"

"Baked goods are made; baked goods are sold."

"Is it making any money?"

"I would have to answer a resounding no to that question. But it breaks even, which I consider quite the feat in this economy, I do. An American success story, you might say. Dad's legacy lives on."

"Cool. I'll go check it out when you get back. I'd like to see if there's anything we could do to up productivity. Maybe change the menu. If we could get it to make a profit, maybe we could—"

Alice retreated into the garage at the same time as the weed-whacking down the street ceased, leaving me with my fluffy sandwich and the distant *snuff puff* of Mom's snoring. A blue damselfly landed briefly on my bent knee, darted a few feet forward, then returned to my knee. It did this again and again until, finally, it returned with a tiny insect in its mouth. And so it goes, I thought as I watched it devour its prey, one minute you're minding your own business and the next you're somebody's lunch.

Alice returned with her bike in tow and proceeded to check the tires.

"Tires were fine last night," I said.

This didn't stop her. Mind you, Alice had a driver's license. She just didn't like to drive. Hence, the bird shit–covered Acura in the driveway.

"Well, what do *you* think we should do with Mom?" I'd given up on discretion. "It's obviously not working now. It's too much for you."

"You moving here would place you in the needed proximity to be helpful."

"Alice, I have my business, my life."

Alice began pumping up her bike tires. *Pfft! Pfft! Pfft!* "Bingo bango. You have a life." Then, in three methodical stages, she flipped the bike up on its handlebars, so as not to get any oil on her kilt or blouse, and began oiling the chain with 3-in-One. "I have to tell you, sisteroo. It's getting harder and harder to care."

"Alice, she's our mother."

"*Was* our mother. What you have in there," she nodded toward the snoring in the house, "is a living organism that shoots out memories willy-nilly. She eats, produces bowel movements, passes gas, walks, and sleeps, but she is unable to learn, unable to recognize the effects of her actions, and while she most certainly does feel emotions—you've seen that, oh boy, have you—she doesn't remember feeling them. Nor are her feelings necessarily appropriate to the given situation. No. No. No. *And* she's getting worse every day, she is, *and* doesn't know it. For a while she did. 'Am I losing my mind, Allie?' she'd say. 'Am I?' But she doesn't say that anymore. No indeedy-doo, she does not. This is not our mother of yesteryear, Lucy-loo. That mother has packed up shop and bought a one-way ticket to La La Land." Alice adjusted her glasses, which, due to the intense delivery of her words, had slipped down her nose a notch. "If we're going to be making plans about what to do with her, you'd best remember that, old sport."

Her frank assessment of the situation made me cry. "Alice, I'm freaking out here," I said between sobs. "Could you cut me some slack? Please? Could you try to be nice?"

She studied me through the whirling spokes of her bike, her brows furrowed with concern. Alice was never very good at reading people, but it seemed to me she'd grown worse, as if shutting herself up with Mom had crippled the few social skills she had. "Well, hey-di-ho, sisteroo, I didn't realize you were on the brink."

"I know," I blubbered. "And I know you want to take your bottles to the bar. And I want you to. I just wasn't prepared for any of this. Wasn't prepared for Mom to be so—Why didn't you tell me she'd gotten so bad when I called?"

"I did, indeed I did."

She was right. She had told me, in her Alice way, giving me reports like *Physically she's in good shape, she is, mentally, not so much.* I'd worry for a few days after each call, then get on with my life, Mom and Alice becoming an abstraction in my mind. I'm an air sign. It's what we do. Our way of circumventing what we're feeling. "Circumventing" because the feelings don't go away; they pile up until Karma comes shrieking her wildcat head off. Then those heaps of passed-over feelings erupt. All of them. All at once.

"I just didn't get it," I bawled. "I'm sorry." I wiped my soggy face with the hem of my T-shirt, my regrets threatening to strangle me. Why hadn't I made the trip down in June like I'd thought about? If I had, maybe then I would have realized how bad Mom had gotten. Maybe then she would have recognized me. Maybe then—

Alice set her hand on the bike's tire to stop it spinning. "Bottles can wait, they can. My sister is in need. Besides, I was just making that up about the manager at the bar. He'll be there till six."

"I don't want to mess you up," I sobbed. "It's just so—"

She signaled me to hush. "I know what you need, I do. A bit of memorabilia." She loped off to the garage.

I couldn't imagine what in there would make a difference, unless it was a time machine. Which, honestly, I wouldn't put past Alice. I took another bite of sandwich and washed it down with a gulp of too-sweet iced tea.

She returned with several of Mom's colorful hatboxes. "Aaaaaand voilà!" She blew dust from the lid of the top box and set the stack before me. "A treasure trove of memories all neatly packed up for your perusal."

"Wait. So you didn't toss everything?"

"Kept these for you, I did. A box chock-full of remembrances." She looked pleased with herself.

I wiped the tears from my eyes and cracked the top box. Inside was a tangle of silk scarves, gloves, and costume jewelry. Mom's most beloved of possessions. *There's not a problem in the world that can't be solved with the proper accessory!* she'd counsel us as girls. I breathed in the scent of her Chanel No. 5, then plucked out a giant, faux-gold sunburst brooch with rhinestone-tipped rays. It was hideous, and beautiful. "Remember this?"

"You bet your bippy I do. Always had it pinned to a scarf, she did."

"Didn't we give it to her?"

"If I do recall, we bought it at Elma Rizzo's garage sale."

"I think it was a birthday present."

"Her thirty-eighth."

"You remember that?"

"It was the year of the failed lemon chiffon cake."

It always amazed me what Alice recalled: dates, random bits of trivia, things we'd eaten at specific family events. "If you say so." We were sitting next to each other, sideways, on the lounger, not quite touching, but close. I pulled a pair of short ivory kid gloves from the box on my lap. "Oh my God, she wore these to my high school graduation. I was mortified."

"If it's good enough for Elizabeth Taylor," Alice said, mimicking Mom's flamboyant toss of the head and backward flick of the wrist, "it's good enough for me!"

I couldn't help but laugh. The affectation looked so funny on Alice. But Mom would say it just like that, inserting into the phrase whichever Hollywood actress served her current purpose.

"Feeling any better, old sport?"

"Yes, a little. Thank you."

"Because I have something else that could raise your spirits, I do."

"Well, you can't just say that and not tell me what."

She made another dash to the garage, returning this time with a half box of See's chocolates. "The return of the Candy Club! From my private reserve."

It was the perfect thing. The Candy Club was our childhood ritual. Each week, we'd spend our allowance on whatever candy we could afford, then prop a sheet between our two twin beds to make the Candy

Club Clubhouse. I was the president of the club; she, the vice president. There were no other members.

I plucked a Milk Bordeaux from the box and bit into the chocolatey goodness. It wasn't the Pixy Stix, jawbreakers, and Swedish fish of our childhood, but it did the trick; I wasn't alone. I had my sister.

We spent the next half hour or so pawing through the remaining boxes and devouring the chocolates. There were so many cherished items: Mom's collection of lace hankies, dozens of photographs, the little figurines that had dotted her dresser top, the perfume bottles… We'd just eaten the last of the chocolates when Alice said, "You okay now, old sport?"

"Why?" I laughed. "Do you have something else up your sleeve?"

"No. I would like to take my bottles to the bar."

"Go! Give 'em hell."

The sun was making short work of the shade. I picked up one of the hatbox tops to use as a fan. "October should not be this hot."

Alice mimed a stogie, wiggled her eyebrows à la Groucho Marx. "Could be earthquake weather, ducky."

There is no scientific proof that unseasonably warm weather portends an earthquake. Still, I will always remember Alice saying that. How she essentially predicted what was to come.

I watched as she loaded her bottles into the bike's saddlebags.

"I love you, Alice," I said.

"Okay," she said.

I walked her around front and waved as she pedaled down the street. "Knock 'em dead!" I was happy for the first time since arriving. Or, if not exactly happy, hopeful. I could do this. *We* could do this. Strolling around to the back deck, I peered into the living room to see if Mom was up yet. She was still conked out in front of the TV. I walked the narrow gravel path around the house to the backyard where I began to clean up the boxes. The knickknacks were lined up on the redwood deck, Mom's scarves laid out over the loungers. I reached for a silk scarf with a Paris scene on it, one I remembered my mother tying around her hairdo back when we'd had a convertible. A stack of letters fell to my feet. They were held together by a thin red velvet ribbon. The envelopes were pretty, feminine. Nothing my dad would have sent. I tugged one out and recognized Aunt Evokia's handwriting. Or Aunt Evie, as we called her. She was the one who'd taught me the meaning of unconditional love. "Salt of the earth and sweeter than sunshine," Mom would say about her. I'd had a crush on her while growing up. Would run to the phone for her weekly Friday night calls and hold on to that receiver until Mom pried it from my grip. *And I made a new friend at school. And my English paper won a prize. And...And...*

I couldn't believe my luck at finding the letters. It was like unearthing a packet of unclaimed love. I was just about to pull a sheet of pink floral stationery from its envelope when I heard Mom bumping around in the kitchen. I returned the envelope to the stack, readying myself to get her cleaned up and fed. Cut her toenails. But how to do it without freaking her out?

CUTTING MOM'S TOENAILS

Hellooooo!" I called, as I opened the front door of the house. "Is this the home of the lucky Euvonda Mae Mustin?"

My plan was to make Mom believe she'd won an in-home beauty visit. I'd snuck around the house into my bedroom to change into a pair of clean linen slacks and the one nice blouse I'd packed—a far cry from beauty specialist wear, but the best I could do on short notice. While changing, I listened to her clunking around in the kitchen, praying she wasn't doing herself harm, then I snuck outside to make my entrance.

"Hello? Anybody home?" I tiptoed through the living room.

She tottered out of the kitchen and into the living room. She looked startled, scared. I carried on. There was no Plan B.

"Are you the lucky Euvonda Mae Mustin?"

She gripped the doorframe to keep steady. "Who-ho wants to know?"

"Just the folks at Cut and Curl Beauty Salon! Because you've won an in-home beauty treatment!"

She looked confused and a little intrigued. With her free hand, she began futzing with her float. "I have?" She patted at her hair.

"Yes, you have! And I'm the specialist here to treat you!"

"Well!" She was smiling now. Truly heartbreaking.

Encouraged, I held up the sack of tools I'd pulled together: nailbrush, clippers, washrag. "Shall we get started?"

"Now?"

I took hold of her arm and steered her back into the kitchen. "No time like the present! Especially where beauty is concerned."

Food littered every available surface. Apparently, once she'd cleared out the fridge, she'd started in on the cabinets: boxes of spaghetti, crackers, Rice-A-Roni. "What a beautiful kitchen!" I crooned, swiping a box of butter from the floor and tossing it onto the counter. "Such taste!" I guided her to a chair at the head of the chrome table and sat her down. "A beautiful kitchen for a beautiful woman! What do you say we start with your hair?"

She looked over her shoulder at me. "This is free?"

I picked some leaf bits from her hair. "Yes, because you're the lucky winner!"

"Wait until Walt gets a load of this! He's never gonna believe I got this for free."

That made me tear up. Whenever someone would compliment her on her looks, Dad would give her shoulder a proud squeeze and declare, "Nothing that money can't buy!" She'd respond by affectionately punching him in the arm. It was their shtick.

There was no styling her hair into its signature poof—even if I'd had the chemicals, she didn't have enough hair—so I tried with a little success to fluff it up, dipping the comb into a bowl of warm water, running it through the thin strands, then crunching it in my fist. I was sorry I didn't have a blow dryer, but the day was so hot it dried quickly. In truth, I was stalling. I was in no hurry to tackle those toenails. "How about a little snack before we start?" I asked cheerily.

She thought about this. "Does it come with the package?"

"You bet!"

"Well, I am a bit hungry…"

I flourished a finger in the air. "Then let me fix you something to eat!"

She only partially ate the grilled cheese I whipped up for her, but at least she was eating. I didn't let up on the act. "Such a lucky woman! So many entries and just one winner," I droned while surreptitiously returning things to the fridge and cabinets. Mostly, she ignored me. She was too busy negotiating her sandwich, carefully nibbling the corner of one half, then moving on to the second half. It was hard to tell when she'd finished. I'd think she was done then she'd pick one of the halves up again. But when she started to look around, as if she were about to get up, I doubled my efforts. "Euvonda Mae Mustin, are you ready for the rest of your prize in-home beauty treatment?"

"My what?"

I explained it to her again. Again, she bought into it. I talked her into letting me help her change out of her dirty float, vaguely implying it was all part of her prize. We made the switch right there in the kitchen, me sponging her off as we went. "This skin treatment will make you look years younger!" I scrubbed her arms and legs, steering clear of her privates. I was afraid it would blow my cover, and I wanted to get to those toenails. I did manage to get her into a fresh pair of waist-high cotton undies and a fresh Cross Your Heart bra. "Has anyone ever told you? You've got the body of a model! I've been in the business for a long time, and I've never seen such natural beauty!" She actually giggled when I said this, giving me no small amount of satisfaction. When it came time for the toenails, I took a deep breath. "And now for our specialty." I returned her to the chair, knelt down next her. I'd already removed her shoes, already filled the roasting pan with warm soapy water. "Are you in for a treat!"

She jerked her foot from my hand. "What are you doing? Who are you?"

"Euvonda Mustin, I am your beauty specialist and I'm about to give you a super-duper A-One pedicure. It's part of your prize."

"My prize?"

"Why, our pedicures are famous worldwide."

She gave me a skeptical look. Clearly, she wasn't big on having her toenails cut. No doubt why Alice had let them grow so long.

"It's sandal season," I said, flashing her a smile. "Time to turn your toes into little jewel-tipped eye-catchers."

She frowned, but let me take her foot. I set it into the roasting pan. "Doesn't that feel good?" She didn't say it didn't, so I put the other one in too.

To take her mind off of the soaking, I filed her fingernails (unnecessarily, Alice had done a good job with them) and chatted her up, inventing juicy Hollywood gossip. It seemed to relax her.

When the toenails had softened, I had to go through the whole "Lucky Euvonda Mae Mustin" routine again, but it worked. Again. She let me rest her foot on my knee, where I, with great gag control, dug out yellow cottage-cheesy stuff from beneath each hooked nail. I tried to be gentle, but it took elbow grease. Each time she winced, I'd amp up the cheerful patter. "Can you believe the gown Meryl Streep wore to the Oscars?" I was flying by the seat of my pants, knowing she might tell me to stop at any minute. I couldn't imagine continuing without her consent.

Cutting and shaping the nails turned out to be more difficult than expected. The heavy-duty toenail clippers didn't have the oomph. So I zipped out to the garage to see what I could find. "Be right back!" I returned with Alice's Dremel, a small drill I fitted with a sandpaper bit, and went at those ten little piggies, producing even more of the yellow cottage-cheesy stuff. I had to go through the whole "Lucky Euvonda Mae" routine again, but by then I was getting good at it. I was also pretty damn good at what I was doing. The toenails were turning out great.

"Done!" I said when I'd sanded the last one into a sweet little crescent.

"What about the polish?" she said.

I panicked. "Well..." Then I remembered having seen an ancient bottle of her antique rose polish in one of her boxes. "Be right back!" I rushed out to get it. It was so old I had to thin it with a few drops of polish remover, which, for some reason, Alice had on her workbench, but it worked. I did her fingernails too.

She couldn't have been happier with the result, fluttering her fingers in the air to dry, just like the old days. Well, I had to coach her a little; she kept forgetting they were wet. But once we were both satisfied, she held her hands at arm's length to admire. "Whaddyathink? Would you be seen with me on a Saturday night?"

I kissed her on the forehead. "Yes, ma'am. You're gonna be turning heads tonight, that's for sure."

I remember that afternoon with such clarity. How badly I ached for real moments with her. And there were several, ones in which I was sure she knew something was off. She'd get a faraway look in her eye, she'd furrow her brow, and I'd be certain she knew in that millisecond that we were only pretending, that I was really her daughter who'd rushed home to care for her. Later, when I shared these thoughts with Alice, she shrugged and said, "Hate to burst your bubble, Bucko, but that's how she looks when she has gas."

I laughed for the first time since Alice's death. Went to check the mail and was accosted by the kid I mentioned earlier, the one who'd offered to help mop up Alice's blood. She's quite a character. Got a haircut since I last spoke to her. Went short short and added platinum tips to her unnaturally black hair. Looks like she did it herself. Choppy. And such gorgeous lashes! Youth! They don't know what they've got. She's skinny as a rail and holds herself like a boy, although dresses like a girl: floral cotton sundress that looks like it's out of the fifties. Quite a contrast to her clumpy black boots and tattoos. The girl seems completely at ease with herself, which I find inspiring.

Anyway, she thought Alice and I were a "cool old lesbian couple." "The real deal," she called us. I howled with laughter. I'm sure she thought I was out of my gourd.

"No, no!" I sputtered. "She's my sister! My little sister!"

She was embarrassed, of course, tugged her lip ring so hard I feared for her lip. I had to wipe tears from my eyes, I was laughing so hard, then explained to her, "Yes, yes, I'm a lesbian. And Alice is just Alice." I was surprised to find out she knew about Alice's bottles. Had interned at the Museum of Art and History when Alice's bottles were showing there.

"What's going to happen to them?" she asked, bending down to tie her boot.

I told her I didn't know.

She lives in the big house down the street. It's crammed with students. They must be sleeping three to a room. They're growing corn and tomatoes in the front yard next to a sign that reads *Food Not Lawns!* They're always very friendly when I walk by. She is not a student. Her parents cut her off when she declared as an art major. This is causing her some angst, although she never said so; the pulling on the lip ring gave her away. Otherwise, she showed no signs of worry. She's what my mother would call *cool as a cucumber.* I'll bet she has the girls swooning, if she even goes for girls. Who knows with these young ones? They seem to be playing by a whole new set of rules. Anyway, she offered her help again, and it made me wonder if there was something she wanted from me. Hopefully, I put her off the scent. I really have nothing to give.

Between her and my beach walk, I was exhausted and wound up conking out for five hours when I'd thought I was just lying down for a quick nap. I woke around 10:00 p.m., feeling muddy with forgotten dreams, and a strong hankering for a glass of red wine. I didn't succumb, though. But really, why shouldn't I have a glass? There's no one left to hurt. Just me, and I take full responsibility for myself. But I didn't do it. Made myself a cup of coffee instead. Now it's 1:00 a.m. and I'm wide-awake.

I'm not sure this could be considered insomnia; I did drink that coffee, and I did sleep. Just at the wrong time. But who cares? The answer is no one. There is no one to care about anything I might do anymore. I might as well be a ghost already. This may sound like a plea for sympathy, but I assure you it is not. This untethered feeling is quite freeing. If Alice were alive, I'd be tiptoeing around the house like a mouse, unable to sit out on the back deck as I did earlier, watching that skunk toodle around the rosemary. I would have been afraid of the sliding glass door waking her. The window in Alice's room, once Mom's room, opens up to the deck, and she is—*was*—a light sleeper. But Alice is not alive and I can do what I want. I could stand in the kitchen and break all the dishes if I felt like it, which I don't, but I could. Perhaps I'll keep these hours: sleeping during the day, owling around at night.

Who am I, now that I don't have to adjust my rhythm to someone else's? What is the essence of the true, unfettered me? How shall I close out this last chapter of my life? Allow myself to slowly deteriorate, my last breath a sputtering death rattle? Or should I, like Alice, take a crazy swan dive into the great unknown: drive my car off the cliffs, take a bath with my hairdryer? But here I am thinking about my death, and I am alive, and awake, and it's 1:00 a.m. and I have so much of my story left to tell.

Truth is, I miss Alice terribly. I keep finding myself in her room, standing there with no purpose besides standing there. Or I poke around in her stuff, which feels so invasive, but I can't stop myself from doing it. She kept her drawers so neat: underwear folded, socks balled, T-shirts sorted by color—work ones in one drawer, good ones in another. The bottom drawer was filled with papers: bills sorted by date, a couple of articles written about her bottles in the local newspaper. I also found that packet of Aunt Evockia's letters. That Alice has kept them all these years was a shocker. I never thought her capable of sentimentality. I snuggled up on Alice's bed with them, her red Pendleton blanket pulled up over my knees. It was comforting to remember my mother through her sister's words, good to be reminded that she wasn't always the confused old woman she was at the end.

July 30, 1934

Dear Euvie,

It's only been a month since you've been gone and I miss you already. But you sure do have everyone stirred up around here. At church today you were all the talk. Daddy, of course, left all the explaining to me and Mama. He's still mad as a wet hen about you and Hugh eloping. (I really don't think he saw it coming. But how he could have missed your all's affectionate glances, I have no idea! Or that Hugh's brush circuit kept bringing him back 'round our way!!!) Anyhow, after how much my wedding cost him, you'd think he'd be thrilled you two eloped! But don't you worry. He'll come around. Mama and I will make sure of that. In the meantime, we're just letting him sulk.

So I thought I should fill you in on a little East Texas gossip. We put Ida Wilkes in the ground on Sunday, God rest her soul. And would you believe, at the gravesite, while the service was going on, John Ward's goats, which had somehow broken out of the pen (no surprise there), sauntered over and started eating the carnations right off the graveside wreaths! I wish you could have seen it! My dear husband took it on himself to herd them away, but as you know, he has about as much sense with animals as an old boot, and wound up with his you-know-what in the dirt when one of the goats reared up. I told him afterwards he should just stick to his tomatoes.

The crop this year has been a good one. Mother Nature is on our side. For once! Now if only the country would get on board. It's truly disheartening to have to sell our beautiful tomatoes at such a pitiful price. It's a wedge between Frank and Daddy. I try to tell Frank that he should take it up with President Roosevelt, that Daddy's packing plant has to make a profit too, but it's hard for a man to put so much into a crop and get so little back. And there are so many men wanting to pick! They come riding in on the train, most of them having hopped freights, and so young! Breaks your heart to turn them away.

But on to much brighter things! Mama and I are going to take the train into Dallas come Saturday. She thinks I need a new dress and shoes, and I am not going to tell her otherwise. Of course, I had to butter Frank up something awful so he wouldn't throw a fit. It's hard on him, not being able to provide the way he'd like to. I told him once he saw me in my new dress, he wouldn't mind so much.

And now the really big news, and I haven't told a soul besides you and Mama. I am once again in a family way. I want to get a little more along before I tell Frank. I don't want to get his hopes up. But I plan to keep this one, if my body will just cooperate!

So that's all the news here. This little town seems so much smaller without you. And you in California! Are there really palm trees everywhere? Have you seen any movie stars?

I miss you so much. Write!

With all my love, your adoring (and slightly envious) sister,

Evie

QUALITY PERFUME

A lice burst through the back door, bubbling over with excitement. "Three cheers! My bottles are moving on to a better life! They've been accepted by the head honcho at the Catalyst, a man with excellent taste and a flair for the eccentric!"

I was examining the contents of the fridge trying to figure out what to make for dinner. I nearly cracked my head on the freezer. "Hip hip hooray!"

Mom looked up from the kitchen table where I'd set a plate of crudités. She been arranging and rearranging the cut-up carrots and celery for the last half hour. "Who's getting married?"

"No one's getting married," I said. "Your youngest daughter has just had a big success in the art world. Her bottles are going to be displayed at a nearby bar." I placed a carton of eggs, a bag of sliced ham, and a Tupperware full of leftover stir-fried veggies on the kitchen counter. "Permanent display?" I asked Alice. "Or temporary?"

"Permanent. He wants me to pick six of my best."

"Hip hip hooray!" I said.

"Hip hip!" Mom said.

Alice knitted her brows. "I just have to figure out the best way to hang them. I have some ideas, I do." She dug her fists into her waist and stood there arms akimbo, legs wide, superhero-like. "I can assure you they will be there to welcome one and all as they enter the bar. Right there on the wall saying…" She made an arc with her hand. "'Greetings, imbiber of alcohol, you have just entered an establishment that offers more than your wildest dreams! Six little worlds in which you can lose yourself—if you so desire. Or you can look upon them as a feat of ingenuity. How did those little worlds find their way into those bottles? What wonder of engineering made such a thing possible?'" With that, she flew out to the garage mumbling something about fishing line.

I went back to figuring out dinner. It felt good to be useful, and cooking was my cure for everything in those days. Still is, but when you live alone there's so little reason to do it. I wound up cobbling together a quiche. Quite tasty, if memory serves.

To fill the forty-five minutes of baking time, I set Mom's hatboxes on the table to go through them with her. I was picturing a nice stroll down memory lane, hoping her stuff might remind her of who she was. I opened the sliding glass door so that Alice could be in on the nostalgia. She was messing around with some hardware trying to create the perfect wall hanger for her bottles. I spotted Mr. Scratch crouching in the shadow of an overgrown rosemary shrub and stepped over Alice's mess to stroke him under his chin. He looked miserable. "We'll figure out something," I told him. "I promise." He tried to purr, but even that seemed to hurt. Sighing, I returned to the house and dug out a compilation tape of country western music. I knew Mom would like that. I slipped it into Alice's boom box.

Kitty Wells started in on "How Far Is Heaven" while Mom gave herself a healthy squirt of Chanel No. 5 I found in the top box. She breathed it in like an astronaut savoring that first lungful of real air after returning from a yearlong mission in space. "There is nothing like a quality perfume to civilize the most brutish of men!" she said.

I clapped my hands to my mouth. She sounded so much like Mom it hurt. "Did you hear that, Alice? Did you hear what Mom just said?"

"I surely did, sisteroo. A little taste of our mother of yesteryear, the old Euvonda Mae."

Hearing her name, Mom grew more alert. "A woman has to be very careful not to give the wrong impression. Men are so easily tempted."

"And you have soooo many gentleman callers," Alice said. "Knocking down our doors, they are."

Mom continued pawing through the boxes, seemingly unaware that Alice was making fun of her, and found a heart-shaped sachet. It was lacy with little silk roses and ribbons. I'd never seen it, but it seemed to have great significance for her. "Do you still have yours?" she asked me.

"Mine?"

"Just say yes," Alice said out of the side of her mouth. "Trust me."

"I made us both one for Christmas," Mom continued. "Made one for Mama too. I stitched the roses myself. Had to roll the silk just so."

She placed the sachet aside, treating it as if it were the most precious thing in the world, then gave herself another squirt of Chanel No. 5. "Quality perfume civilizes the most brutish of men."

"Okay," I said. "That's probably enough perfume for now."

She scowled and placed the perfume just out of my reach.

I got up to check on the quiche. Far from done. I turned to Alice. "You think I could zip over to Safeway and pick up a bottle of wine?"

"I don't know," she said. "Could you?"

"I mean, would you mind watching Mom. I won't be gone ten minutes."

"As you wish."

"Can I get you anything?"

"New brake pads for my bike."

I swiped my car keys from the kitchen counter. "I'll be right back. Promise."

"Never make a promise you can't keep!" Mom chirped.

Walking out to the car, I was feeling pretty good, the domestic scene at the house seeming almost normal. All I needed was that *click* a good bottle of wine would bring. Still, when I got behind the wheel, I had the sudden urge to drive, and I mean *drive* drive, to head off to destinations unknown, on the road for hours, stopping at little towns to pee and refill my coffee, all while mulling over the big questions of my life. I curbed the urge, did the five-minute jaunt to Safeway, grabbed a bottle of Cabernet, grabbed a second for good measure, and turned right back around.

Back at the house, the kitchen table and floor were covered in Mom's stuff, and Dolly Parton was blasting "I Will Always Love You." So was Mom. She was standing by the table, swaying back and forth, a cloud of Chanel No. 5 surrounding her. A large sheer white scarf was draped over her shoulders.

"Use your walker, Euvonda May!" Alice shouted from the back deck.

I turned down the boom box. "Jesus. What the hell happened here?"

"You left," Alice said.

"Where's my music?" Mom wailed.

I put my arm around her. "Still there. I just turned it down a notch."

Mom looked me in the eyes. "Lucy. When did you get here?"

The recognition nearly made me swallow my tongue. "Um. Yesterday. I got here yesterday."

"Well, it's about time you showed up. Your father is waiting for you in the living room, and boy howdy does he have a burr in his saddle. Today was the day you were supposed to help him clean out the garage."

I felt myself slipping into the angry fifteen-year-old who was always in trouble for something. I fought it. I was not that girl anymore.

Mom reached for her Chanel No. 5.

I tried to block her grab but wasn't quick enough. "I think you've had enough perfume, Mom."

She gave herself a defiant squirt.

"Okay. Now, why don't we put that up?"

"No!"

"You're already smelling pretty strong."

"No!"

I glanced at Alice. *Help!*

She sighed, got up from sitting cross-legged on the deck, without the use of her hands—the knees of a teenager, I tell you—and came over. "Okay, Euvonda. Enough with the perfume." She thrust out her hand. "Hand it over."

"No!"

Johnny Cash started in on "I Walk The Line."

Alice pulled me aside and spoke in a hushed tone. "Our only hope is to try and distract her."

"The quiche should be done," I said brightly, hoping food would do the trick. "What do you say we eat?" But Mom dined with the bottle of Chanel No. 5 clamped between her thighs, occasionally stopping to give herself another squirt.

How she could remember her love of the perfume and not how to hold a fork is one of the great mysteries of Alzheimer's. I downed glass after glass of wine, turning Mom's fork over as needed. Meanwhile, Alice seemed impervious to the noxious stench and ate her quiche with gusto, forking bite after bite into her mouth as if she were in a pie-eating contest. "Five-star dining, this is, sisteroo. Five-star!"

Loosened up by the wine, I began making a game of the Chanel squirting, doing fake grabs for the perfume. Mom was thoroughly entertained, giggling and slapping my hand away. Alice not so much.

"It's best not to get her riled up, old sport."

"Oh, come on. It's just a little fun. And she's happy. Look at her."

I think I even told Alice she should indulge in a little wine, that it would lighten her up. I wouldn't put it past me. Not back then. Alcohol made me simultaneously stupid and convinced of the opposite, a winning combination, I assure you.

Alice scraped Mom's uneaten crust onto her own plate, then stacked our three plates and took them to the sink to wash. "When the ship goes down, don't say I didn't warn you."

"Jesus. Does everything have to be so dire?"

"Jesus!" Mom said, "Jesus, Jesus, Jesus!" and gave herself another squirt.

I got up to help Alice, put some plastic wrap over the leftover quiche, picked up the dish towel, and began drying.

"Just like old times," I said.

Alice's lack of response coincided with the country western tape stopping abruptly in the middle of Emmylou Harris singing "Making Believe"—right after the bit about making believe I never lost you. I'm not kidding. Mom pumped another squirt.

"Okay, Mom," I said, reaching for the bottle. "That's enough. It's getting gross."

She hid the bottle in her armpit and stared at me accusingly.

"Just give it to me. So you'll have some left tomorrow."

"It's mine! You can't have it."

"Mom—"

"Get away from me." She pointed at Alice. "Her too! My stupid little goat."

Alice stiffened.

I stood there in shock. Mom had called her "stupid little goat" all through our childhood, but always in a light, teasing tone. This was different. Mean.

"Don't call Alice that!"

"It's okay," Alice said.

"No, it's not."

"Does it all the time, she does. She doesn't mean it."

"Stupid, *stupid* little goat," Mom spat.

"Okay. That's enough." I pried the bottle from Mom's armpits. "Time for you to go to bed."

"Owwwww!" Mom shrieked. "You hurt me."

"I'm sorry, but you've had enough."

Mom shot up from her chair, sending it banging into her walker. "Give me back my wallet!"

"Nobody has your wallet."

"Yes, we do," Alice said slyly. "And if she wants it…" She sauntered out of the kitchen into the hall. "She's going to have to come and get it."

Mom grabbed her walker and started thumping after her. "Come back here. Come back!"

"Alice!" I shouted. "What are you doing?" Everything was suddenly moving too fast.

"Grab a chair!" Alice shouted back.

I hooked the back of a chair with the hand that wasn't holding my wine and took up the rear, dragging the chair behind me down the hall and into the bedroom.

Once in, Alice blocked the door with a tall stool she pulled from the closet. She motioned for me to set the chair next to the stool. "Sit," she said. "You're in for the best show in town." She plucked an empty wallet from Mom's dresser and handed it to her. "Your wallet."

Mom studied the wallet briefly, then tossed it on the bed. "You're a liar."

"No indeedy doo, that's your very special wallet. Pink leather. Snap coin purse."

Mom eyed the two of us like we were a couple of thugs. "Give it back."

"This is it," Alice said, swiping it back up. "Double pinkie swear. Your wallet, Euvonda."

Mom gave her a disgusted look, then zeroed in on the dresser.

"Always goes there first, she does," Alice whispered.

It was a struggle for Mom to open the top drawer, but after a few tries, she managed. She sure didn't want help, not from us. Once it was open, she yanked out a pair of high-waisted panties and tossed them on the floor. "It was in here," she said. "I know it." Next came a Cross Your Heart bra. Then another pair of panties. "Where did you put it?" One after another, after another, her lingerie landed on the floor, all the while Mom accusing us of stealing her wallet. She moved on to the drawer of nighties.

"This is crazy," I whispered.

Alice's eyes were locked on Mom. "She'll wear herself out, she will. Let's just hope it doesn't take too long, old sport."

Mom glared at Alice. "Stupid little goat! Always in the way!"

"Should we let her out?" It felt strange to talk about Mom as if she weren't there, but she wasn't paying us any attention. She wanted to find that phantom wallet.

"Can't let her near the kitchen, sisteroo. There be sharp things in there. Can't trust her with sharp things when she gets like this."

I realized one of the things that had been niggling at me since I'd arrived.

My parents had lived to smoke. Whichever house we resided in, the coffee table was the smoking shrine—dead center, a fancy mahogany box filled with packs of cigarettes: one row of Dad's Lucky Strikes and one of Mom's Winstons. There was also a large crystal ashtray and a Wedgwood table lighter. Mom couldn't walk outside with a lit cigarette because in East Texas that meant a girl was trashy. Dad could because East Texas etiquette deemed it okay for men to smoke on the street. But Mom thought he shouldn't out of respect for her. I can't tell you the number of fights they had around this. More than once while we were out walking, Mom, unable to stand his smoking when she couldn't, plucked his cigarette from his hand and took a drag or two. This made him crazy. "How is it you can smoke *my* cigarette on the street but not yours?" She'd shrug as if it made perfect sense.

I leaned in to Alice. "When did she quit smoking?"

"Four months back, yessiree bob. Left lit cigarettes everywhere, she did. Burned holes in her clothes. The furniture. Didn't want her burning the house down, now did I?"

So, she hadn't quit smoking, like she hadn't quit drinking. Alice had forced it on her, which meant she'd done it cold turkey. It just got worse and worse.

"Sometimes she forgets."

"What, and wants a cigarette?"

"Yep."

Somehow, Mom was in possession of the Chanel No. 5 again and was squirting it around the room like air freshener.

I stood, my intention being to show some authority. "Mom!"

She pointed a crooked finger at me, the nail of which I'd so recently and lovingly painted. "You took it, didn't you? You're the one. I've never trusted you. Not from day one." She gave me a good squirt before throwing a batch of hangers on the floor.

I stumbled back into my chair, suddenly aware of how very drunk I was.

Alice leaned forward, resting her elbows on her knees, and lasered in on Mom. "Got to wait her out, we do. You'll see. Tire out, she will."

This dreadful scene went on for at least an hour, if not longer. Some of the highlights: Mom trying unsuccessfully to unlock the window, Mom fuming at us because there weren't any vacant rooms in the hotel, Mom throwing everything within reach onto the floor. None of her ravings made sense, to me, anyway. Occasionally, she would stand directly in front of Alice. "Stupid little goat. Stupid, stupid little goat." She pretty much ignored me, which, in its own way, was just as painful. As for Alice, she never took her eyes off Mom. She was like a border collie trying to strong-eye a bleating sheep into submission. Watching their strange ritual was both painful and captivating. The two of them had it down: both knew their parts and played them to the hilt.

Looking back, I should have intervened. But I was exhausted, loaded, and nauseated by the stink of that perfume. It's a miracle I didn't pass out. Or, at least, I don't think I did. Not for very long anyway.

Alice was right. Mom eventually did wear herself out and fell asleep. But that wasn't the end of it. Later that night, after Alice and I had cleaned up the kitchen and I'd gone to bed, I woke to the sound of someone bumping around in the kitchen. I rose from my squeaky cot, slipped on a pair of sweats and padded into the kitchen. Mom stood at the open refrigerator with food items all over the counter. Alice was at the table working on one of her bottles. If it hadn't been so bizarre, the scene would have looked domestic. It was 3:00 a.m.

"Sorry, old sport. I was trying to keep her quiet."

I yawned. "What happened?"

"Came into my bedroom, she did. Looking for her keys."

I filled myself a glass of water and chugged it. I had a splitting headache. "I'm starting to get why you cleared out the house." I filled the glass again.

Alice nodded.

"And I'm sorry about riling her up."

Alice adjusted her Clark Kents. "Not to worry, sisteroo. The ways of the mother are a mystery."

I bent down to pick up Mr. Scratch. The old guy was as light as a stack of napkins. I settled the two of us into a kitchen chair and once again tried dropper-feeding him water. He would have none of it. "When was the last time he ate?"

"I got him to eat some tuna about four days ago."

"Four days?"

Alice didn't respond.

I gave him a scritch behind the ears. He shrank away from my touch. "I hate to be the one to say it…"

"I know," Alice said.

"Will your vet come out here to do it, or do we need to take him in?"

"He'll come."

Alice removed her glasses and covered her eyes with her hands. When she took her hands away, they were wet with tears. She studied the tears as if unsure of what to make of them.

Thinking back on that night has me all churned up. It's 2:30 a.m. and the air seems as restless as I am. I should read some of Aunt Evie's letters to quiet myself. They really do work as a calming elixir. The house isn't helping; it's alive with memories.

Alice may have taken over my parents' room, but it will always be their room to me. I was surprised she wanted to move into it. Yes, it's a better room, looks out onto the garden, is closer to the bathroom, but who knows how many of Mom's delusional meltdowns Alice endured in there? Still, she moved right in. I think she felt it to be a kind of victory. But that's probably my projection. Alice didn't attach emotions to inanimate objects the way most people do—though she kept Henry the Coatrack for reasons unknown. A table, overcoat, room, what have you, was one of two things for Alice: helpful or not helpful. The rococo bed set was deemed not helpful, thank God. I didn't ask what she'd done with it. I didn't want to know.

I wound up in her old room. It looks out onto the bamboo hedge in the front yard. That's right, I said hedge. It was the first thing I did upon moving in: rounded up some day laborers and cut that bamboo down to size. It's really quite attractive now. Alice resisted me all the way, of course! She liked her privacy, but opening the place up was good for her too. Gave her a chance to mingle with the neighbors. And the light flooding into the living room and my bedroom can't be beat. I painted my room yellow, Kim's favorite color. "Puts a shine into all the other colors," she'd say.

Tonight, though, the shadows are sprouting shadows as I conjure the past. It's an unseasonably warm night, just as it was that day in 1989, as if the weather's been choreographed to goad my memory.

I just noticed the dragonfly night-light in the hall has gone out. I'll have to pick up another bulb. The old Christmas lightbulbs are hard to find. Everything's gone LED. Progress, I suppose.

RIP, MR. SCRATCH

Alice's mobile vet turned out to be exactly what you'd want in a vet: a kindly bear of a man, middle-aged, scruffy-haired, wearing tan Ben Davis slacks, a clean white T-shirt, and scuffed ropers. He even had hat-head. Once in the living room, he noticed a piece of hay on his shirt, picked it off, then seemed unsure what to do with it.

I held out my hand for the piece of hay.

"Sorry," he said, handing it to me. "It's just—"

"Not to worry. I'm sure it comes with the territory."

He sniffed the air. "Smells like a perfume factory."

"Yeah. We had a little incident."

He chuckled self-consciously, while searching the room for Alice. She was standing by the TV, cradling Mr. Scratch. He reached for his hat, then remembered he wasn't wearing it. "Hello, Alice."

Alice stared at Mr. Scratch as if she hadn't been spoken to.

We were lucky he'd come on a Saturday, and on such short notice. Alice had made the call long before I'd woken up. She'd dug a little grave too, in the backyard, under a bush covered in late-season rose hips.

I held out my hand. "I'm Lucy, Alice's sister. Thank you for coming."

He gave my hand a hearty shake. "Jack."

I held on an extra second, trying, via eye contact, to warn him to move with caution. Alice was in what I used to call *volcano mode*: stone on the outside, spitting lava on the inside. Not that she would do him any harm, but if she did what I was afraid of, she could make my life a living nightmare.

Jack gave me the slightest nod. I got the feeling he, too, was trying to convey something to me. I had no idea what. Meanwhile, Mom sat in her usual morning spot in front of the TV. Some talk show; people laughing, which, under the circumstances, was jarring.

Jack walked over to the bundle of gray fur in Alice's arms and stroked the back of Mr. Scratch's neck. "Hey, buddy. Looks like you're feeling pretty poorly." He was clearly more comfortable with animals than people.

Alice didn't move. She'd been stewing since our conversation the night before about putting down Mr. Scratch. I'm not sure she'd even slept. It had been a rough night for me too. The flowery stench was suffocating, and I was wound up. I got up a couple of times to pee and noticed Alice's bedroom door open, her bed empty. She was likely in her garage crafting her perfect little worlds, though I never checked.

"Alice," Jack said softly. "You ready for this?" The tenderness of his tone told me that he knew how quirky Alice could be. This gave me some reassurance.

She dipped her head slightly. She'd missed a lock of hair while fashioning her ponytail that morning.

"How about we go in the backyard," I said, "where we won't upset Mom?"

"Good idea," Jack said.

Alice walked slowly, deliberately, to the back door; Jack, a respectful distance behind her, the telltale black bag in his hand. All that was missing were the bleak chords of a funeral dirge. At the last second, I dashed out to make sure the front gate was locked. It wasn't. Grateful for the dodged bullet, I locked it and met up with them on the back deck. Alice was sitting on the step, Mr. Scratch curled in a fur nest on the lap of her kilt. Kneeling next to them, Jack kneaded the white patch under Mr. Scratch's chin. He spoke in a soft voice. "Hey, Mr. Scratch, you've done a good job, a really good job."

Alice stared hard at Mr. Scratch.

I thought about going to sit by her, but was afraid it would confuse her more. She was already struggling with the physical proximity of Jack now massaging the back of Mr. Scratch's neck. "You're doing the right thing, Alice," he said. "He's not a happy guy."

I stood off to the side, feeling like an interloper, but I was worried about Alice. Mr. Scratch continued to purr his weak purr. I was sure he, like me, was trying to make this as easy on Alice as possible. I silently thanked him.

Jack reached into his bag with his free hand while continuing to massage the back of Mr. Scratch's neck with his other one. "You've been a good fella, Mr. Scratch, a good friend to Alice." He pulled out a needle, already, thoughtfully, loaded up with whatever it is they use in these situations. "Good boy," he said, then turned to Alice: "He won't feel anything. Just go to sleep. Soon his heart will stop beating."

"I know," Alice said sharply.

Mom appeared in the doorway. I have no idea what she understood about what was going on, but she must have intuited that it was something big because she began to hum "Happy Trails." It was both unnerving and sad, this echo of our childhood. The Roy Rogers classic had been the song she'd sing when she was trying to herd a reluctant Alice out the door for some dreaded excursion, or to go "bump around with other kids her age," as she would put it: an overnight stay at a friend's, summer camp. These always proved disastrous events with Mom getting a call in the middle of the night to come pick her up, but she never stopped trying to socialize little Alice.

"Good boy," Jack said again, and lifted Mr. Scratch's head to expose his white throat. He depressed the plunger a bit, causing it to spit the lethal substance onto his knuckles, said one last "Good boy," then plunged the needle into the roll of skin protecting Mr. Scratch's jugular. He kept the needle in a tad longer than seemed necessary, as if to make sure he'd transferred every last bit of the poison. I didn't realize I'd been holding my breath until he removed it.

Then we waited: Alice's eyes glued to the swelling and contracting of Mr. Scratch's emaciated chest, Jack's too. Mine were on Alice, marking the shallowness of *her* breathing, the emotionlessness of *her* expression. Mom's eyes appeared to be looking at the screen door not two inches from her nose, her humming morphing into an odd series of disconnected notes.

I thought back to the first Mr. Scratch, how Alice chased after him to pull his tail; the second Mr. Scratch, how despite Alice's mauling, he ignored my nightly pleas to sleep with me, choosing instead to put up with Alice's fitful thrashings; the third Mr. Scratch, how he and Dad locked into an alpha male war, Dad declaring nightly, "That damn cat gets his dinner on time more often than I do!" A silly statement. All the Mr. Scratches got their dinners right on time, exactly 5:30. It was Alice's job to feed them. I was much less familiar with Mr. Scratch Number Four. We'd never lived together, but I would have bet my last dollar that it was Alice, not Mom, who got the dead mice placed at her feet. Those Mr. Scratches all loved Alice, and she, in her way, loved them back.

Finally, Mr. Scratch's breathing began to weaken. I could see it on Alice's face, a tightening around her eyes. Then she stiffened and I knew he was gone. She rose, handed me his limp corpse, walked stoically past Jack, slid the screen door open so forcefully it fell off the track, and passed Mom into the kitchen. From there, I could only hear her course: through the kitchen, down the hall, and to her bedroom, where she slammed the door behind her hard enough to make the kitchen windows shudder.

It was the thing I'd been praying wouldn't happen, the thing that could royally screw up the neat plan I'd made to get me through the next couple of days.

Jack looked stunned.

"It's how she deals with things," I said.

Mom seemed to understand what had happened, which surprised me. "She's in her room," she said, using the family euphemism for Alice's shutdowns.

They were as much a part of my family life as my father's wish for Salisbury steak on Friday nights. Triggered by feelings she didn't understand (or that's what I've come to believe), her episodes annoyed me no end growing up. I was sure she was doing it to get attention—in retrospect, it's the last thing she wanted—but once inside her room, she would lie there on her bed, comatose, hands crossed over her chest, staring at the ceiling for hours upon hours, sometimes lasting a full day, sometimes longer.

She'd had them since she was about nine or ten. Before that, it had been tantrums, god-awful tantrums. Horrible sobbing, screaming events that usually included her hurling things across the room, which would throw Mom into a tantrum. Then the two of them would tantrum at each other until one of them tuckered out, usually Mom. Dad would do his best to intervene, but more often than not, he'd get sucked into yelling too. Sometimes, I'd even join in. Then, one day, little Alice figured out to do this instead, to shut down. None of us protested, I can assure you. Her shutdowns were a zillion times more preferable to her tantrums, and, good little enablers that we were, we would tiptoe around the house, whispering, "Is she still in her room?" even though, technically, the room often belonged to both of us.

One incident stands out in my mind. It was my tenth-grade year, making it Alice's seventh. It was a Friday, and I'd rushed home from school because Mom had promised to take me and Alice to the mall. I was invited to a party that night and was going to get something new to wear. I was excited about the party, was sure it was going to change my social status, which was lacking in the extreme. But when I got home, Mom told me Alice had arrived earlier and was now "in her room."

There was no telling what had set her off. Whatever it was had propelled her out of school, sometime between lunch and the final bell, and sent her charging home on foot. Even her teachers had learned to resign themselves to Alice's sudden departures. I'm sure, in a way, they were relieved; she could not have been easy in the classroom: asking questions they were not prepared to answer, pointing out flaws in their logic. Her grades, despite her disappearances, were always good, if not aced, with the exception, oddly, of art, where her teachers found her work too "dark."

"Just leave her here!" I remember yelling at my mother. "She's just lying there!" But Mom would have none of it, understandably. The episodes left Alice vulnerable, like an upturned turtle. I was furious, though, and barreled into our room. "Why are you doing this? Is it because I got invited to a party? Is that it?"

As usual, Alice showed no signs of even hearing me.

I tried every tactic possible that day: yelling, talking softly, begging, bribing. I even tried taking her hand. It was like touching a hand in rigor mortis, only it was warmer. Needless to say, I had to wear an old skirt and blouse to the party. I had a terrible time—not because of the dress, but because I didn't know how to talk to people. Still, I blamed Alice.

That was not the first or the last time I tried to get through to Alice during one of her episodes, but it is a memorable one, and I think it serves to paint the picture. Over the years, I did learn a few tactics. I had to. "See what you can do to get your sister out of her mood," Mom would say, pushing me toward our room. She had the good sense to know she was the wrong person for the job. I reviewed those tactics as I stood there with Mr. Scratch's limp corpse in my arms.

Jack the vet looked as nervous as a rabbit in an open field.

"I should pay you," I said, glancing around for a place to set Mr. Scratch. I noticed a yellow towel by the gravesite, no doubt placed there to wrap him in before burial.

"Well, you can...I mean...But it's fine if you want to..."

"No, let me pay you. Then we can be done with this." I walked over to the rosebush, wrapped Mr. Scratch in the yellow towel, and placed him in the shoebox-sized grave. "And really, don't worry about Alice. She'll be fine."

I was furious. I had a wedding cake to make and deliver in Portland in less than twenty-four hours. Alice knew this. I'd promised her I'd turn right around and come back. And now she'd gone and done this. If I sound heartless, I suppose I was. But I'd been dealing with her shutdowns all my life. They were never convenient.

Mom straggled along behind Jack and me as we walked to the living room to settle up. "Time to go?" she asked, patting at her hair. "Should I go dress?" She always hated seeing a man get away.

"Not yet," I said wearily. "I'll make sure to let you know."

I went to grab my wallet from the bedroom, leaving her and Jack to fend for themselves. I had to keep myself from continuing down the hall to beat on that slammed door. When I returned, Mom was telling Jack a story I'd heard many times: a church potluck where everyone had brought either coleslaw or potato salad. "No meat!" she said. "Can you imagine? All those men to feed and not a single steak!" She smoothed the front of her float when she saw me, fluttering her pretty fingernails like butterflies. "Is it time to go?" Poor Jack must have thought he'd dropped into the insane asylum. Hell, I felt like I had.

"Thank you," I said, handing him the bulk of my cash.

He nodded. "If you…" His sentence stopped there; I suppose he thought better about getting too involved. I didn't blame him.

I walked him out to the street, watched him get into his big white vet truck, then had to keep myself from clinging to the bumper as he drove off. I think I even waved. I was desperate. To this day, walking back into that house remains one of the hardest things I've ever done.

Mom was back in front of the TV watching a bunch of happy people eating breakfast cereal. I poured myself another cup of coffee and made myself walk down the hall to Alice's room. I knew it was pointless, but knocked anyway. "Alice?" I cracked open her door. "Alice? Can I come in?"

As expected, she was lying on her bed, hands crossed on her chest, booted ankles too. She looked like a woman preparing to be shot from a cannon. Her Clark Kents were on her nightstand, her eyes wide open. Back in the day, I'd tried to taunt her into responding, clicking my fingers in front of her face, that kind of thing, until one day she grabbed my wrist, lightning quick, her eyes still fixed in their weird, absent stare—a blind person grabbing a fly midair. "Stop," she'd said, squeezing my wrist so hard she cut off the blood flow. From then on, I used only words to try to unlock her.

I pulled a chair next to the bed, praying I could talk her out of it. I'd done it before, I just had to figure out what had her stumped. See, unlike most of us who, when we hit overload, we're exactly that: overloaded—the impossible work deadline, on top of the neighbor's leaf blower, on top of a crying child, on top of, on top of, on top of... Alice didn't operate that way. Her overloads were a result of a single thing that seemed insurmountable to her. If she could find a way to overcome that single thing, everything else would click back into place and she'd reenter the world. To snap her out of it, I just had to figure out what had her stumped and how to help her deal with it.

That's my theory, anyway. God knows, I should act the expert on Alice's behavior! She was still surprising last week, like when she made us tuna sandwiches for lunch. "I thought you didn't like tuna," I told her. "I do now," she said. My point being, for all I thought I knew about what made Alice tick, I didn't. She remained an enigma until the day she died.

But there I go, jumping time! Honestly, I never understood that whole relativity thing about the past, present, and future all happening at once. I do now. I feel like I'm traveling through wormholes: back and forth between 1989, our childhood, the present... Sometimes I look up from recording the events of 1989 and am shocked to see the house as it is now: my cozy old leather couch in the living room, my collection of Toi's artsy photos on the wall. For all I know, I've gotten as batty as my mother did. I hope not. I don't think so.

This is not a helpful line of thought.

Back to Alice's bedroom, 1989, her lying belly-up on her bed, stubbornly unresponsive; me, sitting by her, freaking out. The bedside clock glowed a green 10:30. As I had it figured, I'd need to leave for Portland no later than 1:00. That would have me baking past midnight, but able to get the two cakes (bride's and groom's) to the noon wedding, maybe even sneak in a nap before I made the delivery. The bride was a friend and wanted me to "man" the cake, so to speak. It was a wedding I simply could not miss.

"Alice," I said, taking a stab at the single thing that might be upsetting her. "We can head to the shelter as soon as I get back from Portland. Or we can go there now." Her lack of a response only egged me on. "There are lots of cats that need a new home." I could hear Mom bumping around in the kitchen. "I'll go with you. We'll get someone to look after Mom. Or we can bring her. It would be good to get her out."

Alice didn't blink.

I wasn't surprised. I rarely got it right.

A loud *clunk* came from the kitchen.

"Be right back." I went to check on Mom. She was rummaging through the fridge like a pirate through fresh booty. I rescued a mustard bottle from the floor and stuck it in the fridge. "Are you hungry? Do you need something to eat?"

"I haven't a thing to feed them. Hugh didn't tell me until ten minutes ago that he was bringing the boys over." She was a ball of worry.

I rested a hand on her shoulder. "I'll take care of it."

"John can't eat eggs," she said. "So no battering the chicken."

"I know. I'll take care of it." She let me steer her to TV. "How about some nuts?"

Mom loved nuts. I was just hoping she'd remember.

I spent the next two hours shuttling back and forth between trying to unlock Alice and refilling Mom's bowl of nuts. I had no idea if nuts caused constipation or diarrhea. If the internet had been around, I would have looked it up, but back then, if you wanted to know something, you went to the library. How archaic that seems now!

In between tending to Mom and pleading with Alice, I considered burying Mr. Scratch, but it seemed as though Alice should be the one to do it. Plus, she would say I'd done it wrong. I placed a kitchen chair over his towel-wrapped body. I worried about some hawk or crow or other wild animal swooping him up, which is ridiculous, I know. I tell you only so that you can understand my frantic state.

Around noon, after all my blathering on about Mr. Scratch and the cruel nature of death, it occurred to me to switch tactics. I was sitting on the chair I'd dragged into her room, my elbows resting on my knees, my head so heavy it was sinking between my shoulders. I'd just explained to her for the umpteenth time that I had to race back to Portland to make and deliver a wedding cake and that I really needed her to step up. I told her about the weird groom's cake, his mother's recipe, a cake that included tomato soup. I thought she'd get a kick out of that, thought it might get her to understand the predicament she was putting me in. Then said, "Alice, I'm not going to leave you to deal with Mom. I'm coming back, I promise. I'm committed to helping."

Alice's brow furrowed, so I knew I was on the right track. Encouraged, I continued. "You can't do this by yourself. I get it." She cleared a bit of mucus from her throat. "Are you hearing me?" I was trying not to convey my total sense of panic. "Do you understand?"

I got a tiny little nod.

"Are you going to be okay?"

Another nod.

So I'd gotten it wrong. It wasn't Mr. Scratch's death confusing her, it was the implications of his death. Now that he was gone, I was the only one keeping her from being completely alone with Mom.

"I'll be back first thing Monday morning. I promise." Even as I said this, I knew it was unlikely. It would mean going without sleep for not one night, but two. "I can drop the payroll checks by the bakery on my way out of town if you want. Would that be good?"

Another tiny nod.

"I'll call you a little later, okay?"

Another.

I am ashamed to say, that was all it took for me to leave.

THE SWEETNESS OF BUTTER

I stood at the apex of the outdoor Pacific Garden Mall where Pacific Avenue and Front Streets merge at a sharp angle, home of the Plaza Bakery. Shell-shocked, exhausted, and perspiring profusely, I was terrified that once I entered I'd find yet another horrible truth, that my dad's business was in complete disarray: employees robbing the till, the place being used to front illegal merchandise, the worst. Meanwhile, visions of Alice lying on her bed, staring blankly at the ceiling, of my mother eating fistful after fistful of nuts, Mr. Scratch unburied in the heat of the day, these thoughts caromed around my head like minnows in a fishbowl. Alongside me in the small triangular park was a ragtag group of transients lounging on the planter boxes with their cardboard pleas for handouts. Seemingly comprised of drug addicts and/or the mentally ill, shoppers strode past them, and me, as if we were ghosts. "You vex my soul!" a disheveled monk with a stringless guitar slung over his back hissed at a pretty young passerby in a short skirt. An older woman, despite the heat, wore nothing but an ankle-length blue down coat and seemed to be suspended in a cloud of sadness, her bare feet calloused and filthy. I felt an odd kinship with this group of misfits. As though one more bit of bad news might tip me over into their camp.

Across the street and through Bookshop Santa Cruz was the Santa Cruz Coffee Roasting Company. My feet started toward it before I'd even consciously made the decision to give in to my sudden craving for coffee. Was I stalling? Probably. Could you blame me?

I tucked the envelope of payroll checks into the woven Greek bag slung over my shoulder and zigzagged through the lively, well-stocked bookstore on my way to the coffee shop, stopping here and there to read a book's dust jacket. How good it felt to do something for myself! To be interacting with a world that made sense!

Much as I adored lazily perusing the aisles of bookstores, the aroma of coffee beckoned. As usual, the quaint brick-and-ivy courtyard cafe was hopping. Spots in the shade were premium, but on that day, a hot Saturday, even the tables in full sun were filled with students and artsy-looking people. A couple of buskers playing mandolin and guitar provided the soundtrack.

To this day, it saddens me to think that three days later, the earthquake would shake the brick bookstore and coffee shop so violently it would collapse on itself, killing the young barista who'd waited on me. Had I treated her with kindness? I've no idea, but I suspect my focus went no further than the slow drip of Steve's Smooth French into my paper cup.

There were no available seats, so I drank my coffee standing under a spray of ivy where I could lean against the warm brick and listen to the music. The everydayness of the scene calmed my frazzled nerves. I was aware of the time, or my lack of it, but stayed one song past my drained cup anyway. Fortified, inspired even, I strode back through the bookstore and across the street, ready for whatever horror might await.

The Plaza Bakery was on the bottom floor of a historic pie-shaped building called the Flatiron building, which also housed a popular bohemian hangout, the Tea Cup, a Chinese restaurant and bar: the locals' haunt for late night snacks and martinis. Quaint, like the bakery, the upstairs lounge had become trendy, which irked my dad no end. He made it his mission to court the younger patrons as they scooted up the red stairway, chatting them up and offering free samples. He loved the history of the building and would bend their ears telling them how it had once served as the county courthouse, that its bricks were made "right here in Santa Cruz." He'd point out the bullet hole in the outside wall. "Shot from the gun of none other than the infamous Californio bandido, Tiburcio Vasquez! Never heard of him? Well…" He'd go on and on. But would he change his recipes to suit their tastes? Don't get me started.

Pushing through the glass door, I was thrown back to 1982, when Dad bought the bakery from the Italian family who'd owned it for sixty years. It looked exactly the same: the glass counter was still stocked with trays of little cookies that could be purchased by the pound; a rack of pies and freshly baked breads was still situated on the wall behind the register; a sign reading "Specialty Cakes Available for Order" still sat atop the counter; and the two ageless gray-haired ladies, Pearl and Tillie, still stood sentinel, aproned and behind the glass counter, ready to greet each customer with a warm smile. It was more than disarming. It was eerie. As though Dad were still watching over the place.

I noted that the morning Danishes had already been replaced by the afternoon fare: Italian rum cream cake, panettone, date bread. It was later than I realized. A large jar of gingerbread men sat on the counter, a plate of broken butter cookies next to it boasting a sign in my dad's own handwriting: "Sweets for the sweet!!! Take a taste on us!!!" His blocky handwriting and overuse of exclamation points nearly brought me to my knees.

It was no secret that my dad had purchased the bakery hoping to win me away from my life in Portland. I was working at a giant retail bakery at the time, a difficult era of my life. I think it's fair to say Dad was devastated that I didn't think a move to Santa Cruz would be an improvement. I even remember telling him it would "make things worse." He was a great believer in the power of family, was always trying to prove that we, the Mustins, could get it right, unlike the stormy Mustin clan of his youth. He purchased each new business not for himself, but "for the family." A guilt trip, yes, and no doubt the reason we didn't sell it upon his death.

I wonder if he regretted that we weren't the family he wanted us to be, one like the Von Trapps in *The Sound of Music,* who faced the world head-on and hopeful, functioning as a single, loving unit. If he did, he never let on, never stopped trying to set the stage for us to break spontaneously into song. But it had to have been difficult for him, our four personalities tugging in different directions; much like his own family that he'd run from; much like Mom's family that she'd run from.

"Lucy!" Pearl said, snapping me out of my reverie. "What a surprise! What brings you down to these parts?"

I popped a butter cookie sample in my mouth then had to talk around it. "Just checking in on Mom and Alice." I would not be baited into admitting that I'd been called down by a worried neighbor, wouldn't give Pearl the satisfaction. I recognized the butter cookie recipe right away. It was my own, one of the many I'd given my dad when he first opened shop, but someone had replaced the butter with shortening. I eyed Pearl suspiciously.

A pint-sized tank, she could have been a mafiosa queen in another lifetime, and had taken it upon herself to manage the bakery since my dad's death. I think we'd even offered her a small raise, which she'd accepted, but it had never been about the money for Pearl. She didn't need the money, or so she said. Her husband had a good job at the high school. She just liked to have the last word, and at the time, we'd been happy to give it to her. Keeping my father's dream alive seemed important. That, or we kept it going out of sheer complacency. Either, both, who knows? It was a horrible time, and I was grateful to Pearl, I was, but I knew she was responsible for bastardizing my recipe. She was always trying "money-saving ideas," like swapping out the butter with vegetable shortening, Vanillin instead of real vanilla. It pissed me off.

Either failing to notice or flat-out ignoring my glare, she was, no doubt, of the opinion that I'd given up my right to weigh in on the bakery, and pulled a bottle of glass cleaner from beneath the counter. "How's your mom?" she asked, squirting the fingerprints on the glass case.

Tillie finished ringing up a pound of almond biscotti for an aging couple and said, "Yes, how is Euvonda?"

I chose not to pursue the butter issue and directed my attention to Tillie. She was everything Pearl was not: sweet, unassuming, and the ultimate codependent. She dressed right out of *The Andy Griffith Show*, wore her hair in a moderate beehive, and had eyes as gentle as a cow's. "Not good," I said. "But I have paychecks."

Pearl took both hers and Tillie's. I think she was annoyed I hadn't handed them all to her. "Alice has really had to step up," she said, her meaning clear, that I'd been neglecting my daughterly duties. For a moment, I thought she was going to open Tillie's check too, but she stopped just short of it and handed it to Tillie.

"She's done a good job," Tillie said, unfazed.

At one time or another, they'd both worked alongside Mom and Alice, so were essentially part of the family, or more like part of my family's family since I'd opted out of this operation.

Pearl went back to wiping down the counter while Tillie pushed around the cookies in the trays, trying to make them look more plentiful—the meagerness denoting that they'd either just had a big run (doubtful) or they didn't have the customer base to justify filling the trays (more likely).

We chatted a bit more, mostly about the unseasonably hot weather until, mercifully, someone coming in to pick up a birthday cake interrupted us. Rather than passing behind the counter to get to the kitchen, I chose to step outside and walk around to the entrance on Front Street, skirting the motley group of transients, afraid their bad luck might pull me under. But for the most part, I was feeling pretty good. The world was making sense again, the challenges before me, doable: pay someone, they are paid. Simple. Easy. I was good at this stuff and admit I even entertained the fantasy that I might move to Santa Cruz and take over the bakery. It was a great location and just needed a fresh approach. I'd change the recipes, get rid of Pearl. I even went so far as to picture a wedding cake and cupcake display.

I flipped through the checks before entering the kitchen. There was only one employee I didn't know, someone named Kim. It wasn't surprising there weren't more new employees; Dad hired people he thought would stick around—all part of the family thing. I considered pinning the checks to the employee bulletin board, but decided to personally hand out those that I could. I wanted to get a feel for the place, let everyone know that the Mustins were back on board.

The room-sized gas oven made the small kitchen that much hotter, but that heat was laced with scents of sugar, butter, cinnamon, and chocolate. The bread and pie bakers would be gone for the day— they arrived anywhere between 4:00 and 5:00 a.m.—so it was the cake decorator, Chastity, who I came upon first. Young, blond, and head over heels for her live-in biker boyfriend, she was busily cranking out sugared roses on a birthday cake for a "Nana Adelita, the Best Grandma in the World!" Her order rack had three more slips of paper, each one an order for a specialty cake. She was damn good at what she did and knew it. She split her time between our bakery and another, setting her own hours, calling in at the beginning of each day to see how many cakes she had to do. She was always in a hurry. Had a high overhead at home.

"Payday!" I said, clipping her check to her order rack.

"Lucy," she said, barely looking up. "Long time, no see."

"Yeah, well—"

"Trust me," she said. "I get it. Life!"

I took this to mean she didn't want to talk. Which I understood. She was in the baking groove, a mode I knew well, where you're measuring sugar with one hand and cracking eggs with the other. It's like a drug, blotting out the rest of the world. I left her to it and circled the large rolling cooling rack to where the majority of baking was done at two butcher-block counters. The one to the left was temporarily unoccupied, but a stack of empty cookie sheets was waiting to be filled. I glanced at the two giant Hobart mixers holding court at the center of the bakery; sure enough, one was filled with cookie dough. I assumed this was Kim's post.

The second counter was occupied by Robert Coppi, who was preparing the puff pastry dough for the next day's Danishes. An odd guy, in his mid to late sixties, he'd come with the business. Standing about my height, five-seven, he had the physique of a bodybuilder, the leathery, tan skin of a Caucasian island dweller, and always wore light-colored cotton drawstring pants, Hawaiian shirts, and a colorful beanie from Tibet or Guatemala. The tan and muscly physique was a product of his daily swims, sans wetsuit, rain or shine, swell or calm, in the frigid bay, thanks to the "voices" that lived alongside him in his head. He was quite frank about his schizophrenia. If asked, would tell you about the man and woman forever trying to get his attention, fighting with one another, bossing him around, throwing obstacle after obstacle in his path for their amusement. "His own personal Greek gods," was how Alice once put it. Needless to say, he was a moody guy; some days all smiles and chatty, other days you could barely get a word out of him. But the guy made *the* best Danishes I have ever tasted: bear claws, cinnamon buns, raspberry custard twists, you name it—no living person could resist Robert's Danishes, especially when fresh from the oven. Like I said, though, he was quirky.

He and I had worked a few holidays together, because "home for the holidays" in my family meant one thing: putting in long hours at the bakery. Easter it was hot cross buns and decorated cupcakes, Thanksgiving was all about pies, and Christmas, well, you couldn't pump out cookies fast enough: Russian tea cakes, butter stars with red and green sprinkles, sugar cookies shaped like mittens, ornaments, candy canes... My point being, I knew Robert. Not well. But I knew him.

I was happy to see him that day. He and my dad had been close, or as close as anyone could be to him. To hear Dad tell it, they'd have long, metaphysical conversations while turning out pastries. He'd come home shaking his head, saying, "That Robert has some nutty ideas, but I'll be damned if some of them don't make a wacky kind of sense." That's how my dad was; he took in the strays. No doubt because he had one of his own. For as lovable as Alice was—and I do hope you love her—she was a hellion to raise, and I salute each of my parents for having done their part with as little aid as they had.

I placed the envelope on the shelf above him. "Your check, Mr. Coppi."

He didn't seem surprised to see me, just continued kneading the mound of dough. "Some heat, huh?"

"Yep." I knew I should be hitting the road, but I wanted a feel for what was going on at the bakery, and Robert would tell me the truth. "So, anything I should know? Is the new baker working out?"

"New? You mean Kim?"

"Yeah. I guess she's not *that* new."

Right then a husky voice boomed from the basement. "Bingo!"

Robert lit up. "Oh, she's a keeper. Got a lot going on, but does her job. Makes a fine cookie."

His appraisal turned out to be spot-on. Kim always did have a lot going on, but there was no doubt she was a keeper. My first vision of her was of one beautiful, strong hand, with three silver and turquoise rings, thrust up through the trapdoor in the floor, clutching a box of parchment paper like a hard-won trophy. This accompanied by her rich, amber voice. "I knew it! I knew if I just took the time to paw through the shelves down here, I'd find another box."

Robert giggled, an emotional expression I wouldn't have imagined in his repertoire.

The hand slapped the box of parchment paper onto the floor. Next came the rest of her gorgeous self as she hauled herself out of the basement and dropped the heavy wooden door shut behind her. Wearing jean cut-offs, flour-covered hiking boots, a sleeveless white tee, and the requisite long white apron, she looked happier about that box of parchment paper than I'd probably ever been about anything in my entire life. Her hair, a riot of bronze corkscrews, was held back ineptly by a red scrunchie.

"Hey," she said when she saw me.

"Hey," I said back.

We held each other's gaze, her warm chestnut eyes meeting mine. It felt like a magical moment, to me, anyway. For all I knew she was just waiting for me to move so she could get back to her post. Whatever the case, my feet would not be moved.

Robert cleared his throat, effectively breaking the spell.

I stumbled backward and nearly slammed into him on his delivery of a lump of dough to the refrigerator. "I'm Lucy," I managed to pry out of my lips. "And I have your...um...paycheck."

"Lucy, as in Lucy's Famous Lemon Bars?"

A ridiculous thrill shot through me. She knew me! Or knew *of* me. "I don't know about *famous*."

She returned to her post and tore off a piece of parchment paper to line the top cookie sheet. "Around here they are. I can't make them fast enough."

I gestured to the cookie dough in the Hobart. "What've you got going here?"

"Peanut butter cookies." She hoisted the mixing bowl up onto the butcher block and began scooping the sticky dough onto the tray with a miniature ice cream scoop. "I'm stoked that I found this parchment paper. It'll save me from having to wash pans."

"She's in a hurry," Robert said. "Has a gig."

"A gig?" I realized I was still holding her paycheck and slipped it between the giant plastic containers of cinnamon and nutmeg on the shelf above her. It was tight quarters. I could smell her shampoo. It was citrusy.

"I just became a member of the local stagehands union." She wiped her hands on her apron and strode purposefully around the empty cooling racks to the oven, grabbing a couple of oven mitts along the way. She pulled out a tray with two almond biscotti loaves, placed the tray on the rack, pulled off her mitt, and pressed one of the loaves with her finger. Satisfied, she pulled out the other two.

Robert angled past me to the utility sink, toting his mixing bowl. "She's only the second woman they've ever allowed in." He ran water into the mixing bowl and began scrubbing it out.

"Impressive," I said.

"Thanks," she said. "Joan Armatrading is in town tonight. I'm working it."

"Joan? Are you kidding me? I love her!"

She was back to scooping peanut butter cookies with those tanned, strong forearms. "Me too."

A trickle of sweat broke free of my temple. I blotted at it with the sleeve of my thermal shirt. When I got back to Portland, I would have to pick up more Santa Cruz–appropriate clothes.

Robert dried his mixing bowl with a clean white towel. "She worked Bonnie Raitt last week." He obviously liked Kim, which told me a lot. He tolerated people at best. Bowl in hand, he squeezed past me and Kim.

I was in the way, I knew it, but couldn't get myself to leave. And it wasn't just because I was enamored of Kim, although that was certainly part of it—a *big* part of it. The rhythm of the bakery was also calming me down.

Robert untied his apron.

"You still swimming?" I asked.

His faced clouded over. "I have to."

I wanted to kick myself. Why had I brought it up? Yes, his daily routine fascinated me, but it had to have been brutal for him, having to swim the cold bay every day to *freeze out the devil*. I glanced at Kim. There was no mistaking her look of compassion. Obviously, she knew about his voices.

"Well, before you leave, is there a good time to talk?" I stammered. "With you too, Kim." I wanted to get Robert's take on the state of the business. My reasons for including Kim were less pure.

Robert paused for a moment, the apron pulled up over his head, then resumed his action of removing it before balling it up and tossing it in the laundry. "You closing the place down?"

I scraped at a bit of dried dough from the counter with my thumbnail. "I don't know what we're doing. But something has to change. Mom and Alice aren't up to running the place and...well..."

"Can't say the writing hasn't been on the wall," he said gruffly.

"I didn't say we're shutting down."

"Then what's there to talk about?"

"I want to do an inventory of what's here. Make a list of equipment and supplies. Like the basement. What's even down there? And I want to get a feel for how you think the kitchen is running, if there's anything we could do to up our profit margin. If Plaza's going to stay open, we're going to have to make some changes."

"Basement is more like a bomb shelter than a basement," Robert said. "Gives me the creeps."

I knew what he meant. The stairway down was rickety, the place itself dark and draped in spiderwebs. It looked as if it had been shored up by brick walls at one time, but the clay-rich soil seemed to be reclaiming it. My dad had installed several metal shelves and had used them to store seasonal nonperishables like the red and green sprinkles used at Christmas. It also served as a junkyard for old equipment. For the most part, though, the basement was rarely used.

"I just want to talk about the business in general, see how you think it's going." I wasn't going to come out and say I didn't trust Pearl, not yet. "I'd appreciate your input too, Kim. I'm heading up to Portland today, and you've got your gig, but I'll be back late on Monday. Maybe we could set up something, say, after five? Close a little early and do a walk-through? You'd be paid, of course."

Kim scooped the last of the cookie dough onto a tray. "Tuesday would be better for me." She walked the three trays of raw cookies over to the oven and placed them onto the rotating racks. "I've got softball practice on Monday."

Any doubts I had about her being gay evaporated. "Tuesday's fine with me. Robert?"

"World Series," he said.

"So, we should do it another time?"

"No. I'm okay with it. Not much of a baseball fan. Just thought I'd mention it."

"How about you, Kim? You okay with missing the game?"

"Yeah. It's too painful. The Giants are getting their butts whipped."

"You sure?"

"Yup. I should tell you, though, I'm not going to be here much longer."

"The stagehand's union is stealing her from us," Robert said.

"I told Alice. She knows."

Kim would say that this was the moment she knew I was interested in her, how I hemmed and hawed something about her opinion being "fresh" and "valued." I don't remember. I just know that we set a date for Tuesday, 5:00 p.m., the three of us, and I felt such a sense of accomplishment, and optimism, and a pleasant anticipation at getting to see her again.

She would also insist I tell you that I questioned her about the shortening in the butter cookies. She always included it when she told the story of how we met; her point being that no matter how smitten I was, I was still unable to let this baking faux pas pass. Turns out Pearl had stopped ordering butter long ago. Kim always says that if Pearl hadn't been the culprit, that if *she'd* been the one responsible for using shortening instead of butter, we might never have gotten together. I'd like to think that's not true, but I was very self-righteous in those days.

Once the meeting was set, there was really no point in my hanging around. I had the long drive in front of me. Still, I lingered, strolling over to the bulletin board to pin up the other paychecks, noting the day-old bread set out for Tom, an arrangement that had been going on since my dad had run the bakery. Tom swept the floors and picked up trash outside the bakery every morning in exchange for day-old baked goods that he distributed among his friends. My dad tried to pay him, but he always declined the money, saying it only got him into trouble.

"You know," Kim said, "they need ushers tonight. I could get you into the concert for free."

How badly I wanted to go! And how encouraged I was that she'd thought to invite me. "Damn! I can't. I have to make and deliver a wedding cake by noon tomorrow—in Portland. Maybe next time?" I added, like I planned to be in Santa Cruz for a while.

"Sure." She smiled. "Next time."

After that, I had no excuse to stick around so said good-bye, feeling foolish that I was so looking forward to seeing her again.

I stopped by the front to tell Pearl and Tillie about closing early on Tuesday. Pearl wasn't happy about it. Nor was she happy when I grabbed a handful of gingerbread cookies to hand out to the group of transients outside. I tell you, visiting the bakery had done me good. For the first time since arriving in Santa Cruz, I thought I might have it in me to fix what was broken.

Sitting here these twenty-some years later, I find myself wondering about the timing of Kim's and my meeting, if the heartbreak I was experiencing hadn't made me more open. Kim would tell you that everything that happened that Indian summer of 1989 was our destiny. She believed we were soul mates. But destiny, for me, has always been a hard pill to swallow. Perhaps if I could believe in this cosmic design, my uneasy conscience could rest. Perhaps.

Egads, I've just learned on the internet that unless I make arrangements (i.e., prepay for my burial) I will be treated as an Unclaimed Person. Apparently, it's a modern epidemic: people dying and no one willing to take financial responsibility. They cremate you anyway, then fold you up in an envelope, assign you a number, and stick you in a drawer until someone coughs up the dough to take you home. I've no idea if there's a statute of limitations on this, whether or not there comes a point where they empty a year's worth of unclaimed ashes into a Hefty bag and toss you in the trash. Any way about it, I find the thought terrifying. I'm going to have to generate some cash. Getting Alice squared away has eaten up my reserve. None of this is cheap! Reverse mortgage? Or I could sell the house and move into one of those retirement places, while away my golden years eating steamed vegetables and boiled chicken.

I never should have looked it up, certainly not in the middle of the night. It's going on 4:00 a.m. and I'm still wired, tired, and now freaked out on top of it all. I think I have it in me to do one more chapter. Anything to take my mind off the vision of my poor little ashes forgotten in some government drawer.

Earlier, I poured myself a glass of Cabernet from a bottle that's been gathering dust in the pantry since two Christmases ago. It was a gift from a neighbor. I didn't drink it, though, just looked at it for a while before pouring the glass and bottle down the sink. Then I did Alice's laundry. I couldn't stand seeing her T-shirts, underwear, and socks looking so sad on the floor of her closet. I didn't know what to do with them after washing them, so returned them to her bureau. I worry that I didn't fold them neatly enough.

MY OTHER LIFE

My mind was filled with plans on the drive back to Portland, all of them contingent on increasing production at the bakery. The bakery was in a great location. It just needed new management and an updated product line. With these simple adjustments, I was sure we could turn a profit. Then we'd hire someone to look after Mom, renovate the garage into a comfortable unit where the nice caretaker would live. It already had electricity and a sink. Throw in a toilet, a shower, some sheetrock, maybe add a skylight, and voilà, it would be perfect. Maybe Alice would want to live out there. Let the caretaker stay in the house. Whatever. It was a plan.

I, the good daughter, would, of course, help Alice and Mom through the transition, thereby providing me the opportunity to get to know Kim better. I would run the bakery while she worked her gigs. I loved that word: gigs. And when we were in a crunch at the bakery, she'd help out. Would I move to Santa Cruz? Possibly. Or, after getting things straightened out, I'd woo her to Portland. She'd love Toi and Dune, I was sure of it. I would sublet my apartment, take a sabbatical from my business. Or maybe I could commute for a while. The drive wasn't *that* bad. Surely with a little creativity…

My Pollyanna attitude started to wear off at about the same time as the caffeine did, and darker thoughts took over. Why hadn't I stopped by the house before taking off for Portland? What if Alice was still in shutdown mode? I pictured Mom emptying the refrigerator, leaving food on the counters to spoil. I pictured Mr. Scratch covered in maggots. Had I locked the gate when I'd left? Would Mom be able to get out?

I pulled over at a gas station outside of Redding. It was roughly 6:00 p.m. I'd been driving five hours. It was dark. I had to piss like a racehorse. Still, I strode straight to a pay phone by the dumpsters and dialed Mom and Alice's number. There was no answer. I left a message. "Alice. Pick up the phone. Alice. Alice!" I dialed again. This time, Mom picked up.

"Hello?"

"Mom, it's me, Lucy. Are you okay?"

"Who?"

"Lucy, your daughter."

"She's not here right now."

I didn't bother clarifying. I was so damn happy she wasn't out wandering the streets. "Is everything okay there?"

She didn't answer.

"Mom?"

Still no answer.

"Would you get Alice for me?"

There was a clunking followed by a shuffling sound, then nothing. I waited, the stench of the dumpsters making me nauseous. I shouted, "Alice!" then waited some more. In the fluorescent light outside the minimart, a cowboy having a smoke gave me a concerned look. I turned my back to him. "Alice!" I shouted again. After a few more attempts, I hung up and redialed. Predictably, I got a busy signal. I rummaged through my bag, hoping by some miracle I'd tucked Emma Buswell's number in there. For once, luck was with me. Or so I thought, until I got *her* answering machine.

"Emma? This is Lucy Mustin. I'm halfway to Portland." I quickly added, "I'm coming back tomorrow. I just had some business to attend to. I was wondering if you might maybe check on Mom and Alice sometime today. When you get back, I mean. I'm sure everything's fine. It would just be a great help—a load off. Anyway, I won't be getting home until after midnight, but you could leave me a message. Or—I mean, *and*—I'll try again later. So, um, thank you."

I got off the phone feeling worse than ever.

Dinner was a couple of Slim Jims and a bag of overly salted assorted nuts. I stopped once more along the way, outside of Ashland, and this time got a hold of Emma. She'd gone over, she said, and everything appeared to be fine.

I thanked her and turned my worries to the upcoming wedding. The bride, Sandra, was a good friend, an ex, actually, who'd gone straight. Well, she said she could never be "straight," but you'd never know it by her demure fiancée act, coddling her man like a Fabergé egg. It was nauseating. Especially since she'd never treated *me* that way. But when Dune accepted the job as wedding planner, and Toi as the photographer, I felt I had no choice but to bake her damn cake, or I should say, cakes. (Is it just me, or does it seem like a bad omen when a bride and groom need separate cakes?)

Let me be clear: what had me dreading the wedding wasn't jealousy. Sandra and I hadn't been together long, eight months tops, and difficult ones at that; our parting was definitely consensual. I was hurt because in 1989, it was still unlawful for gays to marry, and it rankled to see Sandra flaunting her newfound entitlement as if it held no more importance than a new pair of shoes. I, however, was determined to be a good sport, and so reviewed the needed ingredients in my head. I had everything for the main wedding cake, a vanilla chiffon with buttercream frosting and salted caramel filling. But for the groom's cake, I'd have to swing by the grocery to pick up the tomato soup, cream cheese, and who knew what all, meaning I'd have to stop home to get the recipe before heading to the store. This did not make me happy.

It began to rain. I reduced my speed. I was sick of all my tapes, so I flicked on the radio and lucked onto a talk show: two astrologers talking about Saturn moving into the conjunction aspect with Neptune. If they were to be believed, a planetary alignment was the cause for a number of 1989 headlines: the Dalai Lama being awarded the Nobel Peace Prize, the Chinese government crushing the student uprising in Tiananmen Square, the *Exxon Valdez* spilling millions of gallons of crude oil into Prince William Sound, the world's first legally hitched gay couple in Denmark. I can't say I believed that the planets were responsible for all this, but listening to it passed the time, and I do remember adding to the headline list: Lucy Mustin Makes the Trip to Santa Cruz and Finds Her Family in Chaos.

Just shy of midnight, I dragged into my apartment and was greeted by a blinking message machine. Most of them were from Sandra, who was freaking out about the cake colors. She'd seen the bridesmaid dresses and was sure they'd clash. "Are you even home?" she wailed. "Why aren't you returning my calls?" Dune had left a couple, bitching about Sandra, calling her the bride from hell. "How could you have gone out with this woman? Seriously. It has me questioning your taste in women." He asked when I was getting home. He sounded worried. A potential client wanted to know if I could make a cake in the shape of the island of Kauai. The public library's electronic voice told me I had overdue books. And Toi asked me to call when I got back. "No matter what time you roll in, you give me a call. You hear? I've been worried sick about you." You get the gist. I had a life in Portland, responsibilities, overdue library books. I also had friends, thank God. Good friends. I called Toi immediately. The second she picked up, I started to cry.

"I'm coming over," she said.

"No, wait," I managed to get out between sobs. "I have to go to the store. There are some ingredients—"

"Give me a list."

"Toi, that's too much. I can—"

"Go see what you need. I'll pick them up on my way over. I'll call Dune too, let him know everything is under control. The poor guy is, well, never mind. Go find that recipe."

Forty-five minutes later, she was at my house with two bags: one full of ingredients and one with two burgers and a carton of french fries. "First, we eat," she said. "You can fill me in while we bake Sandra's cake."

"Cakes," I said.

"Oh, right, the infamous tomato soup cake."

"In the shape of a hiking boot."

"Good grief! What you ever saw in that woman I will never know." Over burgers and fries, I spilled out the events of the last few days.

"Poor Alice," she said. "Poor you. Poor your mom."

"I don't know about Mom. She seems pretty happy in her world."

"I guess. But doesn't it seem like, on some level, she must know that something's lost?"

Did Toi actually ask me this? Or have I attributed it to her because I've been pondering this very thing recently? Did Mom know she was slipping? Had there been a time when, for a moment, say, between cracking an egg and dropping it into the bowl, that she thought: *Odd, I'm standing here with a cracked egg in my hand and I have no idea why.* Or was the draining of her sanity too slow to notice, like the retreat of the ocean's tide, each wave stealing a bit more: the neighbor's name—*slosh*. The days of the week—*slosh*. The purpose of a fork—*slosh*. More than once, I've entered a room in the house and, for a brief moment, it looks foreign to me. It's an odd sensation, free-floating, but in a bad way. There are other signs that I might be losing my mind. Buying stamps at the post office last week, the fellow gave me a look as if I were daft and asked if I was feeling all right. I've no idea what prompted his concern, but the whole interaction made me uneasy.

Enough worry! I'm seventy-nine, for God's sake. I can't be

expected to remember everything. Honestly, I can drive myself crazy with such thoughts, especially at 4:30 a.m. I just hope I haven't made you question my mental acuity; that would make two of us.

So, back to that rainy night, to my apartment, to Toi helping me with the cakes, listening to me go on and on about my family. I blathered while rolling out the ivory-colored fondant to a perfect nickel-thick sheet, blathered while laying the satiny sheet over the three cake layers, blathered while I coaxed and massaged the fussy fondant over the cake tiers until it looked as smooth as a pearl. And Toi, bless her, listened. She even stuck around while I sculpted the fondant waterfall and wildflowers. Then came the groom's cake. Though smaller, it was much more difficult. Too moist for sculpting, I had to use gobs of cream cheese frosting to get it to look like a hiking boot. But I was happy with the result, and Toi said it was one of my best.

The wedding was like all weddings: wonderful and stressful. Sandra's relationship didn't last, but anyone could have seen that coming. It wasn't for lack of good cakes, I can tell you that. Everyone loved them. And they loved Dune, and Toi, which was all our trio cared about.

Once we'd ushered Sandra and Roger off in a flurry of birdseed, my lack of sleep caught up with me. It was going on 5:00 p.m. Dune, Toi, and I stood together, watching the black-and-white-clad caterers cleaning up. The band was packing up too. A few folks lingered, chatting in small groups. One couple swayed slowly on the dance floor, even though there was no music. "I'm outta here," I said. "Straight home to bed."

Dune brushed some cake crumbs from my white chef's jacket. "You can't. We're coming over to your place to celebrate."

We were back at my apartment in less than an hour, a bottle of filched wedding champagne open and ready for toasting. I never could say no to Dune. Tall, thin, and a true strawberry-blond, he is one of the most charismatic people I've ever met. For weddings, he wore his curly hair in a tight, collar-length ponytail. He was a snappy dresser, too: the only man I've ever known to own more than one tux. He lived to dress.

"To another fabulous wedding!" he said, holding one of my chipped champagne flutes in the air.

Toi thrust hers up to meet his. "Indeed!"

To my embarrassment, I started to choke up. "To you guys!"

"Oh, please. You think you have it bad. The guy I took home from the bar last night thinks he loves me. He's called me three times today."

Dune was never one for encouraging sentimentality, said he got enough of that at weddings.

"You're a cad," Toi said.

"Apparently, a lovable one," he volleyed back, then took a swig and scowled. "I warned her not to skimp on the champagne. But did she listen?" It wasn't so bad, however, that he had to refrain from drinking it. For the record, it tasted fine to me. We drained the bottle, then, as Toi was popping a second, Dune tossed fifty dollars in front of each of us. "Your cut of the tip."

"To cash!" Toi said.

"To cash!" I said.

It was one of our rituals.

Halfway through the second bottle, Toi began taking photos of our socked feet propped up on the coffee table amid plates of half-eaten wedding hors d'oeuvres. There was an ashtray with a good-sized roach from the joint we'd smoked and the empty bottle of champagne.

"You know," Dune said, refilling our glasses. "She was right about the lavender." Which set us off laughing something fierce.

I was so happy—despite the family drama in Santa Cruz, or maybe because of it. Everything seemed more fragile, temporary, precious: my apartment more colorful, my friends even more wonderful.

Then the phone rang. It was close to 7:00. Every cell in my body screamed: *Let the answering machine get it!* Of course, I couldn't. I cast a quick glance at Toi and Dune before picking up. Sensing my unease, they stopped horsing around.

"Had to take Mom to the urgent care, I did," Alice said.

Sobriety hit me like a slap to the face. "What? What happened?"

"Stomach cramps. Doc says her pipes are blocked. We have to give her an enema. When are you coming back?"

Had it not been for Dune and Toi, I would have jumped in my car and set out on the eleven-hour drive immediately.

"You are in no condition to drive," Toi said.

"Agreed," Dune echoed. "You need sleep."

"And to sober up."

"But my mom—"

"Needs you alive," Toi said. "So does Alice. So, go to bed. I'll clean up here."

Dune downed the last of his champagne. "I'll help."

"And by 'help,' he means sit around and watch while I do it," Toi said and clicked one last picture of our debauchery.

"I just never got the knack of washing dishes. It's so tricky."

Toi lobbed a wadded-up napkin at him. "You're so full of shit."

"I think you're mistaking me for Lucy's mother."

"That is *not* funny," I said.

"Of course it is," Toi said, laughing along with Dune. "You're just too tired and stressed to know it. Now go to bed. Get some sleep. Your mom's constipation can wait."

"And if it doesn't," Dune called after me as I stormed to my bedroom, "problem solved!"

I slept like the dead for six hours, then woke in a panic. It was 1:45 a.m. I'm not sure what I'd dreamt, but whatever it was, it had my heart racing. I sat up, blinked a few times, then headed for the shower. I was out the door, coffee in hand, by 2:15.

I have no memory of the drive down.

FIGHTING

Mom was not in her usual spot in the living room. Her choppy snores drifted down the hallway from the bedroom. It was 11:45 a.m. I was exhausted from the drive. I found Energizer Bunny Alice in the kitchen mixing up some chicken salad. "You hungry?" she said.

"Well, hello to you too, sister."

She looked at me quizzically.

"I've been gone," I clarified, "and have now returned."

"Your point?"

I grabbed a couple of glasses from the cabinet. "Never mind." Put the glasses on the table. "Yes, I'm hungry. What about Mom? Is she going to eat?"

"Best to let her sleep. Was up much of the night, she was. Serious abdominal pain, it is."

"So she hasn't...?"

"Nope. *Something* blocked her up." Alice glanced at the almost empty nut jar sitting on the counter.

"I had to do something to keep her busy."

Alice blopped a glob of mayonnaise into the chopped-up chicken and celery and stirred so vigorously the metal spoon clanged against the sides of the stainless steel bowl.

"How was I to know they would block her up?"

Exasperated, she stopped stirring and began to slather the chicken salad onto the bread. "The five main causes of constipation are gluten, dairy, cruciferous veggies, legumes, and nuts."

"Well, thank you for the education; now, will you cut me some slack? Please?"

She set down two plates, a diagonally halved sandwich in the center of each. The crusts had been cut off, exactly the way Mom used to do it.

I filled our glasses with tap water. "So, anything else happen since I left?" I sat at the table. "Besides Mom's constipation?"

"*Besides* Mom's constipation? Let's see…" She sat across from me, plucked a paper napkin from the holder, and spread it neatly on her lap. "I buried Mr. Scratch." Behind her, a ray of sunlit dust motes streamed into the kitchen, giving her a biblical look. "And yet another day passed that I was unable to bring my bottles to the bar."

A car in need of a muffler thundered past.

"Alice, I'm sorry, but I really had to make that cake. I do have a job, you know." It was tempting to call her out on her meltdown, to say: *If you hadn't shut yourself in your room, you could have taken the bottles before I left!* But I held my tongue. The loss of Mr. Scratch was devastating for her. Which is not to say she'd never faked a meltdown.

Once, when I was about fourteen, making Alice eleven or twelve, we were supposed to spend the weekend with some neighbors. Usually, when Mom and Dad headed off for one of their romantic getaways, Aunt Evie would stay with us, but she couldn't that weekend, so we were being pawned off on the Schneiders, who had two annoying boys, one prissy girl, and a mangy mutt who, if you took your eye off him for one second, would try to mount you. Alice faked a doozy that time, was so convincing that Mom and Dad left us alone at the house with me in charge. I remember yelling, "Clear!" when their car disappeared around the corner. Alice bounded out of the bedroom, laughing and clapping. We lived on peanut butter and bananas that weekend, ice cream and potato chips, and watched so much TV it's amazing our brains didn't melt.

I bit into my sandwich and felt the slight crunch of pulverized potato chips: Mom's recipe to a T. I wasn't three bites into my first half when Mom started moaning from the bedroom.

Alice dropped her sandwich onto her plate. "And so it goes."

I took another bite of sandwich. Alice pulled off her boots. I washed the bite down with a gulp of water and followed, lemming-like, out of the kitchen into Mom's bedroom.

Mom's float du jour was baby blue and white. I vaguely remembered having sent it to her for some holiday. Her knotty, age-spotted fingers nervously kneaded the pink blanket, which she'd pushed down around her waist.

"Time for the procedure," Alice said. "Are you ready?" Instead of waiting for an answer, she turned her back on Mom and explained the plan to me. One of us was to hold her up while the other inserted the enema. We'd use the bathtub. Mom let me help her out of bed and down the hall toward the bathroom, a testament to how much pain she was in; she walked slightly bent over, as if she were cramping up.

I uttered reassurances.

Alice hurried ahead and prepared the enema.

"Isn't the doctor coming?" Mom asked.

"Doc said we should do it here!" Alice called from the bathroom.

Mom looked at me, alarmed. "Here?"

"At least to get it started," I said, rubbing the bony hump of her back, "until the doctor arrives." I kicked off my flip-flops at the bathroom door.

"He's coming?" Mom said.

"We need to get her into the bathtub," Alice said.

"You hear that, Mom? We need to get you into the bathtub."

"Who is this woman?" Mom asked Alice. "And why does she keep calling me Mom?"

A hot flush of shame rose in my cheeks. Here I thought we'd been doing so well.

Alice left me to explain myself.

"I'm your daughter, Lucy. Come home to help. Now, let's get you into the tub."

Mom let me help her out of her float, let me yank off her panties, but she wasn't happy about it. Not like she'd been during her free beauty session. It was all happening too quickly, but Alice would not be slowed down. I steadied Mom as Alice guided her into the tub, one leg, then the other. It was difficult for her to get her foot up and over the edge. She didn't have the flexibility. Alice torqued her leg too hard.

"Ouch!"

"Slow down," I said to Alice for the third time.

"You want to do this part?"

She had me there.

Once all three of us made it into the tub, I held Mom by the forearms while Alice squatted behind her. The hot water bottle with enema fitting hung from the curtain rod, its hose snaking down and clipped shut so the water wouldn't spray until just before insertion. "It's okay," I said to Mom as Alice tried to pry open her legs. "We're trying to make you feel better."

Mom tried to squirm out of my grasp.

I tightened my grip.

"What are you boys up to?" she said. "What are you trying to do?"

The implication of her words stunned me. "There are no boys. It's just me and Alice, and we're trying to help relieve your constipation."

Alice tried to spread her legs again; again Mom tried to jerk free of my grasp.

"Maybe we should try later," I said.

"When?" Alice snapped. "When would be better?"

Again, she had me.

After a few more tries, Alice managed to spread Mom's legs enough that she could insert the thin plastic tube.

Mom stiffened, then shoved at me with her forearms.

"Alice," I said. "Are you sure you're doing it right?"

"You're not getting away with this!" Mom said.

"We're just trying to make you feel better," I said.

"I know what you want! It's all any of you boys want!"

"Alice!" I shouted.

Mom was writhing now, screaming, "Help! Help!"

I lost my footing and plowed into the towel rack, causing one side of it to dislodge.

"Alice! Stop! It isn't working!"

"There's still more water in the bag."

"Mom's freaking out!"

It was awful, appalling. It felt as though we were raping Mom. She was moaning a horrible, tortured moan as she twisted and turned, her face covered in tears. Who knew what she was reliving, and who these boys were. "Pull it out!" I yelled. "Pull it out!" But Alice wouldn't.

Unable to stand it another second, I squatted, wrapped an arm around Mom's waist, and flopped her frail torso over my back, giving me a free hand. With it, I reached past Mom, grabbed Alice's wrist, and pulled out the enema tube. The brashness of the move took all three of us by surprise. Mom stopped screaming, Alice stopped the procedure, and all that was left of our yelling was heavy breathing.

Water gurgled from the limp hose in Alice's hand, trickled between Mom's bare feet, through mine, and toward the drain. With Mom still draped over my back, I didn't dare move. My thoughts were still trying to catch up with my actions. Mom's bowels didn't move either, not even a dribble. At least, not at first. Then they let loose in one giant blast. *Blam!* And watery shit splattered across the tub floor.

"Oh my goodness," Mom said, her voice full of wonder. "Would you look at that!"

I laughed. I couldn't help it. The whole situation was so bizarre,

Mom flung over my back shitting her guts out. She started laughing too. She must have felt better. Then I noticed Alice. She was covered in shit: shit in her hair, shit on her glasses, shit all over her formerly clean white tee. "Oh God, Alice, I'm so sorry!" Even so, I couldn't stop laughing, and trying to stop just made me laugh that much more. I tried to convince Alice it was an accident, but Alice had a difficult time making sense of mistakes. I could tell she believed I'd aimed Mom's butt directly at her.

There was nothing to do but move on.

Alice waited in the tub as I sponged off Mom, waited as I rinsed off Mom's feet, waited as I rinsed off my own feet. Then I had to put Mom's panties and float back on. Through all this, Alice waited. I knew better than to offer to help her clean herself up. She was modest to the extreme, and wallowing in a mix of anger and humiliation. As for my thousand apologies, they bounced right off her.

We both had the sense not to pick it back up in front of Mom, but Alice and I weren't done. Me, I couldn't stop thinking about Mom and *the boys*. Had she been raped at some time in her life? Had we made her relive it? And Alice, she was just pissed.

"What boys?" I said to Mom as I followed her down the hallway. "What boys were you talking about?" But her mind was already on the fridge.

I fed her the other half of my sandwich and wrapped up Alice's mostly uneaten one. Alice didn't want it, though. She washed up and retreated to the garage, at which point I went to clean up the bathroom. But she'd done it. I pictured her bent over the tub, naked, scrubbing away Mom's shit. I pictured her hating me.

As for Mom, she retired to her spot in front of the TV, happy as a lark.

I made myself a cup of coffee and sat at the kitchen table listening to the washing machine, then the dryer clunking around in the garage. There was no point in trying to get Alice to talk. She would when she was ready. I hoped it would be sooner rather than later. I hated the feeling of her hating me.

I moved out to the lounger, tried to nap. Couldn't. I grabbed my novel, tried to read. Couldn't. The more I thought about the incident, the more defensive I got; the more defensive I got, the angrier I became. If Alice would have just listened to me…

Alice emerged from the garage around 4:00 and began to rake up leaves from the neighbor's persimmon tree. I got up to help, sweeping leaves into a pile using the kitchen broom.

"You're going to get it dirty," Alice said.

"The broom?"

"It's an indoor broom, it is."

"For Christ's sake, Alice, what do you want from me? I came down to help, but you won't let me! You blame me for leaving the gate open; well, you should have told me. You blame me for the nuts; what was I supposed to do? You were...out. And just now, in the bath, Mom was upset! She was replaying some horrible thing from her past. Maybe you couldn't see it, but I think some boys...hurt her at some time, and she was reliving it."

"Sometimes she plays out parts from movies, she does. I've seen her!" Alice spoke with such force her Clark Kents slipped down the bridge of her nose.

I shut the sliding glass door so as not to involve Mom in our yelling. "That was no movie! You should have seen her!"

"You don't know that! You're not the one here! I'm the one here! I know what's going on! Not you. Me! Me!" Alice shoved a rakeful of leaves into a black plastic bag. Then another and another, until a tine of the rake caught and ripped the bag. She tossed both to the ground. "You don't know!"

She was right, of course. I didn't know, hadn't been around. But I was right too. If she wanted help, she was going to have to let someone help her. And just because it was convenient for her to believe Mom's feelings weren't real, didn't make it true.

I took a deep breath. Our yelling wasn't helping anything. I raised my gaze from the newly raked cement path beneath my bare feet to Alice, who stood, booted feet spread wide, arms crossed at her chest, and mad as a wet hen, as Mom would say.

"So what do you want, Alice? Can you put it into words?"

"To take my bottles to the bar."

"Fine. Go for it."

"I can't now."

"Okay, when?"

"Tomorrow."

"Fine. You can have all day, or until five. Then I'm meeting with Robert and Kim at the bakery."

"Why?"

"To see if we can get it to make a decent profit. You need help with Mom. We need to find a way to pay for it." I figured this was as good a time as any to tell her my thoughts about getting a live-in aide, so I did. It did not go over well.

"I don't see that as a good plan at all. No, I do not. The garage is where I make my bottles. And who would live in my garage? Who would that be, exactly? Would they be in the kitchen? In the house? Would they want to watch TV with us? They're probably going to want me to talk to them all the time, shoot the shit. We'd have to talk about the weather, the price of gas, TV fads…"

"Forget it. It was just a thought." And a good one, I still believed, but it was going to take more convincing. "I still want to see if we can up production at the bakery."

"I want to come."

It was my turn to ask why.

"I just do."

She didn't trust me. That was it. We both knew it.

"What will we do with Mom?"

"Wait in the car, she can. Tillie can sit with her."

How could I say no to such a productive family expedition? Only now, I wouldn't get my time alone with Kim.

Our fighting continued, silently, throughout the evening. I'd laid out my case, she hers, and there was nothing left but for us to stubbornly go about our business. We were used to this; we'd fought all the time as kids. What I couldn't get used to was the look on Mom's face in the bathtub. It whirled around my head as I drank myself to sleep that night in my sweltering room. Who had she been fighting?

If you're expecting the big reveal later in my tale, a shocking disclosure that casts light upon this horrible incident in my mother's life, don't. If it did happen, and I believe it did, the particulars vanished along with her memory. A small mercy, I suppose.

April 28, 1950

Dear Euvie,

    I'm so sorry to hear about the Laundromat!!! Seems like y'all just barely got it up and running. We all thought it was such a good idea, a Laundromat in a college town. I will admit, I'm not surprised Hugh and laundry weren't a good match. I hope you won't take offense, me saying that. But you did marry a dreamer. Half the time I'm so jealous of your life, the other half I'm thanking my lucky stars for my predictable tomato farmer. (Who says hello, by the way.)

    How's it going to work out, the lease on your all's home being up before you can move into the new one? Knowing you and Hugh, you'll turn it into some grand adventure for the girls. I worry, though. Alice is so persnickety! Do you need money? If so, just ask. I've been putting some aside for a rainy day. (Don't tell Frank. He'd want to put the money toward the new barn he's building. Why he thinks he needs another barn, I do not know, but he's set on it. Last year it was his pout house; this year, a new barn. The man just loves to build.)

    Also, and this is hush-hush, Mama says she's gonna sign some of her oil checks over to you and me. Won't Daddy have a fit?! But like she says, the money is hers to do with what she wants. So keep your fingers crossed she goes through with it. She's getting a bit forgetful. I'm worried about her. She forgot Frank's name the other day. Can you believe? Just plumb slipped from her mind. Doc says to make sure she's not taking too many sleeping pills, so I counted them out and check every day. That's not the problem. Anyway, I'll do my best to help her remember about the checks. I know we could all use a little extra.

    Big news around here is the Conways left the church to follow a new fellow that's starting to preach out at the Grange Hall. I guess they're really eager to get to heaven and don't think our Pastor Peters is the man to get them there. Not that I blame them. Last Sunday, it was everything I could do to keep from nodding off as he went on and on about "taking up the whole armor of God." I tell you, that man is so boring he could put the sun to sleep.

What do you all think of Senator McCarthy's list of communists? You know me, I don't pay much attention to politics, but the fact that we could be living next door to a communist scares the heck out of me. Frank says no communist in his right might would be living in East Texas, that they're all in New York and California. Be careful!!!!! I miss you something awful.

Your loving and predictable sister,

Evokia

PS. Please tell Lucy I loved the birthday card and the enclosed short story. Very ingenious!

Time is getting blurry again, as sometimes happens. I walked into the garage expecting Alice's tidy shelves of tools, her clean workbenches and swept floor, and instead, found Dad's clutter of unfinished projects, his buckets of hammers and hook of dull handsaws, even the shiny chrome Cadillac bumper that he lugged with us every time we moved. He'd hang it above each workbench. It was from his first Cadillac, the car that saved his life when he was rear-ended by a delivery truck. It accordioned right up to the front seat, which remained untouched, or so the story goes.

I can't tell you how unnerved I was by this chink in time. I almost expected to see him sitting there, smoking, on what Mom called "his throne," a beat-up green leather chair, surrounded by junk. Dad hated to throw things away, would cart things home he picked up on the side of the road or at garage sales: broken tables, light fixtures, rusted washtubs; he had plans for it all. Ultimately, it fell to Mom to toss the crapped-out stuff. She'd call to have it hauled off when he wasn't around. This process was never talked about, but it had to have been difficult for Dad. He was hard enough on himself without Mom drawing attention to his unfinished projects—although you'd never have known it from his happy-go-lucky public persona. It had to have been hard on Mom too. What a chore to be constantly cleaning up after him.

I stood in the doorway waiting for Alice's orderly collection of rakes and shovels to return, her workbench of bottle-making supplies, the washer and dryer. It gave me quite a scare. It happened again later in the day. I looked up from editing what I've written so far and was thrust into Mom's living room, the collection of souvenir plates of places she'd never been, her bookshelf of Reader's Digest Condensed Books, all of which she'd read. She loved those condensed novels! Would curl up in the living room, cigarette in one hand, novel in the other, a lap blanket across her knees, and shush anyone who bothered her. I didn't have the nerve to cast my gaze toward the door where the gaudy, gold-framed oval mirror used to hang. I knew I would see her reflected there, checking herself out. Even when she'd gone completely gray, when her eyelids were droopy and her skin blotched, when her sight was so bad she'd miss the smear of lipstick on her tooth, she always stopped to check herself in that mirror before leaving. Again, I waited it out, clutching my laptop until the world returned to the present time zone.

Clearly, I am not alone in the house. My telling of this story is calling everyone in: Mom, Dad, Alice. They want to see what I'm going to say next. Alice will want the facts right; Mom, that I make her look good, or perhaps she wants to be vindicated; and Dad, I don't think he cares one way or the other, he's just curious. But the stakes have been raised; no doubt why I've spent much of the day reading and revising what I've done so far. I need to build courage to finish, to get to the Main Event, because everything so far is simply the sauce in which Alice's and my actions marinated. Horrible as those first few days in Santa Cruz were, there was nothing unusual about them. Old people lose their memories all the time, daughters step in to manage their affairs all the time; it's always heartbreaking, the transfer of power always awkward, but it is the natural order of things, and in a way, it was Alice's and my natural order. We'd been negotiating our unpredictable mother all our lives.

Mind, there was more to those few days in Santa Cruz than I've chronicled: endless minutes watching my mother unload the refrigerator, brain-dead minutes half-dozing in front of the TV, Alice and I out on the back loungers laughing at a flock of robins getting drunk on the neighbor's towering pyracanthas—the ordinariness of those moments in stark contrast to the days that would follow. For isn't that what we do after catastrophe strikes? Look back on the moments we barely took the time to notice when they were happening and wish them back? Brushing one's teeth at a clean sink, rolling out the trash to the street.

I didn't wake until noon. Over coffee and toast, I tried to write Alice's obituary again and couldn't make myself do it. The funeral home said the death certificates were ready, so I'll have to pick those up at some point. Honestly, the business of death exhausts me. And knowing there won't be anyone to do this for me, after I've done it for my father, my mother, my lover, and now Alice, well, I'm trying not to feel resentful.

On my daily walk, I once again ran into my little friend. Or should

I say, she ran into me, or nearly did. She came wheeling around the corner on her skateboard. "Sorry!" she said after coming to an abrupt halt, then masterfully flipping the board into her hand. "How are you doing?" she asked. I was touched by her concern and told her I was managing. Turns out her name is Dita. We chatted a bit more about her predicament, that of her parents cutting her off. She said she needed work. So, I was right about her wanting something from me. "I can do all kinds of stuff," she said, whapping the back of her skateboard with her thumbs. "Gardening, I'm good with computer stuff, cleaning; you name it, I'm your gal!" Sees me as an easy mark, I suspect. But I admire her pluck.

I asked about her internship, if that didn't provide her some cash. Turns out it's unpaid work. Shame. Anyway, I told her I'd think on it. Certainly, there are things I need done: the yard is blanketed in leaves, the ivy on the back fence getting unruly, there are a few dead branches that could be cut down and turned into fire wood; things Alice would do if she were alive. I could do them too, except for the dead branches. I can't even look at our ladder, let alone think about climbing it. I haven't much to pay, but I could feed her. She looks like she could use a good meal. I'm just not sure I'm ready to have someone around.

Later, I thought about drinking a glass of wine again, and didn't. Though really, I don't see why I shouldn't. Who could it possibly hurt? I plucked some branches of rosemary from the garden and scattered them around the house, having heard it boosts memory. We'll see. I also surprised myself by calling Dune. I wasn't even sure I had the right number after all these years, but it was his voice on the answering machine. I told him I was sorry to hear about Paul. I left him my number. We'll see if he calls back. For dinner, I ate chocolate ice cream. I never could have gotten away with that when Alice was alive. Her huffs and puffs of disapproval would have taken all the pleasure out of it. I chased the sugar rush with a cup of coffee. It's now 9:54. Outside, the neighbor's cat is wailing at the stars. It's unseasonably warm, just as it was twenty-six years ago, and while most locals love these Indian summers, I always find them unsettling.

PUTTING THE TOP DOWN

Nowadays people talk about humoring those with Alzheimer's, going along with their delusions. I've watched TED Talks about it, listened to NPR specials, and I get it. There's no winning when someone's lost their mind. But they never address how exhausting it is to do this twenty-four/seven, how your brain starts to fizzle, how you feel like *you're* the one going crazy. And they never talk about how much it hurts.

Mom insisted on playing tour guide on the short run to the bakery. She'd point to, say, a liquor store and say something like, "That's where Hugh and I got married!" She was sitting shotgun in the Acura, I was driving, Alice in back. We'd had to take the Acura because Mom wouldn't go near my car. This involved cleaning the windshield of bird shit and dusting off the cobwebs, one more delightful activity in a string of so many.

Neither of us corrected Mom on her landmarks, nor did we engage at all, which bothered her. She wanted attention. She was on an outing and wanted us to get swept up in her excitement, but I was exhausted, functioning on little sleep, grumpy as hell, and Alice was still mad at me from the enema incident.

Mom pointed at a bank. "Oh, look!" We were at a stoplight just seconds away from the bakery. "Look!" she said again. I gave in and looked. "Do you remember what happened there?" I admitted I didn't. "Well…" she said, then lost her focus.

I leaned across her to roll down her window. She recoiled. I didn't let that stop me. The car had no air-conditioning. The light changed. We pressed on. There was a parking spot right outside the bakery on Front Street. I angled the bird shit–covered car into it and shut off the ignition. "Now what?" I was sure Alice had a system that would ease us through the transition.

She shouldered the stubborn car door open. "You stay with Mom. I'll get Tillie."

I can't tell you how badly I wanted *her* to sit with Mom while I went to get Tillie. After all, the visit had been my idea. But I was too tired to even move my mouth. I let my head fall back on the headrest and closed my eyes. Mom opened the glove box and began pulling things out. That's what it sounded like. I didn't look, just listened, and wondered what was taking Alice so long. By this point, I really didn't care. Even the promise of seeing Kim wasn't enough to galvanize me. I say this while having dressed up for her. Earlier, in a stolen moment, I'd slipped into the bathroom and used Mom's nail scissors to tidy up my asymmetric haircut, you know the kind we were so into in the eighties, super short on one side, long, curly mop of salt-and-pepper hair sweeping across to the other. I accented this look with one large silver earring. I had two but chose to wear just the one. (Everything I did was so intentional back then!) I also wore my treasured pair of black carpenter shorts and black Question Reality T-shirt with the cutout neck exposing the strap of my red sports bra. I liked that the T-shirt hid the slight pooch around my middle.

Mom quit her fidgeting. "Evie," she spoke softly, timidly. "Do you know what's going on?"

Being cast as Aunt Evie touched me more than I can say. I opened my eyes, took her hand. "Haven't a clue," I said, because I didn't.

Mom tightened her grip on my fingers. "Sometimes I get confused."

"I know. Me too."

She slid her hand from mine and began fiddling with the radio dial.

"You want some music?"

"I want to put the top down."

She hadn't had a convertible in decades.

"We can't. It's broken."

"That's a shame."

"Yes, it is."

Alice returned with Tillie, who bent down so Mom could get a good look at her through the open window. She had a yellow daisy tucked into her beehive. "Euvonda, how *are* you? You up for a little chitchat?"

Mom lit up like a girl getting asked to the prom. "Why, yes, I most certainly am."

Tillie and I switched out, she taking my seat behind the wheel, me stepping onto the street. I mouthed *Thank you* to Tillie, who, in her modest way, waved it off as though it were nothing. I didn't say good-bye to Mom, a detail that would haunt me for the next sixteen hours.

THE CHOOSER

Kim was cleaning up her baking area. Robert was sitting on his, legs dangling off the butcher block. They both had cups of coffee from the Santa Cruz Coffee Roasting Company, Kim's on the shelf above her, Robert's in his hand. It struck me that even the staff wouldn't touch the stale, Farmer's brand coffee served at the bakery, choosing instead to stroll across the street for a cup of fresh-dripped French roast, Colombian, Italian roast, what have you. I made a note to install a better coffee system in the bakery makeover. I also remember finding Kim every bit as fetching as I'd found her the first time.

"Hey, Alice," she said. "Didn't know we'd have the pleasure of seeing you today." She'd dressed extra cute, her shorts rolled up an extra fold, her T-shirt sleeves too, highlighting her tan, muscular limbs. I hoped she'd done this for me.

Alice pulled a few outdated notes from the employee bulletin board and tossed them in the trash. "Yes. Thought it best I be in on the meeting, I did." She spoke in her professional voice, pitched lower, words clipped and overly enunciated, all of this to let me know that I was trespassing, which hadn't occurred to me until that moment. For better or worse, on top of everything else, she'd kept the bakery operational too. No small feat. Maybe Pearl hadn't been responsible for the shortening in my butter cookies, but Alice. That made even more sense.

Amused, Kim glanced from Alice to me. "Cool." She clearly liked Alice, and knew her, which always made the going easier. I wondered what it was like for her, or any of the employees, to give Alice the last word.

Robert raised his cup by way of greeting. I couldn't imagine him taking orders from Alice. He was as set in his ways as a Zen monk.

"And, Lucy," Kim said, one cheek dimpling, "nice to see you

again. I trust all went well in Portland?" She used the back of her hand to push a wheat-colored curl off her forehead. A simple, unconscious gesture, pushing back a lock of hair, but she might as well have placed that beautiful, strong, tanned hand with its beaded leather wristband on my crotch. That's the truth of it. Because what I felt between my legs was an unbolting of sorts, a release, as though my long-dormant libido were springing back to life. And believe me when I say it had been dead and buried—under heaps of disappointments and layers of excuses.

There'd been no lover in...I don't know how long, and I'd all but stopped masturbating. It left me feeling lonelier than ever. Indeed, menopause had brought with it the Big Dry Spell. I thought I was okay with that, welcomed it even. It made life so much simpler. That is, until Kim brushed that lock of hair from her forehead. Suddenly, I was game for whatever complications a roll in the hay might include, because that's all I could think about. Not love. Not happily ever after. Sex. Hot monkey sex. And it surprised me so much that I started to laugh.

"What?" Kim said. "Do I have flour on my face?"

"No, no! Portland was fine," I got out between giggles. (Yes, giggles. The woman made me giggle.) "Great. I was just...I didn't...I was thinking..." I could feel Robert and Alice looking at me, making it that much harder to make words. My eyes started to tear up, my nose to run. Thankfully, Pearl chose this moment to stick her head into the kitchen.

"I'm just about to close up." She put out a few loaves of day-old bread for Tom, said to Alice, "Anything you need from me?" only glancing at me for a second.

Alice, ever helpful, handed me a paper towel, then used her professional voice to say, "Everything's shipshape, it is. Carry on."

Making changes to the bakery wasn't going to be as easy as I'd hoped. Alice was invested. I blew my nose, wiped my eyes, and used *my* professional voice. "We'll be talking with you at a later time. Just want to get a feel for the kitchen today. Thank you, Pearl."

Pearl clearly didn't like being excluded from the meeting; she could tell change was on the horizon, and that woman resisted change with the fervor of a backwoods preacher. If she teamed up with Alice, I'd be sunk. "I see," she sniffed and returned to her post out front.

"So!" Robert clapped his hands together and slid from the countertop. "I got some friends I got to meet up with. How long is this going to take?"

I blew my nose. "Not long." I could barely look at Kim. Undoubtedly, she thought I was a nutcase. "Shall we, um, start in the basement? What do you think, Alice? Shall we go see what's down there?"

"I know what's down there."

"Okay, well, I don't, and I think I should."

Alice marched over to the basement hatch and hefted it open.

"Sounds good to me." Robert followed.

I was a step away from joining them, when Kim rested one of those gorgeous hands on my shoulder. "Could I have a word?"

"Sure."

I yelled to Alice, already partway down the rickety stairway, "Down in a minute!"

Kim pulled a backpack from under her workstation, unzipped the front pocket, and produced a signed copy of Joan Armatrading's latest cassette. It had my name on it. *Lucy,* it said, *Wish you could have been here. Joan.*

I began to tear up, even though I already had the tape.

I know what you're thinking: This woman is a basket case! Laughing and crying at the drop of a hat! But I cried more in that week and the weeks to come than I'd probably cried in my whole life. Growing up, I'd been stoic. I'd had to be. My parents had their hands full with Alice; there wasn't room for any theatrics from me. So I learned to tone it down, accept what was, and in my twenties, I learned to drink.

Eyes brimming with tears, I clutched that tape I already owned as if it were a lifeline to a world where my mom still recognized me, my sister didn't hate me, and I wasn't in way over my head.

"Hey," Kim said, softly. "You okay?"

I don't remember exactly what I said; I think, between gulpy sobs, I tried to explain to her what was going on with Mom. Whatever it was, she took me in her arms and held me, and I let myself be held, and I let myself cry while being held, which, back then, was a new experience for me. I liked to do my emoting in private. All that would change with Kim; she was big on feeling your feelings. But I didn't know that then, just knew how good her arms felt, how I clung to her.

For those who've been told relationships take hard work, let me offer you this: they don't have to—not if you don't try to change each other. I've had plenty of those relationships, worked my little butt off trying to change someone into my vision of the perfect partner, or change myself into *their* vision of the perfect partner, but I didn't feel

I deserved to be truly loved for the person I was; I didn't feel I was enough. And I was never the Chooser; always the Chosen—the path of least resistance, the path with the least amount of risk. If someone wanted me, and they were halfway decent, I made the effort to want them back.

But on the evening of October 17, 1989, at 5:01 p.m., in the kitchen of the Plaza Bakery in Santa Cruz, California, weeping my eyes out, I, Lucy Louise Mustin, chose Kimberly Ann Knight to be mine. She had no idea I'd chosen her, and I'm quite sure she didn't choose me, not then. She was just being her usual, wonderful, caring, capable self. The point is, I chose her. I didn't know if I could *have* her, but I admitted to myself that I wanted her; a big move for me, unheard of, really.

She handed me another paper towel, the one Alice had given me now soaked with snot and tears.

"Thank you."

"My pleasure."

"I'm usually not—"

"I can tell."

"It's just been...I don't know..."

"A lot?"

"Yeah, a lot."

She had her hands on my shoulders now and was regarding me tenderly, something I was unaccustomed to, and I was struck by an odd thought: all the terms Toi and I used when checking out women at the bar, or wherever—hot, gorgeous, sexy—were irrelevant, although Kim was all these things. What mattered in that moment, though, was a sensation: two puzzle pieces clicking into place, creating order from chaos.

Alice poked her head up through the hatch. "Chop chop, sisteroo. Miles to go before we sleep."

"In a second!"

Her back to Alice, Kim whispered, "You okay?"

"Yeah."

"Sure?"

I nodded.

"Okay then. I'll be down in a minute. Just let me get my station cleaned up."

"Okay." I took in a lungful of air and headed for the hatch, the gift cassette tucked comfortably in the side pocket of my cargo shorts. I'm sure I had a stupid grin pasted on my face. It was as though the powers that be, whatever, whoever, they are, were throwing me something bright and shiny. God knows, I needed it.

The stairway down to the basement was constructed with planks and two rod rails that descended into the center of the dark, dungeon-like room. A bare bulb with a pull chain hung from a ceiling joist by the stairs and cast an eerie, shadowy glow over the small living-room-sized cavern. I hesitated three-quarters of the way down, letting my eyes adjust to the dimness. I fumbled in my pocket for my pen and palm-sized notepad to jot: *Electrician—see if we can wire for more light.*

To my right, Alice was stacking what looked like baking racks against the brick wall. I remembered my dad saying he'd replaced the racks in the big gas oven upstairs. He'd no doubt had some un-manifested plan for these old ones. The rest of the room's walls were also brick with areas that had been cemented over. I had no idea why. There seemed no rhyme or reason to it. Figure the place was built in 1859, the basement itself a product of shovels, pickaxes, and Chinese sweat. The floor was dirt but you could see remnants of a rotted-out wood floor. The ceiling, along with the sturdy joists, was a maze of copper pipes and wiring.

Robert was gazing impatiently at a row of canned goods on one of the four freestanding metal and wood shelves. He used the flashlight kept down there to augment the crappy lighting. "We'll have to order more canned peaches," he said. "Only a few cans left."

I remember him saying that. I remember being about to reply when a loud rumble, like the groan of a huge, sleeping creature, began rolling toward us through the earth.

Alice, who was bent over with her back to me, jerked up to standing. Robert reached out to steady the rack by him. I grabbed the rail so I wouldn't fall off the stairs. The basement was shuddering violently; things were crashing from the shelves, the lightbulb flickering on and off, turning the whole scene into an old movie reel. A cascade of cans came clattering down on top of Robert. He held up an arm to protect himself. One of the shelves listed to the side. I tried to pivot on the steps to get the hell out but couldn't catch my footing. Then a thunderous roaring ripped the stairway from the wall and slammed the hatch shut, missing my head by inches.

I was falling, flailing and falling. Robert was shouting something I couldn't make out over the din. I think I was shouting too. I landed on my hip, hard. Something cracked into my shoulder. I covered my head with my hands, squeezed my eyes shut. Finally, after what seemed like minutes of being pummeled by debris, the dreadful shaking came to a stop. I opened my eyes. I'd gone blind! That's what I thought, it was that pitch-black, and save for the shrill ringing in my ears, and the accelerated thudding of my heart, quiet as a tomb. I took a deep breath to calm myself, and broke into convulsive coughing. The air was eighty percent dust, but I was breathing; I was alive. There was a stink of vinegar.

I believe I was slightly concussed, because I wasn't thinking clearly. For instance, I did not call out to Alice or Robert, as you might expect, or like they do in the movies, screaming frantically for loved ones moments after whatever disaster Hollywood has cooked up for them. No. I just lay there feeling the frantic *thud-thud-thud* of my heart, my breath's timid *in-out in-out*. I was a scared little mouse in between bats of a cat. Shock? Probably. Resigned? Not so sure about that. Resigned implies recognition of a future, and the present situation was so inconceivable, it blotted out any thoughts of future. Indeed, my mind was still reacting to what had happened moments before the earth moved, as if these thoughts might be helpful somehow, might even apply to my current situation. I remember wondering if I'd thanked Kim for the cassette. Wondering if I'd mentioned I'd like to take her up on ushering sometime. I thought about the bag I'd left on the counter with my car keys in it. Wondering how I was going to drive now that I was blind.

Another explanation for my failure to call out to Alice and Robert: I was not ready to face the horror that I might be the sole person buried alive in that sightless world, that were I to feel around, I might bump into their corpses.

I remember listening for their breathing, remember the ringing in my ears being too loud, remember lifting my right arm to see if I could, my lack of vision making it difficult to know for sure. Had I moved my arm at all? Or did it just feel as though I had?

Then, from out of the inky blackness, came Robert's soft "I'm sorry."

For a few long seconds, his words hung there in the nothingness, my addled brain trying to make sense of them. Was there something I'd missed? Something he'd done to cause this horrible situation? Then, just like that, I was jump-started back into the land of the living. "Robert? It's me, Lucy. Are you okay? Alice? Are you okay? Can you guys see?" The words came out rapid-fire, crazy, my breathing so shallow the air barely made it past my throat. "Alice? Alice? Are you there?" I coughed. "Alice?" Coughed again. "How about you, Robert, are you okay?" I spoke to hear myself speak, to assure myself I was alive.

"So far so good," Robert said, "and no, I can't see. The light must have gone out."

So I wasn't blind! What a relief! I listened to the shift and scrape of him moving; cringed involuntarily, afraid he was going to set things falling again.

He grumbled, "One of these shelves came down on my foot. I don't think my foot's broken...no...not broken. But I need to get this shelf off me."

The ordinariness of his voice helped me focus. A fallen shelf. A foot. Robert. These were things that could be dealt with.

"How about you?" I listened to him say. "You okay?"

I mentally scanned my body but was too frantic to make sense of its flurry of messages. "We have to find Alice," I managed before starting to cough again. I tried to sit up and cracked my head on something. Saw stars. Pushed past them. "Alice! Alice!" I shouted. They say adrenaline keeps a person from feeling pain. This must be true, because the bump to my head caused no pain, nor did what I would later learn was a torn rotator cuff. I just babbled on and on, oddly unmoved by the ghastliness of our situation. "I think we had an earthquake. Do you think? It couldn't have been a bomb. No, I don't think so. It rumbled toward us. Did you feel that? Did you *hear* it? Alice! Alice!" I began to crawl out from under whatever it was I'd hit my head on. I moved slowly, so as not to crack into something else, the palms of my hands feeling their way across the uneven earth to where I imagined Alice to be. But who knew if I was even going in the right direction?

"Be careful," Robert said, his voice tight, straining. "There's probably broken glass. Smells like a jar of your dad's sauerkraut busted."

My dad's sauerkraut. Was it possible there was still a jar down here after all these years? Did it matter? No. What mattered was glass. And Alice. I had to get to her. But Robert was right. I had to move carefully. I stopped in my tracks, calmed my breath. This was Alice we were talking about, Alice who panicked if a spoon was out of place, a bedspread wrinkled. I could only imagine what she was going through—if she were alive.

"Alice?" I said again, only this time as calmly as I could. "Can you hear me?"

Robert started to speak. I shushed him.

"Alice? If you can hear me, please make some sound." I waited, stock-still, the gravelly floor pressing into my hands, bare knees, and tops of my feet. Finally, it came, half whimper, half warning. She was alive! Now I had to figure out if she was hurt. "I need you to talk to me. Can you do that?...Are you okay?" My throat was scratchy, dry, but I was able to control the coughing if I kept my breathing shallow. I needed water. "Alice, use your words. Are. You. Okay?" I rested back on my heels. Took a breath. Bowed my head. Waited.

A grating sound came from Robert's side of the basement, accompanied by his grunts and wheezing. There was a loud clunk and some clattering. "Careful!" I hissed. "We don't want to—" I couldn't finish my sentence. Don't want to what? Without the use of my eyes how could I know what we did or didn't want to do? I remained still while he fumbled around, as if it were too dangerous for two people to be moving at once. I returned my attention to Alice. "Alice. Do you hear me? Can you talk?" I resumed crawling in the direction of her one whimper, brushing imaginary glass aside. Was she hurt? Or just shut down? Shutting down? "Light," I said. "We need light. Robert, you had the flashlight."

"I'm looking." He sounded irritated. There was more scrabbling from his side of the room.

I was about to shout for Kim when he said, "Wait."

There was the strike of a match, and suddenly what was unknown was known. "Holy shit," he said.

I could not have agreed more. It was bad, really bad.

SIXTEEN SECONDS OF LIGHT

When a match strikes there is an initial flare that lasts less than a second, turning the inky blackness into high res. In that less-than-a-second, by coincidence or some cosmic sister connection, Alice and I were looking directly into one another's eyes. Quite something really, considering Alice was phobic about eye contact. I cannot say for sure that she actually saw me in those milliseconds that passed between us. I, though, locked on to her huge trembling pupils through the lenses of her skewed glasses, my fervor that of Dorothy in *The Wizard of Oz* clicking her red shoes, wishing like hell to be back in Kansas. I was about five feet from Alice, still on my hands and knees, the oven racks she'd been stacking now strewn between us. She was huddled by the brick wall, gripping her knees to her chest, revealing the bike shorts under her kilt. There was a large scrape on her right arm, but otherwise she appeared to be okay, at least physically. Her eyes, though, told me another story: she was on the verge of shutting down.

The initial flare dimmed and Alice was consumed by the shadowy darkness. But in that millisecond of eye contact, I knew my first priority had to be talking her down. If she went into shutdown, whatever we were going to have to do to get ourselves out of there would be that much harder. I used the rest of that precious matchlight to scan the fix we were in. The stairway had ripped completely from the wall and fallen into one of the shelving units, setting off a domino effect with two of the others. The fourth remained standing but was surrounded by cake and cookie pans. Canned jams and other sundries littered the rest of the floor. Robert was right. Broken glass was everywhere. I was lucky not to have been cut yet. We would have to be careful. I looked up to see what I'd cracked my head on. The stairway, it was at an odd angle.

I used the last lit seconds to check in with Robert. He was searching the ground, I assumed for the flashlight. He looked remarkably unscathed sitting there with one leg stretched out and the other bent, like the wizened old man a spelunker might find living in the back of the cave—save for his leathery skin from a life spent in the sun. His gray, two-day stubble and comically bushy eyebrows, the faded Guatemalan beanie he always wore, his canvas surf mocs, cotton shorts, and sleeveless tee revealing muscular arms and legs, all covered in a soft gray dust.

No question, I was sizing him up. Who knew what we were in for, or what we were going to have to do to get ourselves out of that hell? For a guy pushing seventy, he was in excellent shape. It was his mind I was worried about. Who was he apologizing to? What was his phantom's agenda? Robert had told me once that the two main voices who talked to him were a man and a woman. The Woman would try to keep him out of the trouble that the Man urged him into. She made him swim in the frigid bay, every day, without a wetsuit, to freeze the devil out. "But it's more complicated than that," he'd said to put an end to my prying.

I studied him as he let that flame burn down, how he let it lick his calloused fingertips before letting it drop to the floor. In that last millisecond of light, he met my eyes, and I got the feeling that he, too, was sizing me up.

After that, blackness.

MATCHES

How many matches do you have left?"

"Two."

"Okay." I tried to keep the panic from my voice, to slow the thoughts pinballing around in my head. Maybe things weren't as bad as they seemed. Maybe up top hadn't been hit so hard. Maybe all we needed to do was shout for Kim to flip a breaker and we'd be back in light. Did I even remember where the breaker box was? Surely, Kim would know.

"I'm going to call out to Kim," I said to warn Alice I was about to get loud. I didn't want to set her off any more than she already was. "We need to let her know that we're okay. All right?"

"Let's hope *she* is," Robert said.

I hadn't let myself consider that Kim might be hurt, or dead, that the whole building might have collapsed on her, on us. A violent shiver shot through my bones. I steadied myself. "Kim?" My shout came out like a squeak. I tried again. "Kim!" It wasn't just Alice I worried about: there was the feeling that my yelling might set off another avalanche. I braced for it and gave it another go, this time as loud as I could. I yelled over and over, Robert joining in. "Kim! Tillie! Anyone! Help! Help!"

The silence that met our cries was deafening.

"Holy shit," Robert said softly. "What the fuck happened up there?"

"Maybe they just can't hear us." Even as I said this, my eyes welled with tears. I brushed them away. I could not succumb to fear. If we were going to find our way out, I had to stay strong, for Alice, for myself. I thought of Mom, left in the car, told myself it was a blessing she wouldn't understand what had happened. Hell, I didn't understand what had happened. I prayed Tillie was with her. Prayed she wasn't hurt.

Matches, I told myself, focus on the matches. I worried Robert was going to strike one without a plan. I don't know what plan I was thinking of: *you look left, I'll look right?* But I could hear him fidgeting.

"Robert's harmless," Dad had said one time after I'd voiced my concerns about his dark moods. "Poor guy goes through life getting scolded all the time. Personally, I think he's to be commended. How many schizophrenics do you know who can hold down a job?" All well and good in the light of day, but in the pitch-blackness of that underground cavern, it made me damned uneasy. Who knew what his voices would say to him, what they'd make him do?

"Okay," I said. "We need to think."

Although still ringing, my ears became more attuned, distinguishing between Robert's breath with its glottal hitch and Alice's shallow butterfly breaths. My other senses ratcheted up to hypersensitive too— my fingertips probing the landscape, feeling for level spots and jutting obstacles, assessing danger, and confirming what I'd seen during those sixteen seconds of light; my nose searching through the yummy stink of Dad's sauerkraut, the ripe tang of Robert's body odor, the musty scent of the basement's mildew for possible clues as to how we might free ourselves.

Another rumbling thundered around us. I flung my hands over my head as pans and other unseen things clattered to the floor. A loud crack exploded from the stair unit. One loud clunk. A spray of debris. I stayed huddled and cowering until the shaking subsided, then started screaming like a Banshee. "Help! Help! Help! Anybody, can you hear? Help! We're trapped! Help! Heeeeeeeelp!" I was crying, sobbing, gasping for breath. "Help! Help!" I had no thought of Alice in these moments, nor of Robert, nor of the people aboveground. I had no thought at all, only a fierce will to survive.

Once again, my cries were swallowed up by the terrible darkness. Then the strike of a match. I was too distraught to protest and watched passively as Robert prolonged the flame by setting fire to what looked like a pile of tissues. How he'd managed the clearheadedness to scrounge them up I've no idea. But it was brilliant. I spotted the small notepad I'd been using pre-quake, snatched it up, and tossed it to him. If need be, I would strip off my clothes to burn. Anything to keep us in that blessed light.

"Keep that flame going and I'll find the flashlight," I said and began crawling toward him, gingerly, the shifting shadows dancing around me. "We can burn the labels off the cans. Alice? Can you help with this? Rip some labels off the cans?"

She didn't respond. Not a good sign. But there was no time to worry about her mental state. We had to find that flashlight. *I* had to. Robert was busy feeding the flame. My knees ground into the grit, my shoulder started to throb, but I kept on scanning, sweeping the broken glass from my path with a rusted cookie sheet. After a few false alarms, I saw the black shaft sticking out from under a cake pan. It wasn't lit. With trembling hands, I snatched it up, afraid its bulb had busted. I flicked the switch. Light!

Robert whooped. I started breathing again, but there was not a peep from Alice. Knowing better than to shine the beam directly at her, I caught her in its peripheral glow. Her legs were still pulled to her chest, her focus still turned inward.

"Alice. We found the flashlight. We're gonna get ourselves out of here."

She acted as though I hadn't said a word.

I swept the beam up to the trapdoor. It was easily fifteen feet above us. With the steps out of commission, we were going to have to find another way to reach it. "Anybody up there?" I yelled, forcibly steering my mind away from Kim's well-being, from the well-being of the world. There was nothing we could do to help, not until we could get the hell out, and then, who knew what we'd find?

"If we move the shelving up against the wall," Robert said, "I can climb it and test the door."

I crouched next to Alice. "We're going to need your help for this, sisteroo. I know you're scared. We all are. But it's going to take all three of us to get out of here." It's no wonder she didn't respond, my words were literally hiccoughing through the panicky clog in my throat. "Can you hear me?"

Robert came up behind me. "Leave her. We can do it ourselves."

The open plank stair unit, too cumbersome and broken to move, was like a twisted ship run aground—and in exactly the wrong place to be useful, planted on its side smack under the hatch, the right supporting stud snapped in two like a toothpick. And there were baking supplies everywhere, begging to twist your ankle. We didn't take time to clear it all away; we were too eager to get out. It didn't help that my shoulder had begun to scream with pain, making it impossible to lift my right hand much past my waist, nor that Robert was limping and had a nasty gash on his shin. But through sheer will we managed to drag that shelving unit and prop it up against the cement wall. I held it steady while Robert scaled it up to the hatch. I can't tell you how much I regretted having chosen my cute, flimsy bamboo flip-flops over my sturdy walking sandals that morning. I remember thinking that if Alice was just going to sit there, I should annex her boots.

Robert pushed up on the hatch with his hands, repositioned himself so he could push it with his back. I had to dig in my heels to keep the rack from sliding out while shining the light up so he could see. The hatch door would not budge. I worried that if it did open suddenly, it would bring with it a landslide of rubble; worried about what we were going to find when we got the door open; worried that the flashlight batteries would give out; worried about the dust-filled air we were breathing. Was it possible we'd suffocate? Mostly, I worried about Alice. She looked to be okay, but I worried about internal bleeding, or that she was concussed. All the while, Robert pounded on the door with his fist, causing blankets of dust to spill down into my eyes, and I yelled, "Help! Help!"

Then, out of the blackness, a hand snatched the flashlight from me. "Not working, it isn't. We need to try the tunnels." It was Alice, obviously. I hadn't heard her approach due to Robert's and my racket, but what a surge of relief I felt. She was okay! And could help us get out of there! For that seemed to be her plan, to do what we lesser individuals couldn't. She did that sometimes, went rigid and dictatorial instead of shutting down.

Moving into a new home comes to mind. Already at her wit's end from having dismantled the old house, she would charge from the U-Haul into the new house, stake out a bedroom, and start feverishly setting up her stuff. Meaning I'd get stuck with the room she hadn't chosen, given the house was even big enough for us to have our own rooms. "Rise above," Dad would say, "she's doing the best she can." I tell you, there were times I felt like I'd *risen above* my whole childhood.

I snatched the flashlight back and returned to lighting Robert. "He needs to see what he's doing."

"Not working, it isn't."

"She's right," Robert said and crab-walked down the makeshift ladder to us. "Doesn't seem like anyone's up there. The tunnels are our only chance."

"Tunnels?" It was the first I'd heard of them. "What tunnels?"

Taking advantage of my confusion, Alice reclaimed the flashlight and stomped past me in those sturdy boots of hers, stepping over a fallen shelf to what looked like a piece of plywood leaning against the back wall.

"Tunnels?" I said for the third time.

"Run under the street, they do, and connect the basements of some of the downtown businesses."

Robert cleared our path by kicking a batch of cake pans aside. "They were built during Prohibition."

"Incorrect," Alice said. "They were built in the mid-eighteen hundreds for deliveries." She slid aside the board that I'd assumed was nailed to the wall and shined the flashlight into a double-door-sized opening. "If we're super-duper lucky, daylight bricks will be up ahead."

"Daylight bricks?" I was beginning to feel like a parrot. Tunnels? Daylight bricks?

"In the sidewalk," Alice said, as if this explained anything.

I didn't take the time to follow up. There was a magic tunnel that was going to lead us to safety! What did I care of the history of it? As it turns out, the history is interesting, as well as pertinent, or so Alice thinks. She's all but looking over my shoulder as I tell this part.

As mentioned, the tunnels were built in the mid-eighteen hundreds, a product of a growing population, a lack of planning, and one stubborn Mrs. Williams, who refused to sell her apple orchard next to the river. The downtown was prevented from expanding its run down the levee because of her, so it did as a river does when trying to skirt, say, a fallen boulder, and moved its course over a notch to skirt her apple orchard. The previous back doors of the businesses were refashioned into front doors; the back alley and delivery road became the new Main Street with businesses popping up on its other side. The result was no viable delivery entrances for the riverside businesses. Hence, the tunnels where goods could be transported without disrupting commerce were created. Over the years, they also served as an underground railroad for the persecuted Chinese, getaways for the speakeasies that popped up during Prohibition, a haven for curious spelunkers, and who knows what else? But in 1989, most Santa Cruzians had no idea they were there, walking on the daylight bricks (thick glass bricks in the sidewalk) without a second thought. Nor did the businesses use the tunnels anymore; they'd become too unstable. But ghosts wandered those tunnels, oh yes, drifting through the cobwebs, hanging out in the shadows. I could feel them tickling the back of my neck as we made our way down the dark, claustrophobic passageway. As we inched our way forward by the light of the flashlight, it occurred to me that one of the ghosts I was feeling was my dad's. I couldn't imagine he'd let the bakery take his daughters' lives too. I begged him to lead us to safety.

We'd gone about fifty feet when we came upon a cave-in blocking our way.

"Fuck!" Robert said.

Alice skimmed the flashlight's beam over the heap of bricks. My heart sank. My hysteria rose. There was no telling how deep into the tunnel it went. Then I spotted what appeared to be an opening at the top of the pile. "There!" I said. "At the top."

Alice directed the light where I was pointing. "Bingo bango!" Taking the flashlight with her, she scaled the rubble. "It goes all the way through. We just have to get past this pile, which looks to be ten feet or so."

Robert scaled up after her, then called down to me. "It shouldn't be too hard. All we have to do is make the opening big enough to crawl through."

So we made a plan: two people would work at removing the rubble, the third would sit in the dark under the hatch and call for help. We'd rotate every half hour. Alice strapped her watch around the flashlight, making the flashlight-bearer the timekeeper as well. It was now 5:25. Twenty-one minutes from when the earth had begun to move.

SYRUPY PEACHES

We used the tools we had: cake pans, a large metal bread paddle, a piece of rebar. As you can imagine, forging a passageway through the caved-in wall of the tunnel was exhausting, dirty work. My shoulder throbbed, my head ached, I jonesed for alcohol, pain relievers, fresh air; still, I preferred the work of digging us out to sitting in the pitch-black basement with who knew what crawling around. Rats? It was a living nightmare, I'm telling you. Especially when those aftershocks hit, and there were many. Some as big as the original quake, or that's what it felt like belowground. In those moments, the darkness itself roared to life. All you could do was protect your head from the pelting debris. So this is how it ends, I would think as cake pans rattled to the floor, Alice and me going together, beneath our father's last business venture, the very one that had taken his life. Or I'd be convinced that a cave-in would bury Robert and Alice, leaving me to die alone in the dark basement. But we stuck to our plan: two digging, one sitting beneath the trapdoor calling for help, although with no response from the outside world, the basement shift was starting to feel futile.

We were down there a total of sixteen hours. And while the official timekeeper was whoever was in charge of the flashlight, it was really Alice. "Lucy," she'd say, if it was my turn to call for help. "The shift should be over by now." I don't know how she did it. For me, down there, time was totally wonky. The half-hour shifts either crawled by or happened in a blink. Not for Alice; she was spot-on every time. I began to think of her as our foreman.

But we each had our roles. One of my duties was to call out after each aftershock, "Everyone okay?"

Alice would respond, "Aye aye, Captain!"

Robert's responses ranged anywhere from "Still digging!" to a loud grunt. Hearing their responses, I would return to worrying. Raw fear is not sustainable. The adrenal system gives out, leaving nothing but anxiety and despair. Or so it was with me. And so, in between aftershocks, I maintained a constant state of worry.

Early on, my worries were centered on Robert. I had other worries, of course I did, a whole heap of them, the flashlight batteries top on my list. What would we do if, when, they gave out? And Mom. I pictured her wandering around what I imagined was a wrecked world, confused and scared. I was sure that Kim was dead. It was the only explanation I could come up with for her not trying to save us. But I had no control over any of those things.

Except Robert.

I'd just finished working a shift with him. He'd been locked in an argument with his voices the whole time, grumbling things like, "I'm trying!" and "She did not!" and other stuff I couldn't make out. I was afraid he'd give out on us, or turn on us. I had no idea if he was on medication normally, and when I tried to broach the subject with him, he just gave me a pained look and went on slamming the bread paddle into the pile of bricks and dirt. I began thinking of his voices as the Scolders. I resented their presence.

I wanted to voice my concerns about him to Alice, meaning I had to climb up to where she was working. Due to my bum shoulder, whoever I was teamed with worked high, digging out what was to be our narrow passageway at the top of the cave-in while I kept the tunnel clear of the bricks, dirt, and chunks of cement they threw down. I stacked it alongside the tunnel walls. I hated that I couldn't help dig the shaft. I did try, but we all agreed my injury slowed me down too much, and time wasn't something we had to spare. We kept the flashlight balanced on a jutting brick to maximize the spread of light so both people could see what they were doing—sort of.

Climbing up the pile in flip-flops was not an easy task, but I didn't want Robert, currently on basement duty, to hear what I had to say.

"Would you stop? For one second?"

"Why? My shift's not over."

She worked like a machine down there, wielded that bread paddle like a miner's shovel. *Chuck! Chuck! Chuck! Scrape. Scrape. Scrape.*

"I'm worried about Robert."

"How come?"

"His voices. They might make him do something…strange."

"They haven't so far."

"Don't you think it's disturbing he *has* voices? Just a little?"

Alice thought for a moment. "No stranger than Elwood P. Dowd."
"Who?"

Alice let out an exasperated breath. "In the movie? Harvey? Jimmy Stewart's character?" She examined a bit of dried blood on her elbow. "Now can we get back to work?" She handed me a cake pan full of dirt. Apparently, in her mind, the conversation was over.

Angry, I negotiated my way back down the pile of bricks and dirt. Was it too much to ask that Alice and I might grow closer in this situation? That our last breaths might be taken in unity? My thoughts were disrupted by the sound I had come to despise: the awful groaning that preceded an aftershock. I leapt out of the way so that Alice could jump clear of the pile, a safety measure we employed in case the cave-in caved in more. The hand-hewn redwood beams twisted and trembled like blades of grass. The flashlight shook from its perch, its beam helter-skeltering as it plummeted to the floor. I lunged to grab it, my arm shooting white-hot pain, but missed it by inches and *BAM,* we were back in pitch-blackness. Panic-stricken, I dropped to my knees and frantically felt around for it, jamming my finger in the process. I felt a horrible responsibility. Alice was doing her job, Robert was doing his, how could I have let the flashlight fall? Then, by some miracle, I set my hand down upon it, felt the wristwatch still wrapped steadfastly around its base. Terrified the bulb had broken, I whacked it into the palm of my other hand, once, twice. Mercifully, it turned back on.

"Everyone okay?" I called out shakily.

"Aye aye, Captain," Alice said, though she was giving me a mutinous look.

"Good," Robert called back from the basement.

I was terrified to let go of the flashlight after that, but it was too impractical not to. It had to sit high for both parties to get the light we needed. I used a piece of found rebar to gouge a nook into the side of the tunnel, then stuffed it with paper napkins to hold the flashlight in place. But you can imagine how I lunged for that light at each subsequent aftershock.

At the end of the shift, we gathered in the basement to partake of our meager rations: four large cans of syrupy peaches (for crisps), a large tub of peanut butter (for cookies), and two ancient jars of my dad's sauerkraut (there because he'd run out of storage space at home, then forgotten all about them, no doubt.) Alice used her Swiss Army knife to pierce and pry open the peaches. (She kept a knife in all of her kilts, in a hand-sewn pocket inside the waistband.)

Between the sauerkraut and the peaches, we were able to keep relatively hydrated, Alice and I relishing the sauerkraut, Robert tolerating it. It had gotten too vinegary; you could barely taste the caraway and Dad's signature dill, but our memories supplied what it lacked. My dad would eat a cupful at every meal, championing its healthful benefits. There was also a large bottle of imitation vanilla, twenty-six percent alcohol, which we passed around like hobos keeping warm by the fire, only our fire was a flashlight, powered by two batteries—life expectancy unknown. We were careful to divide the meager provisions equally.

Alice handed the can of peaches to Robert. "Had a mini cave-in, we did. Set us back some."

Robert flexed and clenched his hands before taking it from her. I watched him tip the can back and drink, watched as he took the exact three gulps we'd agreed on, then glanced over his shoulder as if his exactness were being scrutinized by someone besides me or Alice.

"There was some action in here too," he said, handing me the peaches.

"What? Where?" I said.

He took the flashlight from me and aimed it past the stair unit. The wall had caved in.

"Shit."

"Has it occurred to anyone that maybe it isn't an earthquake?" he said grimly. "That maybe it's something bigger?"

I won't say I hadn't thought about it, that we might dig our way out only to find Armageddon, or that Santa Cruz, for some unknown reason, had been the target of an attack. But the thought was not helpful and I didn't appreciate the Scolders conjuring it up.

Alice didn't appear to be listening. She was too busy tightening the laces on her boots, yanking at them like reins on a runaway horse. It was a territorial move. The next shift was hers and Robert's. She'd been allowing me to wear them on my shifts with Robert, though they were a size too small. I'd had to talk her into it, appealing to her logic: it made more sense for me to wear the boots while she did her basement shifts. The flip-flops flicked pebbles under the soles of my tender Portland feet. Plus, I couldn't get any traction in them, and I kept banging my toes. Alice finally agreed, but she hated flip-flops, hadn't worn them even when we were kids. Throughout our time down there, she never stopped reminding me the boots were hers.

Suddenly, I was so tired of all of it: Robert and his doom and gloom, Alice and her persnicketiness, my scaredy-cat worries and judgments. "Can we not do this?" I said sharply. "Can we not call in the end of the world? Can we hold off on that cheery vision? Cause it's really not helping me motivate. Really, it's not." I completed my point by dramatically tipping back the large can and taking my allotted three gulps of that sugary sauce. It wasn't easy with just the one arm; I had to grip the rim of the can. A little syrup ran down my face. I set down the can and caught it with my finger. Licked it off. Its tang cut like a fine malt whiskey.

We sat in silence for a few moments after that. Then Alice said, "We need to tighten the ranks."

"No," I said. "It's me. I'm being a jerk. I'm sorry, Robert. I didn't mean to lash out. I'm just—"

But that wasn't what Alice was getting at. "Getting unstable in here, it is," she said. "We should move our operation to the tunnel. Rations, all of it."

Giving up on the trapdoor was a bleak thought, but she was right. Someone would have heard us by now if they could have. If we were going to get out, we were going to have to do it on our own.

That move saved us, or more accurately, one of us. An hour later, a huge section of wall collapsed, cutting us off from the basement entirely.

THE SCOLDERS

About halfway through the tunnel, Robert was working the passageway, his legs dangling out of the narrow shaft, the *chuck! chuck! chuck!* of his bread paddle rammed into the dirt and bricks. I'd say it was about one in the morning—although without the sun to mark time's passage, the hour of the day had little meaning for us. We marked the time by cans of peaches and peanut butter, and were down to dregs of both. That, and Alice's "Shift!" on the half hour. We still had a good six feet to go. Keeping the flashlight in our nook no longer worked. The light wasn't reaching Robert. I'd had to climb the pile to light him. He was using the rebar to pry out the more ornery bricks, grumbling to the Scolders as he repeatedly rammed the metal spike into the blockage. "No...No...No, you can't...You can't...We made a deal...Yes, we did...She was there...Yes, she was...Weren't you there?...Oh, come on...You were...Tell him! That's not what you said to me..." It was agonizing to listen to. Once he had a small pile, he shimmied backward through the shaft, dragging it with him, then held the light for me while I collected and stacked the bricks, cake-panned the sand and dirt. It was slow moving.

Our new accommodation was a stretch of tunnel about twenty-four feet long. Cozy. Suffocating. But we were together. That one of us could have been stranded in the dark basement alone was terrifying. I tried not to think about it.

Alice was on break, lying on a pallet of bricks she'd set up for our rest station. It was as far from the action as you could get in that tiny space, and if you kept your knees bent, you could lie on it, which is what Alice was doing, on her back with her knees pointed toward the ceiling. When we'd reconvened our operation in the tunnel, she set up an area for provisions, an area for resting, and an area for our tools. It reminded me of back in the days when we moved into a new house, how she had to have everything just so. Only I wasn't whining about it this time.

"What time is it?" Alice said.

I checked the watch. "Five minutes to shift."

She sighed loudly.

Alice hated taking breaks, choosing instead to fire-line the bricks to the sides of the tunnel, but I made her. If she didn't break, Robert wouldn't, and he needed it. From the sound of it, the Scolders were torturing him. I needed my breaks too. Every muscle in my body pulsed with pain. There was also the issue of the boots. Alice would want to keep working, but it would be my turn for the boots, only she wouldn't want to give them up. One of the flip-flops was now broken, so the boots were a vital part of being effective. On my shifts with Alice, I'd wrap my feet in strips that I cut from my Question Reality T-shirt, leaving me wearing my shorts and sports bra. The wraps didn't help much, but it was something.

"Now?" Alice said. Then coughed. We coughed a lot down there. So much dust, especially after that wall collapsed.

"Alice, it's only been thirty seconds."

"I could do it ten times faster than you."

"Probably, but rest is good too."

"Not if I don't need it. And if I could do it faster. Haven't got all day down here, Bucko."

Robert shimmied out of the shaft with an armload of bricks for me to deal with, only he lost his footing and began scramble-hopping down the cave-in toward me. Instinctively, I raised my arms to break his fall. My shoulder exploded with pain, my ankles got pummeled by the bricks that came with him, but I managed to keep us both upright.

Robert jerked away from my grasp and dropped his head between his knees. "Fuck! Fuck! Fuck! Fuck! Fuck!"

Alice joined us. "You okay, old sport?"

He said, "Fine!" but he was panting, clenching and unclenching his hands.

"Seriously, are you okay?" I was worried, and frightened. Not of him, of the Scolders. They seemed to have him in their grip.

"I'm sorry," he said.

"You're tired. You lost your footing."

"Not for falling. For this!" He flicked his hand toward the ceiling, indicating the whole of our predicament.

"Robert, no. It was a natural disaster. Or maybe a manmade one. We won't know that until we get out of here. But it sure wasn't caused by you."

"Can't believe everything they say, you can't," Alice offered.

It took me a moment to realize she was talking about the Scolders. Such a presence they became down there, for all of us.

Robert rubbed his face, his knuckles covered in scratches. "I shouldn't have listened to him. He told me not to swim, said the water was too choppy, said I shouldn't let her push me around. I should have known better. Known he was setting me up. Now she's mad. And he fucking left. Like he always does." His filthy cheeks were streaked with tears.

I laid my hand on his shoulder. "Robert—"

He jerked away. "I should never listen to him! He's full of bullshit!" He was spitting his words out between sobs.

"They're not real. You know that."

The look he gave me kicked my hubris in the butt. Who was I to tell him what was real and what was not? Just because I couldn't hear the Scolders didn't mean they didn't exist. In retrospect, the choice to wear my Question Reality T-shirt that morning was prophetic.

"Is she talking to you now?"

He nodded.

"What's she saying?"

"She doesn't like me talking to you."

That did it. Imaginary or no, she'd pissed me off. "Well, I don't like her talking to you. And you can tell her that. You can also tell her that I refuse to believe that any of this is your fault. I could just as easily say the reason we're in this mess is because I've been a shitty daughter and left Alice to deal with Mom!"

Hearing those words come out of my mouth shocked me. Psychotic as it sounds, it seemed I too had voices in my head that were blaming me for our predicament. They may not have been as strident as Robert's, but they'd made their presence known, indeed they had.

"Is this that karma thing you're always talking about?" Alice asked.

I laughed. "Yeah, I guess so." I turned to Robert. "What do you say we get back to work and dig ourselves out of this hell?"

"It's my shift," Alice said. "Now give me the boots."

To this day, I have to remind myself that the earthquake was a simple natural disaster, uncaring of the lives it destroyed or rerouted, Earth settling her hips into a more comfortable position, but in that fragile, shadowy purgatory of shifting angles, our futures anything but certain, we too became unmoored.

ESKIMOS AND ICEBERGS

I'd say we were about twelve hours in, around 5:00 a.m. The flashlight batteries were starting to go, the beam getting duller. I was exhausted, had a pounding headache, my mouth was varnished in dust, my shoulder throbbed, my jammed finger felt like it was swelling, I was covered in scrapes and scratches that stung like hell, and my feet, oh God, my feet…I was in no hurry to get back to work, but Alice and I had just finished a shift, and Robert and I were up next. I'd gotten to where I could lace the boots by feel.

I was glad my shift with Alice was over. Her manic pace was hard to keep up with. Not that working with Robert was easy. The Scolders had full hold of him by then, had convinced him, I'm pretty sure, that he deserved to die. The only reason he kept on was for us—and because I wouldn't let him stop. "You'd do that?" I'd say, playing the guilt card. "Leave me and Alice to die?" If the Scolders weren't going to play fair, neither was I. But he was definitely slowing down.

I hated that I couldn't climb up there and dig myself, but there was no way I could inch my way through our shaft, walking on my elbows the way Alice and Robert did. When the time came to make our exit, I was going to have to go through on my back, pushing with my feet. I was already worrying that I wouldn't fit. The two of them were thin hipped. Not me. I stuck to my job, though, keeping them lit, moving the debris from the lip of the shaft to the walls of the tunnel, and cheering them on. I was still hanging on to the hope that someone might find us, and called out regularly, although I was getting hoarse. I figured rescue crews, if there were any, probably wouldn't have worked through the night. But morning was approaching.

We'd just had another aftershock. Robert and I were going to have to clean up the tunnel before we could proceed. Two stubborn steps forward; one crushing step back; that was the way of it. Although we did get lucky sometimes, hitting a sandy section. Apparently, much of the downtown was built on sand. Who knew? But those good moments were rare. Mostly it was knee-scraping, muscle-aching determination that got us anywhere.

"He won't get up," Alice said.

Having just secured the second boot, I was resting on one of my stacks of bricks, eyes closed. I was thinking about Mom. As far as I knew, she'd had no ID on her.

"Is the registration in the car?" I asked.

"What? Why?"

"Something to ID Mom, in case…"

"In the glove box it is."

So maybe, if something happened to Tillie, if Mom didn't wander from the car, if someone happened to find her, if the world wasn't completely destroyed, if if if if…maybe she'd be okay. Not all my thoughts were so selfless. I remember thinking, *The lengths I will go to avoid a relationship!* It was a tongue-in-cheek thought, sure, but it cut to the bone. Here, someone, Kim, had finally made me feel something deeper than casual interest…

"Robert," Alice barked. "Get *up!*"

I opened a single eye. Alice, standing over the golden, shadowy lump of a curled-up Robert, appeared to be seconds away from poking him with the flashlight. I didn't think that would go over well. I heaved myself off the bricks and dragged myself over, running my hand along the side of the tunnel to mark the way. The lack of light, the sheer exhaustion, was getting to me. I felt like I was walking through a dream. Robert lay curled in a fetal position facing the wall, his hands over his ears, mumbling what sounded like, "Nonononononono," as if it were taking every bit of energy he had to block out the Scolders. How I hated the Scolders! They worked against us every step of the way.

"Robert, it's me, Lucy. You doing okay?"

He kept on with his mantra, building his cocoon of *no*. I didn't blame him. I tell you, I was ready to lie down on that hard pallet and curl up next to him. We weren't going to get out of there, so why *not* go to sleep, never to wake up? It seemed as good a plan as any, but I knew Alice wouldn't let me.

"Robert? Can you hear me?" I reached out a hand and set it on his back.

He froze. Stopped murmuring.

I was too tired to interpret his sudden change in behavior. I just wanted him to get the hell up. If for no other reason than to appease Alice, who was standing behind me and breathing down my neck. I shook him. "Robert? We need you, man. Can you—"

Quick as a cat, he turned toward us, swatting blindly into the dark, clipping my arm. "Leave me alone! I'm done. Done!" Alice and I both jumped back; me, stepping my booted foot on Alice's naked one, the beam of flashlight in Alice's hand ballyhooing around the tunnel.

"Alice, I'm sorry!"

"Okay, old sport," she got out between gritted teeth.

"You sure?"

"I'm fine."

I returned my attention to Robert. He was back in his cocoon. Did I dare push him? He seemed like a man on the verge of exploding, and frankly, he was scaring me. The way he'd swiped out at me told me he didn't understand who I was; I was just another voice nattering at him. I turned back to Alice. "Looks like it's up to you and me."

"Then I get the boots back."

"Can we just take a break first?"

"Don't see this as a good time to take a break, I don't."

"A few minutes isn't going to kill us."

"But we've just had a cave-in."

"I know! And I'm a little discouraged, okay? We all are. A break will do us good."

She tucked the flashlight between her legs to fix her ponytail. She was not happy.

"Alice, I'm sorry. I'm just tired, and freaked out. Can we just sit here for a minute? Two minutes? Please?" I headed down the tunnel toward my newest stack of bricks, conveniently the size of a small bench, Alice lighting the way. "Doesn't this pile of bricks just call out to you? Say, *hey, Alice, take a load off!*" Regardless of her decision, I sat. I had to, if for no other reason than to settle myself. I was worried about Robert. Had we lost him? Leaning against the cool wall of the tunnel, I rested my forearm against my chest.

Alice checked the time. "Throw off our schedule, it will."

"I'm asking for two minutes! To talk. You haven't said two words to me in the last few hours. We might die down here. Don't you care?"

She plopped down onto the pile of bricks. "Then we have to turn out the light."

"If we die?"

"If we *talk*!"

I saw her point. But what if it wouldn't turn back on? Still, we had to preserve the batteries; she was right about that.

Typical Alice, she didn't wait for my response, just flicked the light off. I steadied my breath—slow inhale, slower exhale, slow inhale, slower exhale—a trick I'd learned in a yoga class to calm the adrenals, which, at the moment, were banging their little drums like mechanical monkeys. The dark wasn't the problem. It was the possibility that there would never be light again, the possibility that Robert had tipped over the edge of sanity. Of course, there was that last match—*if* the Scolders would let Robert give it up. They were getting increasingly pushy, and they did not like the Mustin sisters.

I could feel Alice's body heat. "Okay, what?"

Her words floated in the dark, searching for something to latch on to. I had nothing. We'd speculated every possible outcome, reviewed strategies for staying alive, planned the first thing we were going to do when...

"Stay awake!" Alice said.

My eyelids jerked open. "I am!"

"What do you want to talk about?"

"I don't know! Something meaningful...Like, I love you. How about that? We might die. How about that? Might die right where Dad died, how about that?" My heart was slamming in my chest. It was the first time I'd spoken it out loud.

"I love you too," she said. Though her words were stilted, I could feel that she meant it. Alice, in her Alice way, loved me.

Suddenly, I was transported to one of our childhood bedrooms, a blanket was stretched between our beds, a bowl of candy between us. The Candy Club meeting was about to begin. I wiped the moisture pooling in my eyelids and sucked it from my finger. Was this the end of it? Were the Mustin sisters coming to their end? I can't tell you how badly I longed to lean into Alice, to feel our skin touch, the beat of our hearts meeting. Life touching life, that is what I craved. But there was no touching Alice, not deliberately. She tolerated the occasional brushing of knuckles or bumping of shoulders during our desperate excavation, but a deliberate touch was different. It would be harassment. So I did what I used to do when we were kids, when Mom and Dad would be having one of their pot-flinging fights. I reached over and grabbed hold of the hem of her kilt. She either didn't notice, which I doubt, or was too tired to care. Or maybe it made her feel good, the way it did me.

"Another thing," Alice said.

"I know. You want the boots."

"Something else."

I could feel her fidgeting. She was worked up over something. "What is it, Alice? What's bothering you?"

"Eskimos and icebergs," she said, and, just like that, I was fifteen, Alice, thirteen, and we were riding to Aunt Evokia's house in East Texas after Mom and Granddaddy Paps had gotten into a fight.

It was Christmas Day, late. We were cruising on a stretch of rolling hills, the kind where the car in front of you keeps disappearing and reappearing. Mom and Dad were passing a thermos of vodka back and forth. Mom was driving. It was raining. She was spitting mad. She was all right to drive, though, or that was the story my parents told themselves. "Did you see how he was treating Mom? Did you?" Her accent always got stronger after our visits to Texas. "And what about what he said to me? About being high and mighty! Trying to make me feel bad for looking after Mom. And poor Evie. Did you see? She'd cooked that whole meal and not one word of thanks from him! Not one! If I were Frank I'd call him out, I would, tell him to show some respect for my wife!"

We'd driven straight through to East Texas from our home in Southern California, because Aunt Evie had said our grandmother, Lady, was losing her mind. "If you want to see her before she's all the way gone, you'd best come," she'd said. "She's one thought away from forgetting her name." We arrived late Christmas Eve in a station wagon filled with presents, but we'd "missed the deadline" with Lady. That's how Dad put it—privately of course, to me and Alice, who were confused and frightened by her decline. Sweet as always, she didn't have a clue as to who we were or what was going on. This infuriated the hell out of Paps, a self-made man and proud of it. He'd yell at her, "Don't you even recognize your grandchildren?" and "Didn't you hear? No one wants coffee!" It made Mom boiling mad. You could tell because she got really quiet at Christmas dinner. Then, predictably, later that night, as Alice and I were climbing into the foldout bed on Paps and Lady's sun porch, we heard Mom and Paps going at it in the living room. We both started changing back into our clothes. The visit to Lady and Paps's was going to end like they all did. Five minutes later, Mom came charging into the sun porch. "Pack your things! We're leaving!"

Now Mom was driving too fast, and Dad was starting to doze and we were going to spend the night at Aunt Evie and Uncle Frank's place the next town over.

"The way he treats her!" she ranted. "As if she were losing her mind on purpose!"

Dad spoke with his eyes half-closed. "Aw, Euvy, the man's scared."

"Mean is what he is! Meaner than a hot skillet full of rattlesnakes!"

Mom pulled into the oncoming lane to pass a truck. It sprayed our windshield, and for a moment, you couldn't see where we were going. Dad started snoring. Mom took another snort off the thermos. "Are you girls awake?" She'd waited for Dad to go to sleep because he would have stopped her from saying what she was about to say.

"Roger roger," Alice said. She was focused on sharpening her new set of personalized pencils in her new turtle-shaped sharpener, a gift from Aunt Evie.

I grunted my acknowledgment. Mom wasn't the only one who was mad. I didn't much care for Paps, he scared me, and now Lady scared me too, but Aunt Evie had promised to take us out for catfish the next day, and that meant going out to the lake, and I loved the lake, and I loved Aunt Evie. But Mom said we were going to leave first thing come morning, that she couldn't spend one more day in Texas, that Paps ruined the whole state for her.

Mom's driving was scary.

"I need you to promise me something. You listening, Lucy Loo?"

"Yes, I'm listening."

"When the Eskimos know they're too old to be of any use, their tribe sends them out onto an iceberg and they just float away."

"Mo-*om.*"

"For once in your life, Lucy, just listen, will you?"

"Did you know that icebergs are made of fresh water?" Alice said. "That's one of the reasons they float."

Dad let out a big snore-snort and adjusted in his seat so his head rested on the window. Mom waited until his snoring returned to its rhythmic sucking and blowing. "What I'm saying is, if I ever get like Lady, if I ever get to where I don't know my ass from my elbow, you girls need to help me find my iceberg."

"You're never gonna get like Lady," I said.

"Typically, icebergs are found in Antarctica, they are. Although some can be found off Alaska and Siberia and in the Barents Sea. Might have trouble finding one in these parts, we might."

"That's not what she's talking about," I said. "She wants us to off her if she turns crazy like Lady."

Alice looked up from her pencils, stunned.

"Thank you for that, Lucy. Now you've upset your sister."

"You're the one who brought it up! Talking about Eskimos and icebergs! It's not something *normal* mothers ask their children to do. Anyway, I'm not going to do it. If you get crazy like Lady, I'm just going to let you wander the streets."

"Well, I wouldn't count on you anyway. You're too sensitive."

"Am not!"

"Alice will do it. I can always count on my little Alice. Isn't that right, Alice?"

Alice knew this game. We both did. Mom playing us off one another.

Mom reached into her handbag and, using her lips, pulled a smoke out of the pack, then talked out of the side of her mouth. "You hear that, Alice? Lucy doesn't want to help." She touched her Winston to the glowing circle of the car's lighter. The windshield wipers went *squeak-thump, squeak-thump.* "You going to help your mom?"

Squeak-thump. Squeak-thump.

"You don't have to," I said.

"I'm going to pull this car over and make you walk to Aunt Evie's if you don't."

"She's lying, Alice. She's not going to make you walk. She wouldn't. She's just drunk. That's the only reason she's saying this."

Mom reached back to swat me. The car swerved dangerously close to the ditch by the road. "You stay out of this, Lucy. This is between me and Alice. You promise me, Alice?"

Alice stared ahead at the windshield wipers. She was afraid of walking the dark roads at night.

"Do you?"

Alice thought for a moment longer. She took promises seriously. Finally, she nodded.

"Say it," Mom said.

"Don't do it," I said to Alice. "She's using you."

"Say it," Mom said.

"I promise."

"Promise what?"

"That I'll find you an iceberg."

"There you go." Mom polished off the vodka and tossed the

thermos on the floorboard. "I can always count on my little Alice, can't I?"

Mama Hyde. She didn't play fair.

"I'm ready for the boots," Alice said.

Like that, I was back in our current nightmare, my hand gripping her kilt, my back pressed against the wall of the tunnel.

"Alice, you know you don't have to honor that. Mom won't remember. And it was wrong to make you promise; you were only twelve."

"Thirteen."

"Okay, thirteen. Still, it was wrong. Mothers don't ask their children to do that."

We count on the earth not to move. When it does, more than houses and bridges topple. Sitting in that terrifying blackness, I felt my outer shell breaking apart, a slow splintering starting at my head and branching its spiderweb fissures throughout my body, the very assumptions about who I considered myself to be shattering at my feet. First went my ideas about the kind of person I was. *Smash!* Next came my beliefs about right and wrong. *Smash!* Until finally all I was left with was cold hard logic. Alice was right, our mother would hate what she'd become, and she'd want us to do something about it.

But we had to save ourselves first, and that seemed close to impossible. I tuned into Robert, who was still grumbling at his imaginary voices. "Poor guy," I said quietly, although even had I spoken full volume, I'm pretty sure he wouldn't have heard. "Talk about psychological warfare."

"That's not what psychological warfare means," Alice said.

"Maybe not, but it applies."

Alice thought for a minute. "True enough, old sport. True enough." Then she flicked on the flashlight. "Boots, please."

That tiny bit of light did me a world of good. "Can't I wear them for a shift? Please? If it's just going to be you and me? We can switch back and forth."

"They're *my* boots," she said.

"True enough." I began unlacing.

The cleanup from the aftershock went faster than expected. Did I think a whole lot about our conversation? No. Not until way later. It was too hypothetical. Who knew what we'd find on the other side of the cave-in—if we ever even made it that far. Freedom? Another cave-in? Meanwhile, the flashlight's beam was down to a dull amber.

Just Alice and I working was a relief in some ways. Yes, we were down a man, but we got a second wind, singing musical numbers to keep our spirits up and to make sure if someone were passing by above us they'd hear. We were all but feeling our way through the process, but kept on. When the flashlight's beam was down to nothing but a spark, I had to approach Robert again. I was nervous, after the last time, when he'd swung his arm out trying to hit me, but we needed that last match.

In between hauling loads of debris, I'd gathered up everything I could find that would burn: the labels off cans, a roll of paper towels, napkins, a short cardboard box, some shelving paper; all stuff Alice had insisted we take with us when we'd moved our operation to the tunnel, saying, "Never know what might come in handy." (Was she right about that!) But we needed that match.

"Robert," I repeated as I felt my way toward him. I didn't want to surprise him. That seemed like a bad idea. "We need the matchbook."

"She wants the match," he muttered. "I told you she'd want it... Shut up! You're not allowed to say anything. Not after what you did!" He went on speaking gruffly, incoherently, to someone other than me, and I wasn't sure what to do. I couldn't see him at all. Alice had the flashlight in the tunnel. He was just a disembodied voice arguing with people who seemed to me to be about as real as he was in that pitch-blackness.

"So can I have it?" I said, "The match? We need light, and the flashlight is close to dead."

"Shut up. Shut *up*!" he growled. "You think you know so much. But you don't. You *don't*. All this bullshit you keep laying on..."

Clearly, my voice held neither more weight, nor less, than those of the Scolders. He'd drunk their Kool-Aid and believed he deserved to die. I didn't like them, and they didn't like me. Yet I had to go through them to get to him. Our survival depended on it. I reached a terrified but determined hand into the blackness and made contact with what I think was a thigh. "Robert, don't listen to them. They're not helping. They're—"

A hand grabbed my wrist. I pulled back, nearly losing my footing, pulling Robert with me. We tussled, or maybe we were just falling, or keeping ourselves from falling. It was hard to tell without being able to see. Alice yelled, "What's going on?" My response was short-circuited by Robert pressing something into my palm: *the matchbook!* Meanwhile, he kept on with his angry muttering. "You're a liar! That's not true! You can't make me!"

I backed away, reaching a hand out behind me for navigation purposes. I was afraid to turn away from him, afraid he might jump me. I've no idea if this was a well-founded fear, if he'd have gotten violent. Down there, robbed of sight, anything seemed possible.

"You okay?" Alice aimed the non-beam at me, which did little to help me find my way.

My heart thundered in my chest. "Fine. Here." I thrust the matchbook at her. I didn't trust myself to light the small pile of wadded-up napkins in case I had one of those failed strikes in which the match head pops off and doesn't ignite. But Alice, she wouldn't do that. Alice negotiated the physical world with a finesse I'd envied my whole life, a finesse I was betting on.

The strike of the match was a blessed moment, the flame that rose when match touched crumpled napkin, a goddamn Jesus, Mary, and Joseph miracle!

I called, "Thank you!" over to Robert, but I'm pretty sure he'd gone back to his cocooning.

After that, we worked by firelight; me, keeping the tiny flame going in the mouth of our tunnel within a tunnel; Alice, burrowing farther and farther in. I no longer needed to retrieve what she unearthed, as whe was able to push it through a small hole to the other side. She worked like a robot, ramming with the bread paddle, scraping with the cake pan. The air grew smoky. There were just six peaches left, a bit of peanut butter.

"Still with us?" I'd call over to Robert every now and then. He'd grown quiet. Too quiet. I was afraid he was dying, or even dead, but I was more afraid of leaving the flame unattended—even for a second.

I wiped the sweat from my palms onto my cargo shorts and felt something square and plastic in the side pocket. The Joan Armatrading cassette tape! I'd forgotten all about it. I slipped my hand in to caress the plastic casing, trying to feel if Kim was still alive, trying to send her the message that I was. I imagined Alice, Robert, and me being found years later, the meat of our bodies gone, the way they find dinosaur bones, Robert's curled in a fetal position, Alice in the tunnel, and me gripping onto that cassette tape.

If you've ever had a near-death experience, you know how quickly your life flashes before your eyes. It was the same down there, only my life crawled past. "Remember when you, me, and Mom got stuck in the snow? In the car?" I called to Alice, who I'm sure couldn't hear me over the *Chuck! Chuck! Chuck!* of rebar hitting brick. "How she took us to Lake Tahoe because Dad was hosting a poker game and she was *damned if she was going to spend her Friday night serving beer to a bunch of card-playing fools?* How we sat in the car until the snowplows finally came in the morning?" I counted those who would care if I died: Toi, Dune, the bride whose cake I was supposed to make the following week. I fixated on what would happen to Mom if Alice and I didn't make it out. Who would care for her? I pictured her wandering the green halls of a state-run facility, her toenails curling into her skin, dried food plastered on her chin. I begged Dad to help us out of the nightmare.

Then there was nothing left to burn, and with it went any hope that we would make it out alive; at least for me. I slumped down onto the rubble and began to sob. Alice, though, kept working. I have no idea how. I was so tired, so disoriented, I barely even understood that she *was* still working. The *Chuck! Chuck! Chuck!* of her hacking away at the cave-in might as well have been my heartbeat. I said good-bye to my mother, to Toi and Dune. I said good-bye to Kim, to the future I'd hoped to have with her. I asked them all for forgiveness as I drifted off into a troubled sleep. At one point I thought maybe I heard a jackhammer. Then decided it was just Alice, and drifted back to sleep.

I woke to her saying, "Lucy! Lucy! Light! I see light!"

I can't say I leapt to my feet. I will say the legs that moments before had been unable to support me now hoisted my aching body to standing. I felt my way through the dark over to the pile and crawled up to see what she was talking about. Sure enough, there was light at the end of the tunnel—no metaphor. A soft glow that was enough to make out Alice's silhouette and the edges of the shaft where she'd broken through. We had a chance!

"A few more minutes of digging and we should be able to squeeze through," she said.

"You think it opens to outside? It looks like sunlight."

"Probably a daylight brick. Laid them in the sidewalk to light the tunnels, they did. Thick glass bricks. Can see them around town, you can."

I didn't care. Not about the tunnels or the daylight bricks. I just wanted out from that underground hell. "Robert!" I croaked. "We've hit light!"

I left Alice to punch through the rest of the way and felt my way down the tunnel to Robert, presumably, on the pallet. I was afraid I'd find him dead, or gone. (Irrational, I know.) Afraid he'd attack me. We hadn't heard a peep from him for hours. What, I wondered, would have killed him? A heart attack? Sheer inner loathing? But as I got closer, I heard that deep inhale with the glottal hitch. Then a snort. He was alive, and snoring! "Robert! Robert!" I said, as I inched my way toward him, bare feet testing each step, hands out in front of me like a zombie. My toe jammed into the pallet. I fell forward onto him. "Ouch! Sorry!"

He wriggled beneath me. "Wha—?"

"I'm sorry. I'm sorry." I tried to heave myself off him, but wound up shoving my hand into what I think was his chest.

"Lucy?" He sounded confused, but who wouldn't be under such circumstances?

"Alice hit light!" I said, managing to stand.

"Wait. What?" He sounded like himself, and like he was talking to me.

"We can get out! We're going to be okay! Alice just has a bit more to go—"

I didn't have to finish what I was saying. He pushed past me toward the passageway to relieve Alice in the shaft. I've no idea what flicked the switch, what brought him back to us. Maybe the Scolders were still conked out, or the sleep had brought him round. But he went at that blockage like a battering ram and cleared the rest of the way in no time.

The way Alice and he described it, the descent from the shaft was going to be tricky. Especially for me with my shoulder. After shimmying through, we were going to have to maneuver down a short, steep pile of debris on the opposite side. Alice and Robert would be able to crawl down on their hands since they were going belly down. My descent was going to be trickier since I was going belly up. I was already concerned about ripping my back to shreds as I pushed my way through with my T-shirt-wrapped feet, but sliding down a five-foot pile of debris, head first, on my back, sounded uncomfortable, to say the least. We decided it would best if I had Robert on one side and Alice on the other; they could assist me.

"Through!" Robert said when he'd made it. What a feeling of triumph those words carried!

Alice anchored me by my forearm as I climbed the pile and leaned back into the shaft, one of the few times in my life when she deliberately touched me. She also let me push my feet off her hands until I could propel myself through the shaft by digging my heels into the floor. I couldn't get much purchase due to the narrowness of the opening, and it was hell on the exposed skin of my back, but I hummed "Always Look on the Bright Side of Life" as I inched along. When I was close to the edge, Robert grabbed me by the armpits to drag me the rest of the way. It hurt like hell, but it got the job done. Alice, who'd crawled in behind me, grabbed my ankles as Robert shouldered me down the embankment. Once Alice made it down, we stood together for a moment, misted in that single illuminated ray of dancing dust motes.

"Daylight brick," Alice said.

"Daylight brick," I echoed gratefully. There appeared to be one every half block or so, marking our path forward. The tunnel itself was like a miner's shaft, all redwood beams and earth. But those daylight bricks were like windows from heaven.

Robert, still limping, continued to lead while Alice took up the rear, sandwiching a grateful me in the middle. I chuckled to myself about how worried I'd been about being stuck with the two of them, thinking *I* would have to be taking care of *them*.

When we spotted our first door, I steeled myself for the inevitable: it would be locked or otherwise inaccessible. But it wasn't. Robert pushed it open like any ordinary door and we were standing in a basement that was like any other basement, this one lit from above. There was a hatch! It was leaking light! Save for a bunch of toppled cases of canned goods, this basement seemed largely undisturbed. We picked our way through the mess to the stairway. Alice climbed the stairs and pushed open the hatch, which flooded us in a delicious blaze of light and buckets of fresh air.

7.1

The three of us stood in the bright kitchen of Zoccoli's Deli, between the walk-in refrigerator and the large industrial sink, shell-shocked and blinking like moles. Impulsively, we formed what I've heard called an "alert circle," a positioning used by pack animals to protect the group. Clustered together, each gazelle, wildebeest, what have you, faces out to protect the heart of the group, assuring there are eyes on all sides. I was facing the shop where boxes of crackers, cookies, olives, and other gourmet items littered the floor. A glass-doored display fridge gaped open, its sodas and single-serving milks having spilled out and rolled everywhere. The place stank of vinegar and food going sour, but I breathed in the stink greedily, one long breath, then another, vowing never to take air for granted again.

I had a narrow view to outside, where Santa Cruzians trolled the streets, public servants and pedestrians alike, all with dumbfounded looks on their faces. I'll admit, down in the tunnel, there was a part of me that believed Robert was right, that the End of the World was upon us, but what I saw did not look like the End of the World, just a badly shaken-up one. I turned to face Alice and Robert.

Alice had a gash of dried blood on her face, and the elastic of her ponytail had come partially loose, shooting the short rubber-banded spray of hair at a jaunty angle. Her arms and shins were covered in scratches and scrapes, her clothes filthy and torn, her glasses covered in dust. There was a streak of ash on her neck. She flipped the faucet on the sink to check for water. There was none.

Robert looked like a man who'd been buried alive: body slack as a mop, eyes sunken, shirt ripped to shreds. He too was covered in scrapes and scratches, a particularly painful-looking gash across the bridge of his nose. He was squinting up at the light flooding through a skylight.

Both looked as though their brains were trying to catch up with the moment. There's no other way to explain it. I'm sure I looked that way too. The world had just been returned to us—and it was amazing.

I felt I should say something profound to mark our salvation, or come up with a gem that would express how grateful I was to the two of them, *for* the two of them, but those sentiments were merry-go-rounding in my head with a cavalcade of questions: Had Mom survived? If she had, was someone caring for her? What if the house was destroyed? The bakery? What were we going to do then? And, of course, I thought of Kim. Oh man, did I think of Kim, praying she was alive. Never had it been clearer to me that second chances were a gift, and that I was going to put mine to good use.

"I have to go," Robert said.

He was right. We all had to. It was the next leg of the journey: to find out what was left of our earthly cares. We moved as one, picking our way through the crackers and fancy vinegars, stopping only to swipe those Crystal Geysers off the floor. Oh, that water tasted good! Standing there, we each drank a full bottle, then took another. I left a filthy five-dollar bill on the counter. Had it been a fifty in my pocket, I would have left that.

Alice led the way outside. Robert went next. We hung together outside the deli, surveying the scene in the early morning light. Whole buildings had toppled, while others seemed to have sustained little visible damage. A car was crushed beneath what had once been the brick wall of Shockley's Jewelers. A broken tree lay across the road. A fire truck was parked down the street, its ladder extended up to a second story. Wide-eyed people were everywhere, emergency workers, business owners, gawkers. And it was loud. Sirens. Helicopters. Pounding sledgehammers. I spotted one man leaning out of an upstairs window. He was lowering a garbage bag of goods down to someone on the street. A police officer shouted to him, "You need to evacuate the building! Now! It isn't safe!" Another officer was cordoning off a building with yellow tape. A woman sat on the curb crying, a black and white dog nuzzling her ear. The smell of natural gas was everywhere. A man strolled by with a surfboard under his arm. I felt as though I were watching TV. All I could think about was how fresh the air was—even though I'm told it wasn't, that the dust didn't settle for days. And the light! The world was so shiny! I cracked open my second bottle of water. To have two whole bottles to myself seemed gluttonous!

But there wasn't time to revel in this sensation of rebirth. With life came responsibilities, and we had a bucket-load of them. I turned toward the bakery, the sweep of my gaze pausing at Bookshop Santa Cruz. Half standing, the rest of the brick building had collapsed. People were combing through the rubble, shouting, not heeding the officials telling them to stop. A small group of young people held hands with their eyes closed and were singing something I couldn't make out. A helicopter was beating overhead. All very desperate, but not my cause. I continued my surveillance. The bakery appeared to be in good shape. I turned to mention this observation to Alice and Robert, but Robert was already limping off into the crowd.

It was the last time I would see him. I think of him, though, from time to time, when I pass a person wrapped in blankets, pushing a cart of stuffed animals or standing on a hot street corner wearing three overcoats and spitting obscenities. What a remarkable man he was, able to negotiate life with those cruel voices nattering at him all the time. I suppose he's dead now, like they all are.

"Crikey," Alice said, and took off for the bakery at a quick clip. She had the boots. I hobbled after her, trying to catch up, hugging my arm to protect my shoulder. It was like moving through a dream. Noticing the glass on the sidewalk outside the bakery, I thought, *Huh. The plate glass window shattered. Watch where you step.* Noting that the building itself remained standing, I thought, *Huh. It's standing, but there are some very big cracks.* As we got closer, it was: *Huh. The inside of the building appears to have imploded on itself.*

We paused street-side of the broken window, me standing back a ways to protect my bare feet. The wall between the kitchen and the shop had partially given way, causing the tall glass display case to pitch forward onto the front glass counter. Between the open beams of the ceiling, I could see directly up to the Tea Cup Lounge. Plaster chunks, broken glass, and baked goods were everywhere. And there was so much noise! The crisp *thunk! thunk! thunk!* of sledgehammer, men shouting, someone sawing, all of it coming from the kitchen. *The kitchen! Kim!* My heart began slamming in my chest. This wasn't a movie I was watching. This was no dream. This was life. My life! I scanned the area frantically.

"I'll check for Mom," Alice said, and took off toward Front Street, where we'd left her in the car talking to Tillie—leaving me to pick my way through the broken glass, and over the piece of yellow tape cordoning off the entrance to the bakery, to see what was what—by myself. Only I could not do it. Could. Not. My feet refused. Despite what, moments earlier, had felt like an abundance of air, I was having trouble drawing it into my lungs. I pressed my arm to my chest, trying to calm myself, but the noise, the glass, the general chaos, had me shaking like a leaf. I took one step, two steps, then had to steady myself on the outside wall of the bakery, right next to Tiburcio Vasquez's gunshot hole. I had to get a hold of myself.

A flash of movement by the smashed display case caught my attention. A woman, disheveled and squatting, was picking through the broken glass for cookies. She was like a kid on an Easter egg hunt, eyes hungry for the next find. She seemed oblivious to the banging around in the kitchen behind her, to the man yelling, "Can you hear us? Can you *hear* us?" I decided it would be easier to walk around to the Front Street entrance where hopefully there would be less broken glass, and where I could summon someone's attention without having to actually enter the building, which I seemed unable to do. Just then a hard-hatted, orange-vested man strode in from the kitchen. A strapping fellow, he wore a Santa Cruz Firefighter T-shirt, shorts, and boots, and was dusted in plaster—everything you'd want in a rescuer.

"What did I tell you?" he barked at the woman filling her pockets. "This building is not safe!" It was a compassionate bark, more motherly than official. The woman looked up from her hunting and pecking to hiss something back at him, her hackles raised like a cat's. She wanted those cookies. I understood. They were Dad's almond biscotti, a comfort food if ever there was one. I felt I should tell the rescue worker that it was okay, I was the one of the owners of the bakery and she could have all the cookies she wanted, but again, my thoughts refused to convert into words. He took a step toward her. "I mean it!" She scampered out the broken window, nearly cracking into me.

"She's been at it all morning," he said to me apologetically. "I don't know how to get it through to her. This structure is not safe." He took a deep, tired breath then seemed to see me for the first time. "Whoa. You don't look good. Do you need some kind of assistance?"

I shook my head. "No. Yes. I'm one of the owners." I clarified, "Of the bakery, not the building." It seemed important to distance myself from *that* aspect of the disaster. "I need to know if—"

I'm sure I looked frightful in my filthy torn shorts and jog bra, my hair a rat's nest, my feet scraped and raw. Who knew how many street urchins he'd had to deal with? But he treated me kindly, even if he didn't believe me. Or maybe he was simply overloaded, because he said, "Still no luck. They've been trapped down there close to," he glanced at a rugged wristwatch, "over sixteen hours. But we're not giving up. If the basement didn't collapse, there's a good chance—"

A police car blaring its siren roared down Front Street.

"You misunderstand!" I yelled. "It's me you're looking for. We found our way out!"

"What?" he yelled back.

"I was one of the people stuck down there. Me and..." I looked over my shoulder for Alice, who was rounding the corner, guzzling her second bottle of water. "The car is there. But no sign of Mom."

"But the car looks okay? Nothing...fell on it?"

"Wait," said the firefighter. "*Who* are you?"

"We're the owners of the bakery," I repeated distractedly. Surely Tillie had thought to care for Mom, or so I hoped.

"Who?"

"The ones you're looking for. We escaped through an underground tunnel." Even to me, my words sounded implausible.

The firefighter seemed to know exactly what I was talking about. "Holy shit! You found the tunnels!" He turned toward the kitchen. "Guys!" he shouted at ear-drum-breaking decibels. "Guys!" I started to ask him about Kim, but he'd already begun tramping back to call off the rescuers.

A helicopter pounded overhead.

"You still have the car keys?" Alice yelled over the thump-thump-thump.

The car keys. It seemed like a million years since I'd tossed them on the butcher block and headed down into the basement. I gestured toward the bakery and shouted, "In there somewhere!"

Alice looked as if she were about to step over the broken window to get them. I grabbed her forearm. She froze. I didn't care. "It's not safe."

Too stunned to pull out of my grip (although she certainly could have), she snapped, "Let go!"

"No."

"Then I'll walk."

"Home?"

The look she gave me said: *Where else, you idiot?*

"Please, Alice. Don't make me do this by myself."

"Do what?"

"We need to find out about Kim. And Mom. Tillie. Maybe somebody knows something."

A woman wailed in front of what had once been Bookshop Santa Cruz. A black Lab trotted purposefully toward us, gave us a sniff, and trotted on. The lids of my eyes felt like sandpaper; my legs like noodles. The whole *I'm alive!* adrenaline rush had given way to sheer exhaustion. "Please, Alice. Just a few minutes to thank these people and ask a few questions?" I understood her desire to get home, to a bath, to a bed, and, in my case, to some shoes and a T-shirt.

She squinted across the street where a young couple was handing out bottled water on the steps of the post office. "Okay. A few."

I released her forearm just as Kim charged out of the kitchen. "Lucy! Alice!"

If ever there were a time for the soundtrack to swell, this would have been it. Kim and I slow-mo rushed toward one another, her hard hat wobbling comically on that cloud of curly hair, her orange vest swishing side to side. Once she was through the door, we fell into each other's arms, or almost into each other's arms. I had just the one arm; my other got squeezed between us. That's what it felt like, a movie moment. Huge. Although admittedly, a very confusing moment for Kim. "But you were…How did you…?"

I squirmed. She held me at arm's length, cocked an eyebrow. "You're hurt."

There was a thick white bandage above her eye. "So are you."

"I'm fine," she said and took me in her arms again, this time gently.

I will never forget the feeling of my frantic *pitter-patter* against her steady t*hud-thud thud-thud*. It felt like coming home, like fate, like life. I wanted to stay in her arms much longer. It was so hard to pull away. It was for her too. Or so she always said when she told the story, how it took almost losing me to know how much she wanted me. Meanwhile, Alice, tugging at her kilt, shifting her weight from boot to boot, clearly wanted to bolt. "Where's Mom?" she asked.

"She's fine," Kim said. "Tillie took her. Said she'd hang on to her until we found you. But how about you, Alice? Are you okay? You looked pretty banged up. You both do. Lucy, where are your shoes? Your shirt?"

"Long story," I said.

Alice took off her Clark Kents to blow the dust from them. "Things could definitely be better, they could."

Kim smiled. "I don't know about that. You being alive just turned this day into one helluva miracle."

Alice returned her glasses to her face and stared at her boots, but I swear she blushed a little.

"And Robert...?"

"He's fine," I said, "Went home to check on..." Then realized I had no idea what, or who, Robert cared about.

"Screech," Alice said.

"I hope he finds him," Kim said. "Lots of cats took off before the earthquake and still haven't come home."

I let go of her arm, which I'd been clutching as if it were a buoy in the middle of a stormy sea. "But how did you guys..."

By now, a small group of curious bystanders and rescue workers had formed around us. We were a big deal. Survivors! And with survival came responsibility. People needed hope, and we had it to offer. That's what I felt. Not Alice, though.

"Time to vamoose, it is," she whispered out of the side of her mouth.

I ignored her. People had risked their safety to rescue us, and they deserved our story. Surely, I thought, Alice could cope for a few more minutes. "The tunnels!" I said triumphantly. "We found the tunnels."

A flurry of questions followed. I answered them as best I could, despite Alice's standing by one of the city's planters—giving me that border collie look she used on Mom. As it turned out, I *needed* to tell the story, to put the whole traumatic experience in the past. It didn't hurt that Kim held my hand throughout. At some point, someone handed me a bottle of water. Someone else was snapping photos. Miraculously, a sling appeared for my arm; another pair of flip-flops, too big; and some man's extra-large Hawaiian shirt; all of which I welcomed. There was lots of hooting and clapping, and other people recounting their near misses. Our firefighter, whose name I learned was Steve, laid a meaty hand on Kim's shoulder. "And this gal was damn lucky! When the bar upstairs fell through the ceiling, it got caught on the joists. If not for that, she would have been crushed."

"Wait. What?" I said. "The bar...?"

Kim squeezed my hand. "I'm fine."

"You should come take a look," he said, beckoning us to follow.

I glanced at Alice. She was glaring at me. "Just this," I said, "and then we'll find a way home. I promise."

"You said just a few minutes. It's been longer than that." But she joined us as we hiked around the building to the kitchen entrance. I had to force myself to step up to the doorway to see the wreckage, and I never let go of Kim's hand. It seemed to me that as long as I held it I would be safe.

The damage was worse than I could have imagined. Like a flimsy house of cards, the floor of the upstairs Teacup Lounge had given way and crashed down on top of the butcher block and baking area—right where Kim had been standing. "Oh my God," I whispered. One end of the large mahogany bar was planted next to the Hobarts, the other hung precariously from the ceiling joists. A minefield of broken liquor bottles, cocktail glasses, and napkins was strewn about, all coated in a fine layer of white, due to a fifty-pound bag of flour exploding. I gestured to the protected area beneath the bar. "So you were standing…"

Kim nodded. "That bar saved my life."

One of the rescue workers joked, "That's what they all say."

I couldn't get myself to laugh with the rest of them.

"We found her knocked out and bleeding," Steve went on. "But that didn't stop her from wrangling together the rescue mission once she'd come to."

"There was *no* stopping her," another guy chimed in. "She's one tough cookie."

"I just knew you were alive down there," Kim said shyly. "I could feel it."

They told us that even when nightfall had forced them to stop digging, she'd stayed up much of the night to keep the vagrants out. That only after everyone insisted she go home and deal with the cut on her head had she gone home to rest, first rounding up a couple of her nephews to stand guard until she returned at the crack of dawn to continue digging. This act of faith meant so much to me, to think she'd been willing to risk her life for us…All these guys had.

Alice stepped up to the doorway for a look, her arms wrapped around her middle. "Oh boy, oh boy, oh boy."

"It's okay," I said. "No one was hurt."

My gaze strayed to the hatch door—or to where it should have been. The adjacent wall had tumbled down upon it, burying it under a huge pile of rubble. An involuntary shiver ran up my spine. What if I'd been standing farther up on the stairway and the trapdoor had slammed down on my head? Or if the trapdoor hadn't slammed shut and the debris from the caved-in wall had come crashing down? Or if Kim had been standing by the Hobarts instead of the counter and the bar had crushed her? The near misses made me giddy, and weak in the knees.

"They're calling it a seven point one," Steve said.

"San Andreas Fault," Kim said confidently. She was not one of these women who went dopey around men. "Folks up by Nisene Marks got hit bad."

Other people chimed in.

"A bunch of houses down on Myrtle Street."

"My wife's sister said Watsonville got hit hard. St. Patrick's came down."

"San Francisco too."

"A damn blessing for the Giants!"

"They say Bush is coming."

"Sure! Now that there's a natural disaster!"

They were filling in each other, as much as telling us. With the phones and electricity down, word of mouth had become the way to keep each other informed. I rested back into Kim. The celebrity of having defied death was starting to wear thin. "How's Pearl?"

"Fine. And get this. Seconds after the quake, she charged back into the building for the register."

"That's our Pearl." I chuckled. "Anything to keep costs down."

I let her guide me away from the building. She could tell the scene was stressing me out. That we were walking over what I now realized was a series of tunnels didn't help. Then I noticed Alice slipping through the door and into the kitchen. "Alice!" I screamed. Paying me no mind, she squatted beneath the large fluorescent light, dangling precariously and skewed by just a single chain, and started pawing through the rubble. I screamed a second time, but just then, the ground beneath us began to shake. I watched in horror as plaster rained down, the light swayed, the bar groaned. "Alice!" I shouted for the third time. I was hysterical. To lose her now, after all we'd been through!

She snatched up whatever it was she was looking for and darted outside to safety—at which point I unleashed upon her a torrent of panicky, big-sister scolding. "What were you thinking? Are you nuts?" I was shaking all over, my knees playing the castanets.

She waited for me, and the aftershock, to subside, then held up her shiny object. "Car keys!"

"Are you insane? You could have—"

Kim gave my hand a short, sharp squeeze. She was right. I was on edge. And Alice's need to be home *right now* wasn't helping. Wasn't it enough that we'd escaped the jaws of death?

"I'll drive," Alice said.

Apparently, it wasn't.

Sighing, I turned my back on the bakery. There was nothing to be done about it now anyway, except to thank the people who'd spent time trying to dig us out. So I did that. A motley group, they nodded and scuffed their heels, laughed, said it was the least they could do. Then they picked up their sledgehammers and pickaxes and headed over to Bookshop Santa Cruz where, it was believed, there were still some people trapped. They were heroes, those men and women, every last one of them.

"We need to board the place up," Steve said. "It's not safe to leave it open like this to the public."

I glanced at Alice. I could not imagine having the wherewithal to find a hammer, nails, and a board. She was halfway to the car.

"Is she okay?" Kim asked.

"Who knows? But yes, I think she is."

"Well, don't worry about this. I'll take care of boarding it up," Kim said.

"But you—"

"Have had a night of sleep, which you haven't. I've also had a chance to check out my house. Now go."

I called out to Alice, "Do you even know where Tillie lives?" She did. Of course she did. The ever-capable Alice.

In retrospect, it is amazing how quickly life's complexities robbed me of that intoxicating feeling of having cheated death. All I could think about now was: *If the house is destroyed, what will we do with Mom?* I flashed on Alice's and my earlier conversation, about the Eskimo solution to old age, then shook the thought from my head. I was in no condition to be rational on the subject. I was exhausted, in pain, hungry, and in dire need of a glass of wine and a handful of painkillers.

Alice honked the horn.

It was time to leave Kim's side. I didn't want to. At all.

"After I get this boarded up," she said. "I'm going to make sure they don't need any more hands at Bookshop. Depending on how that goes, you want me to drop by?"

"Yes. Definitely, yes," I said and made myself release her hand.

All this talk about the earthquake is giving me bad dreams. Last night, I was trapped in a car, a schoolroom, and a bad relationship. I tossed and turned until the trash truck clunked down the street, at which point I bolted out of bed, threw on a robe and slippers, and charged out of the house to pull the can to the curb. I wanted those dead tree limbs of Alice's gone. They were too painful a reminder, and a damned nuisance poking out of the can, keeping me from filling it.

I made it to the curb just in time, but the sudden drama of racing out at the crack of dawn made it impossible to go back to sleep. I lay there, looking up at the cracks in the lath and plaster of my bedroom ceiling. A few hours of this, and I got up, threw on some sweats, put on a pot of coffee, and went to get my morning paper. I spotted Dita sitting out on the curb next to her bike, counting change. She looked like she'd slept in her clothes. It could just be her "look." Hard to say. Before I had a chance to sneak back into the house, she waved. "Morning, Ms. Lucy!"

"Morning! You okay?"

I had to ask.

"Just seeing if I have enough for a cup of coffee."

I thought of the pot brewing in my kitchen, and about what a rough time I'd had when I was her age. "If you feel like hanging out with an old lady, I'll cook us some breakfast. I have a pot of coffee brewing now." It would be my first decent meal since Alice's death.

She all but jumped to her feet. "That would be awesome! Can I park my bike in your yard?"

What have I done? I thought. *What can of worms have I opened?* But I said yes. Fixed us a green chili and cheese omelet, some sourdough toast.

Poor girl is drowning in student loans. "I just don't see how I'm ever going to be able to pay them back," she said, fiddling with one of her dime-sized ear holes. "Not if I plan to make art for a living." Which I thought she was smart to consider. I asked about her parents. She said they "didn't approve of her focus—or her life." Had "pulled the plug" on funding her "abnormal choices." It didn't take a mind reader to know what that meant. She asked about Alice, if there was going to be a service. I told her no, that I really didn't have it in me to put one together, and that I didn't know who would even come.

Then she brought up the bottles. She was concerned about what's going to happen with them. Told me Alice's work shouldn't die with her. I took her out to the garage. She was fascinated! Pored over Alice's materials and tools. She asked if she could put together a video of her work, kind of a tribute, and post it on YouTube, or maybe turn it into a documentary. She'd want to interview me and anyone else who knew her, she said. Her enthusiasm was infectious. Before I knew it, I was offering to fund the project. See what offering someone a cup of coffee and hot breakfast will get you into?

After she left, I was exhausted, but happier than I've been in days. And as if that weren't enough, I got a call back from Dune. We had a long talk, filled each other in on the last twenty years of our lives. He's heartbroken about Paul, and rich beyond words. (No surprise there. He always had a way of attracting money.) He made me promise to come visit him, either in Portland or in Italy—Italy!—where, apparently, he now owns a small villa. "Nothing too ostentatious," he said. "You'd approve." I suspect I would. Especially if it was sitting in some wonderful old garden with lots of trellises and walkways. We'll see. It was wonderful to talk with him again, wonderful to laugh.

ARMAGEDDON

A lice and I argued the whole way over to Tillie's. She didn't see why we had to check on Mom before checking on the house. I said, because we did; it's what you do with people you love, you check on them. Alice countered: Mom probably didn't even remember the earthquake. I came back with: Still, Mom was in new surroundings, and she wasn't so dim that she wouldn't know something was up. She said, wouldn't it be hard on Mom to come back to the house if it was in shambles? I said, we didn't have to bring her back; we were just checking on her. The argument was a continuation of the war we'd been fighting our entire lives: me trying to get Alice to care; she, not caring. Or so I thought.

"What's so important at the house anyway?" I said. "It's just stuff. And we're alive! That's what matters. Stuff can be replaced. Besides, people said the West Side wasn't hit that hard. Chimneys, dishes, that kind of thing. We can handle that. We'll be fine. Everything will be fine."

"Dishes," Alice said coolly.

She might as well have hit me over the head with one of her bottles. "Oh my God! Alice, your bottles! I'm sorry! I didn't even think!"

It was too late to change course. Tillie, whose house we'd just pulled up to, spotted us and rushed down the perky, daisy-lined pathway to the street. She wore a lightweight pink tracksuit and white fluffy slippers. "Lord have mercy! You're alive!" It must have occurred to her that if Alice and I died, it would be up to her to figure out what to do with Mom. Even for a saint this would be cause for concern.

I turned to Alice. "I'll make this quick. Promise." I spoke with confidence, clinging to the absurd notion that I had control over my life, as if a natural disaster hadn't just proven otherwise. Alice wouldn't even look at me.

I shouldered the car door open, jangling every part of me that hurt, and stepped responsibly out onto the sidewalk, emotions slinging around inside me like nuts in a blender.

"Prayers answered!" Tillie's intention to throw her arms around me was thwarted when she noticed my sling. "You're hurt."

I waved off her concern with my good arm. "It's nothing."

"But you're alive."

"That I am."

She peeked into the car, her perfect pearl pink fingertips resting on her knees. "Alice! It's so good to see you! What a blessing!"

Alice stretched her lips in an attempt to smile. "Made it, we did. And now we need to return to the roost." She drummed her fingers on the steering wheel. Kept the engine running.

"Of course you do." Tillie then asked me quietly, "Is she all right?"

"For the most part. We're both pretty banged up, and tired."

"How about Robert?"

"He's fine. Took off the second we got out."

"Probably went to check on his cat. But how did you—"

We were interrupted by Doug, her husband, yelling, "Euvonda!"

Mom had hold of the wrought iron rail and was tackling two porch steps. She was so unsteady, I was afraid she was going to topple into one of the rosemary bushes flanking the stairs. I made a move to go to her but was beaten to the punch by Doug, who, like Tillie, was wearing sweats and slippers, only his sweats were gray with Giants insignias. He charged out of the door and grabbed her by the armpits, and slowly flung her around, as if she were no heavier than a sack of feathers. "Oh no you don't, lady!" He plopped her gently on the porch.

The little whirl totally disoriented Mom. She looked this way, then that, her gaze finally settling on Doug. A man. A handsome man. A handsome man who seemed to be waiting for her to…what?…She had no idea. She slapped his arm coquettishly and laughed.

"It's been a long night," Tillie said.

"I'm sure."

"I really had no idea how bad she'd gotten."

You and me both, I thought to myself. It felt too negligent to say so out loud.

Mom, having spotted the car, patted at her hair, and then, from what I could make out, started explaining to Doug how she had to go. She took his arm, expecting him to escort her. The pink and green float we'd dressed her in the day before now seemed to accentuate her sagging neck, her toothpick ankles.

"I tried to change her into one of my nightgowns," Tillie said. "But…"

"No need to explain. I'm sure she was very confused by all this."

Alice leaned over to the passenger's side and whispered, "Time to vamoose, sisteroo." She revved the motor.

"Alice seems pretty upset," Tillie said.

"We've had a very long night. I think she'll feel better when we've seen the house."

"Of course," Tillie said.

I waved to Mom. I admit, some part of me was still waiting for her to recognize me, to raise her hands and say, *You're alive! You're alive! My daughter is alive!* But the only thing she recognized was the car, and she wanted in it.

"You can't make me stay one more minute," she said playfully to Doug. "Now, take me to my ride, mister!"

I couldn't very well say, *No, let's leave her here. We just stopped by to check on her.* Doug was already herding her to the car, she clinging to his arm like Miss America to Bert Parks. Nice as Doug was acting, I could tell he couldn't wait to get rid of her. Who knew what earthquake issues of their own they were dealing with?

Alice groaned, just loudly enough for me to hear.

"But how did you get out?" Tillie said.

I propped my tired self up against the car. Alice was going to have to adjust; Mom was coming with us.

"Have you heard of the tunnels?" I said.

"I'll be damned!" Doug said, joining us. "You found the tunnels?"

"Language," Tillie said teasingly. "Ladies are present."

Mom reached for the car door handle. Doug, ever the gentleman, or the guy who couldn't wait to get rid of Mom, beat her to the punch and opened the front passenger door.

"He's so good with her," Tillie mouthed.

I nodded.

The morning was warming up. Tillie tucked a stray hair into her do. "Personally, I never set foot in that basement. The steps down give me the creeps."

I pictured the steps, unmoored and twisted. There'd be no going down them any time soon, if ever. "Yeah, well. We came out at Zoccoli's."

"Sounds like *Indiana Jones* stuff," Doug said.

"How about you guys? Everything okay?"

"Plenty of cracks in the plaster, but all cosmetic. Roof's another story. Took a ladder up this morning. Chimney knocked a good-size hole in it. That's the only real structural issues I've found—so far." Doug clapped his hands together and looked at Tillie. "Anyway…"

"Go!" she said to him. "I've got this covered."

"Thanks, love." He mock saluted and bid us adieu.

"He's going nuts about his freezer of salmon," Tillie said when he was out of earshot. "Just got a hold of a friend's generator. We're going to see what we can salvage. It was a tough season to begin with and now this! But tell me, what's the news on downtown?"

I could feel Alice's fingers gripping the steering wheel, her foot itching to press down on the accelerator. "Um…"

Tillie rested a hand on my arm. "Bless your heart. You've got a lot on your plate. We can talk later."

"I'm fine. It's just—"

Mom whapped the dashboard. "Time to go! I have lots to do to get ready for tonight."

"I should tell you, she didn't get much sleep last night, and she had a rather explosive bowel movement early this morning." Tillie spoke quietly, so as not to embarrass Mom. "We didn't have any diapers, and the stores were all closed, but my daughter brought over some sanitary napkins and those seem to be working. At least for now. My daughter is a nurse; she was a great help. Now, you go. And don't hesitate to ask if you need anything."

"Thank you," I said and meant it.

I went to fasten Mom's seat belt. She reared back. "I don't know who you think you are, Missy, but you need to take your hands off me."

I had no defenses left. Her reprimand shot straight into my heart and stuck there.

Tillie, ever helpful, bent down so Mom could see her. "Don't you recognize your daughter? Lucy, all the way from Portland, who came down to take care of you?"

I made sure Mom's limbs were out of the way, and shut her door, perhaps a little too roughly, reasoning that if we could survive an earthquake, she could survive a car ride home with no seat belt. "It's okay," I said weakly. "She's just really confused. Sorry…" I slipped into the back seat.

"For what?" Tillie said, closing my door very gently. "And get someone to look at that arm."

"Will do."

The ride home lasted forever. Fine by me. Riding in the back seat, I was free to stare out the window. I looked for clues as to what to expect when we reached the house. This offered the added attraction of keeping my mind off Alice's jerky driving. She'd speed up between stop signs and blinking red lights, then slam on the brakes when she reached the next intersection. The streets were almost empty. I made an effort to reassure her a couple of times, to say I was sure her bottles would be okay, that Tillie's house hadn't looked so bad, but my reassurances sounded empty—even to me. Mom's endless "Where are you taking me?" and "Why are you so dirty?" didn't help.

She was even more disoriented than usual. The night at Tillie and Doug's had to have been confusing for her. I wondered if she'd found the refrigerator. She kept calling Alice Waltine, the name of one of her cousins. Went on about the "hotel" she'd just stayed at. "It was just as clean as could be. And they were just the nicest people. Cooked us grits and eggs for breakfast." I recognized the hotel, the story. She'd shared the childhood memory with us countless times. Her parents had taken her and Aunt Evie on a road trip, and somewhere along the way, Louisiana, I think, they'd been unable to find a "white" hotel with any vacancies, so my grandfather had asked a "negro" hotel to put them up for the night. (As though they could have refused!) The story always concluded with how they were "clean as could be. Just the nicest people. Served us grits and eggs." I hated the story, hated what it said about the way they grew up.

"Glad it all worked out," I said wearily.

Mom jumped at the sound of my voice. She'd forgotten I was sitting in the back seat. She looked at Alice. "Where are you taking me?"

"Home," Alice said for the zillionth time. It was the only thing she said the whole way. Home. Home. Home.

"What's going on?" Mom asked at an intersection. "Why are all the stoplights out?" And when we passed the Safeway, "Why are they all standing in line to get in the store? Why are the lights out?"

"The electricity is out all over town," I told her. "But they're working on it." I said it the way Alice said *home,* a one-size-fits-all answer. It seemed to satisfy her—until the next time she asked.

Meanwhile, I gazed at the world outside where all that needed to be fixed were simple things, like collapsed porches and fallen chimneys. Anything brick had gone the way of the bakery. So that was one thing we'd likely have to take care of, not that Mom's brick chimney was functional anymore, but its toppling would likely have caused roof damage. Some areas showed little external damage, which gave me hope. Maybe we'd been spared. Maybe, by some miracle, Alice's bottles had been too.

We passed another market with a long line out in front. The stench of vinegar and rotting food permeated the warm air. People were everywhere, filling each other in on what they'd heard. I longed for Toi and Dune. I wanted them to be worried about me.

By the time we pulled up to the bamboo fortress, I was worn to a nub by Mom's questions and worry over Alice's bottles; the bottles would be fine, or they wouldn't; somehow, we would survive. Aspirin and a shower were my priorities. That and the two bottles of Cab I'd brought back from Portland—if they'd survived. But as it was only about 10:00 a.m., I was going to have to wait. I wasn't that big an alcoholic.

Mom perked up at the sight of the house. "I knew it!" she said. What she knew, I had no idea. I didn't ask.

A small cluster of neighbors were gathered a few houses down; someone was handing out cups of coffee. Emma Buswell broke from the group and came rushing toward us, bracelets clank-clank-clanking, Birkenstocks flop-flop-flopping. "There you are! I've been worried sick!"

Alice flung open the car door and charged for the house.

Emma looked at me questioningly.

"It's been a long night," I said.

"I guess. Jesus! What happened to you? You look terrible. You both do. I hear downtown is a disaster. What happened to your arm? Is it broken?"

For some reason, Alice chose this moment to chime in. She stopped at the gate, turned primly toward Emma, and said, "I'm sure you'll understand if our current priorities are not on the recounting of our story but on checking in on our abode." She looked hilarious standing there, filthy as a coal miner, ponytail sticking up, shins and arms covered in scrapes and scratches, kilt and T-shirt ripped. I would have laughed if I hadn't hurt so much. I had a pounding headache. I must have looked ridiculous too, in my oversized flip-flops and Hawaiian shirt.

"It's fine, Alice," I said through the open car door. "I'll bring her up to speed." It was the last thing I felt like doing. The cushion of having survived was now as flat as a motel pillow. Just getting out of the car seemed a Herculean task.

"I've been worried about you," Emma said. "I saw you loading Euvonda into the car yesterday afternoon and then when you didn't return, well, I…What happened? Are you okay? Is there anything I can do?"

I believe I mentioned earlier my disinclination to interact with Emma. She was the kind of overly helpful person who shed light on your weaknesses by offering assistance before you yourself even identified the need. But on that day, her unsolicited concern meant the world to me. Somebody cared that I was alive, and was offering help, and I felt such tenderness for this woman who wore too much jewelry that I would have hugged her, if I could have, would have clung to her bangle-wearing body like a tear-soaked tissue to a tabletop.

"Alice and I were trapped in the bakery basement—" I sniffled.

Her hands flew to her face. "Oh my God!"

"But we're okay. Just tired and hungry."

Mom beat a weak fist on the car door, trying to get out.

"Let me," Emma said, and opened Mom's car door. "You poor things. You poor, poor things."

I stood by, exhausted, grateful, as Emma reached in to help Mom out. "Fortunately, we'd left Mom in the car. One of the gals from the bakery took her home."

"Oh, Euvonda, you must have been so scared."

Naturally, Mom had no idea what she was talking about. "What do you want from me?"

"Just for you to go to your house," Emma said. "Right here. Don't you want to go to your house, Euvonda?"

Mom shrank back from the bigness of Emma's personality. "I don't know who you think you are…"

"Your neighbor, Emma Buswell. Remember?"

Mom looked at her like she was nuts, then said, "Somebody give this woman a drink."

That made me laugh—even though it hurt like hell. That was my mama, all right. When in doubt, bring on the alcohol. "Let me try," I said. "Not that I'll have any more luck."

Emma withdrew, bangles a-bangling. "She seems really confused, more than usual."

Not really, I felt like saying, then reminded myself that Emma knew a lot more about my Mom's recent "usual" than I did.

"Oh, and Mr. Mendoza turned off your gas," Emma said. "You might thank him when you see him. He went around to everyone's house to make sure they knew how. Also, folks have been congregating in the Barretts' backyard. That's the blue house, there. They have a fire pit out back. We all brought food over. Made a big pot of chili last night. Coffee this morning—we still have water; although some people don't. Someone brought donuts. In fact, there are probably some left. I'll go grab you a few. You must be starv—"

A painful wail rose up from behind the wall of bamboo. We stood—or, in Mom's case, sat—motionless as the wail intensified.

"What on earth?" Mom said.

"Is that Alice?" Emma said.

I rushed toward the house. "Stay with Mom!" Would the drama never end?

I charged through the gate, through the yard, up the porch steps, through the door, through the living room, down the hall, each footfall setting off a wrenching pain in my shoulder. When I got to Alice, she was on her knees in the guest room, amid a pile of perfect miniature worlds, shattered, and strewn across the floor. That picture will remain burned in my brain for the rest of my life: Alice, the Great Creator of Tiny Worlds, looking down, helpless, on the mass devastation of her handiwork; the heels of her hands dug into her thighs, her rocking forward back, forward back, her face a mask of agony. While the world at large may have escaped Armageddon, Alice's worlds had not. All but four bottles had crashed down and exploded on the hardwood floor, mixing up *The Munsters* with *Little House on the Prairie*, *Night of the Living Dead* with *The Brady Bunch*. Her knees were bleeding, her wailing turning into a low eerie moan, one you might hear from a fox kit lost in the woods.

Unwilling to risk my knees, I maneuvered myself down onto a corner of the cot where I could more or less face her. "Alice," I said softly, but could no more figure out what to say next than I could magically put it all back together for her. I've never been good in these kinds of situations, never known how to calmly sit by when someone is hurting. I couldn't touch her, or hug her, like I would do with anyone else. I came up with this: "At least it didn't get all of them. At least you have these four, and maybe the ones at the bar too." I know. I know. It was a stupid thing to say. In my defense, I'd been stuck underground for over sixteen hours, had a torn rotator cuff, banged up feet, was filthy, thirsty—and, at the same time, feeling damned lucky to be alive at all. At the sound of my words, Alice stopped her keening and rose in one fluid movement from the floor. Thinking I'd somehow gotten through to her, I shoved my foot down my throat a few inches more. "Mom's outside with Emma. I was thinking once we get her inside, I'll try and scrounge us up something to eat."

Alice responded to my heartless return to normalcy by walking over to *It's a Wonderful Life*, taking it from its shelf on the wall, and hurling it to the floor.

"Alice, no!"

Glaring past my right shoulder, but clearly aiming her wrath at me, she reached blindly for the next bottle, and the next, flinging each one to the floor. *Rear Window. Mary Poppins. Jaws.*

"Alice..." I said lamely. "No. I'm sorry. Stop."

"Hel-looooo!" Emma called from the living room. "Is everything okay? I've got your mom here and she seems to think you have some people coming over for dinner?"

I couldn't let them find us here, couldn't subject Alice to Emma's attempts at being helpful, couldn't let Mom around the broken glass—although, if I knew Mom, she was heading for the refrigerator, where there was probably more broken glass. Who knew what condition the kitchen was in? I dashed down the hallway and met Mom and Emma by the front door.

"My God," Emma said, "is everything all right?"

"Yes. No. I don't know."

She glanced around the living room. "Alice sure did clear the place out." She shot a look toward the hallway. "Is she okay?"

Mom tottered toward the kitchen. Alice started back up with her keening.

"Not really," I said, chasing after Mom.

Emma followed me, making it a conga line. "It's a blessing in a way. Not Alice freaking out, but her clearing the place out. All those plates your mother used to have on the wall. They all would have come down. Can you imagine?"

Mom stopped abruptly at the doorway into the kitchen. I nearly cracked into her; Emma did crack in to me; Keystone Cops stuff. It would have been funny if it hadn't been taking place to the soundtrack of Alice's moaning.

The kitchen was strewn with dishes, some broken, mostly not.

There was stuff from the refrigerator and cabinets all over the floor. The large green glass popcorn bowl of my youth lay in three pieces on the floor, a box of cereal had exploded. One of the chairs was knocked completely over. And the place stank of the fermented smell of a freezer defrosting.

"Goodness gracious!" Mom exclaimed, overenunciating the words like an actress in a silent movie. She even flung her fingertips in the air to demonstrate her shock. "I've got some cleaning up to do. Those girls left this place a mess!"

Emma turned in the direction of Alice's low moans. "Should I go check on her?"

"No!" I blurted. I believe I even stuck my arm out, crossing-guard style. Then I swooped up Mom's walker, by the TV, and placed it in front of her, my shoulder shooting spasms of pain. "Use your walker, Mom."

Emma, ever helpful, said, "But it sounds like—"

"She's upset. But don't go back there. She needs to be alone."

"You want me to stay with your mom so that you can?"

I considered this for a millisecond. "No." Then reconsidered. "Yes."

"Okay." She took hold of Mom's hand. "We'll clean up the kitchen. How's that, Euvonda, you and me?"

"What's that sound?" Mom said. "Who's making that noise?"

"It's just a cat," I heard Emma say as I headed down the hall to Alice, "just an old alley cat making a fuss."

May 15, 1954

Dear Euvie,

You must be thrilled Lucy's going to college!! Mills College!!! To think we've come so far that a girl can choose college instead of marriage. Not that a pretty girl like her won't get married, too. Remember how Mama used to say, "A man thinks you're too smart, he'll grow cold as a banker's heart." Ha! Your girls will prove her wrong. Speaking of Mama...Oh, Evie! It would break your heart! I'm not even sure she knows who I am. Just some nice woman who comes around with groceries. She forgot where the bathroom was the other day and wet herself. It was awful. Daddy got so mad. Like she did it on purpose! What they say about men being the stronger sex, don't believe it. He's scared to death of what's happening to her. Can't figure to do anything but yell. That's how I see it.

I spend a few nights a week with them now, cook up some casseroles, do a little cleaning that Ruby doesn't get to. Poor Ruby, Daddy hasn't given her a raise in who knows how long! If ever!!! I know Daddy appreciates my visits. Not that he'd ever say so. Threw a fit yesterday when I served grocery-bought butter rather than creamery-bought. Can you believe? I don't know how Mama's put up with him all these years!!!! Sometimes I want to tell him that too, but Frank says leave it alone. Says nothing I say is gonna change Daddy. I'm sure he's right. He just makes me so mad!!!!!

But enough about all this! How are you? Hugh is selling insurance now, is that right? I couldn't quite tell from your letter whether he was actually selling it, or just fixin' to. I know the oil checks being up must be a big help. It sure is around here. We put a new roof on the house—finally!!! And guess who got a new Buick Riviera!!!!! I tell you, driving around town, I feel just like the cat's meow. Frank's awful disappointed I didn't buy him a new truck, but if Lucy can go to college, I can get me a new car.

Speaking of, I worry about Alice not having Lucy around. Lucy's always so good about looking after her. If you need me to come out for a spell, just give a jingle. I could drive my new car! Wouldn't Frank just pitch a fit?

We were all so sorry you couldn't make it back for Dulia's funeral. Everybody asked about you. You might give Halbert a call or write him a note. He's beside himself with grief. So far as I can tell, he hasn't been down to the donut shop since her death, and that's not like him.

One last note, a coupla drunks stole one of Emory Wilkes's heifers. They shot it then hitched it to the bumper of their truck and drug the poor, half-dead thing a half a mile to their place off the highway. All Sheriff had to do was follow the drag marks. Poor cow was still hitched to the truck, while the fellows that killed it were passed out on the porch.

So, that's the news here. Write me!!!! It's been too long.

Your loving and new-car-owning sister,

Evokia.

PS. Tell Alice that Uncle Frank still wants a chess rematch. He still can't believe she beat him when she'd only just learned how to play.

NATE THE NURSE

O nce again, I was the one helping Alice cope, while Mom was off in *her* perfect little world, where the dinner parties never ended, where a glance from a good-looking man was *as good as a pocketful of folding money*. It sounds harsh, I know. Mom couldn't help it this time; the world everyone else was living in had gone missing for her. Nor was she sitting at the kitchen table, puffing on a Winston, stewing, like she used to, leaving to me the hard part: helping Alice to find her way back. As far as she knew, there *was* no hard part, just the annoyance of a stranger in her kitchen. Still, the déjà-vu-ness was disturbing.

I stood, propping myself in the doorway to the guest room, trying to suss out the best course of action. Leave Alice alone? Join her? She sat on the floor, her butt resting on her crossed booted feet—a position I couldn't have managed even if my calves and thighs hadn't been covered in scratches and cuts—staring unblinkingly forward and rocking ever so slightly, her keening now more of a high continuous whimpering. My poor little battered toes recoiled at the moat of broken glass surrounding her, warning *Turn back! Turn back! Unsafe territory ahead!* while my arms, or my good arm, longed to comfort her. I didn't even know if she knew I was there. Then she grew quiet and I knew that she did.

I waited for another signal: go or stay?

She didn't move, just kept staring forward at my unmade cot.

I grabbed a broom from the hall closet and began gently sweeping some of the tiny people, tiny houses, tiny cars and broken glass into a pile, careful not to break any of them but out from underfoot. Alice turned her head, owl-quick, and glared at me. I took this as a good sign. She was acknowledging me. I kept sweeping. After clearing a path, I made a trip to the bathroom for a bowl of soapy water, a washrag, a pair of tweezers, a tube of antibiotic ointment, and a box of Band-Aids. I set them next to Alice so she could tend to her bleeding knees. She glanced at them briefly.

I can't tell you how much I longed to give in to my exhaustion, to say, *To hell with it,* and stretch out on the cot to unkink my body. But I didn't. I grabbed the pillow and lowered myself down onto the scratched hardwood floor next to her, using the pillow to prop up my tired back. Every aching muscle in my body screamed, *Cease and desist!*

"Alice, I know you can hear me," I said. She didn't let on that she could; I didn't let that stop me. "We're lucky to be alive, and it's mostly due to you. You got us out of there. Robert was ready to give up. So was I. But you kept going, because you're strong. I know you're upset about your bottles. How could you not be? But you can make them again, better ones."

When someone is so utterly bereft, what, really, is there to say? I did my best and segued into, "And I know you feel alone with Mom. You've done more than your share. And now I'm here to help. I have a few things to figure out at home, so I'm going to have to go back to Portland at some point…" I had no idea I was going to say this until it popped out. I regretted it instantly. But the pull to sleep in my own bed, to eat soup on my own deck, to be surrounded by my own friends was strong as a riptide. "I won't leave until the electricity's back on and we've gotten the house in order," I added hastily. "And the phone. I'll come right back, I promise, and we'll figure out what to do next. Together. You and me. Just like we always have."

Alice continued staring at the unmade cot. She was angry, or looked it. It was hard to tell; strong emotions expressed themselves in a one-size-fits-all pinching of her facial muscles. I counseled myself that she wasn't angry at me, even though it seemed like she was, which put me on the defensive. I might have been a less than perfect sister, but I sure as hell hadn't caused the earthquake. Aboveground, I was pretty clear about that.

"It's all going to work out," I said. "Somehow, it will."

I don't think she was even breathing at that point. I considered that maybe she didn't want me there. Or maybe she did. Either way, Emma couldn't stay forever; she had her daughter and husband to get back to. "Look, I'm going to go check on Mom and Emma. If you need me, let me know." Using my good arm, I boosted my exhausted body off the floor. Tossed the pillow onto the cot. "What do you say we wash up and I'll fix us something to eat? I'm sure I can find something to throw together."

I didn't expect her to come; still, I was disappointed when she didn't. It made me feel even more alone.

I popped my head in on Emma and Mom. The toppled chair was righted, all trip hazards off the floor, and the glass was swept up, meaning Emma had found the "outdoor broom" on the back deck, which would have irked Alice so. "You're an angel, Emma, really."

Emma twisted a trash bag closed. Mom looked on suspiciously. "It's nothing. You guys actually made out good. Your mom got upset about that green bowl, though, didn't you, Euvonda?"

"What are you doing here?" Mom said.

Emma set the bag of trash by the back door. "Helping you clean up after the party. Remember? You had a big party and everyone made a mess."

Mom shuffled over to the fridge to open it. "It's not plugged in. You forgot to plug it in."

"Electricity's out, remember?"

I wasn't ready for Mom yet. I needed just a few minutes to myself. "Could I talk you into staying while I take a shower?" I asked. "I'll make it quick."

"Take your time," Emma said. "But don't expect hot water."

To this day, that shower remains one of the highlights of my life. By some miracle, the water wasn't completely frigid. My skin soaked it up like a thirsty cactus. I used Mom and Alice's shampoo and conditioner, some knock-off brand that smelled like green apples, lathered my body with a white, fresh-smelling soap. It felt so good! I had to force myself to turn the shower off. I felt I should leave some of the tepid water for Alice.

Towel-wrapped and feeling so much better, I walked down the hall to "my" room. "Sorry," I said to Alice, who, I was relieved to see, was off her knees and picking through the carnage, "but I need to get some clean clothes."

She picked up the tiny trailer from Lucille Ball's *The Long, Long Trailer* and set it on the windowsill with a few other pieces she appeared to be salvaging. Her knees were starting to scab over.

"Oh, good," I said. "Maybe all is not lost." My suitcase was on the other side of the room. There was no way I could get to it without risking cutting my feet or stepping on some miniature person or thing. "I left you some semi-warm water. You might want to shower before it goes completely cold. Who knows when we'll be able to turn the gas back on?" I continued to stand there in my towel, dripping onto the hardwood. "I'm so sorry, Alice. I know this has got to hurt. You've put so much time into these."

"O-*kay*," she said. "Jiminy Cricket, what do you want?"

I was so happy to hear her talking I almost laughed. I took a careful step into the room. "My suitcase?"

"Why didn't you say?" She picked her way through the mess, grabbed my suitcase from the dresser in the closet, and held it out to me.

"Thanks. I'll just grab some clothes and aspirin and take them to the bathroom. I'll leave my suitcase in the hall so it's not in your way. And don't worry about Mom. I'll take care of her. You do what you need to do. I love you, sis. And if you need some aspirin, I'll leave the bottle in the bathroom."

She pointed to a miniature cactus by my foot. "Watch where you step."

I had no idea if she was worried about my foot or the cactus. Most likely, the cactus.

I returned to the kitchen in a pair of fresh shorts, clean tank, and my wonderful, wonderful Ugg boots, even though it was too hot for them. Oh, it felt good to have my feet covered!

Emma handed me a cup of hot coffee. "Welcome back to the land of the living." She gestured to a small plate of donuts on the table. "Compliments of the neighborhood." I couldn't thank her enough. Didn't ask if she'd brought Mom with her for the donut run, or left her alone. Didn't care. Whatever she'd done, I had coffee. And Mom, sitting at the table, a half-eaten donut in front of her, seemed more or less content, although she pursed her lips when I entered.

"You okay if I leave?" Emma said. "Martin's hankering to walk the neighborhood, see what's what."

"I've got caffeine," I assured her. "I can take it from here."

"All right. But if you need anything, you know where we live. And like I said, the Barretts down the street have set up sort of an outpost."

I walked her to the door, thanked her again, then called out to Alice, "There's coffee and donuts if you're interested!"

Mom was back at the fridge. "Why's it turned off?"

I settled my weary bones into a chair and took a sip of coffee. "Electricity's out."

She set a sack of limp celery on the counter. There seemed no point in trying to make her use her walker. She seemed to have the refrigerator routine down. She took out a few other items, then seemed to finish whatever it was she was doing and tottered toward the living room.

"Where are you going?"

"Well…I've just been busier than a moth in a mitten today! Think I deserve a little relaxation now that all is said and done."

I went after her. Reluctantly. I didn't want her bothering Alice. She stopped when she got to her spot in front of the TV. Settled into her chair, picked up the remote, and punched the on button. "It's not working."

"Electricity's out."

"That's a nuisance."

"Yes, it is."

"Well, what are we going to do, then?"

Good question, I thought to myself. "Want me to read you something?" Growing up, she'd liked me to read to her while she prepared dinner. She'd pull me from homework or friends and hand me her *People Today* magazine. She loved the stories about the stars.

"What a good idea!"

This meant I had to find something to read, which, in a house that'd been stripped of damn near everything, was a challenge. I didn't think she'd appreciate *The Color Purple*, which I'd brought with me for a second read. I knew I could dig something up in the garage, but I didn't want to leave Mom alone, lest she go after Alice. In the end, I lay on the floor, belly up, knees bent, a favorite position of mine to this day, and began improvising a bodice-buster, the kind she loved. "Evelyn Moro stood on the cliffs above the blustery sea, her velvet gown flapping in the wind…"

"Get me a cig," Mom said.

"Just a sec," I said. "She'd come to the small cottage by the water in hopes of forgetting her broken heart, but the humiliation of having been left at the altar by the cruel count was not so easily cast off…" I went on this way, praying it would put Mom to sleep—if it didn't put me to sleep first. Luckily, Mom was first to go, her eyelids growing heavy about the time Evelyn Moro's carriage broke down at the edge of the forest, and snoring outright by the time Blaise Everritt's white horse came galloping by.

I thought about checking on Alice, but I was sleepy too, and tired enough that the hard floor felt great. I was just nodding off when Alice came tramping through on her way to the garage. I made an effort to look bright-eyed, but Alice paid me no mind, and Mom kept on snoring.

Fine, I thought, and began to drift off again, this time to be startled awake by the sound of footsteps clunking up the creaky steps and onto the front porch. I considered not getting up. I was sure it was Emma, or some other concerned neighbor, and I didn't want them to wake Mom. There was a light knock. Mom didn't wake. But whoever it was was sure to knock again, and then she would be awake. I heaved myself up, tiptoed to the door, and cracked it open.

Kim and a flamboyant fellow dressed in black-and-white parachute pants and a close-fitting hot pink T-shirt stood on the porch. "Oh my Goddess!" the guy got out before I had the wherewithal to put my finger to my lips. "Kim told me about you in the tunnels," he continued in a whisper. "That is *so* intense."

"I hope it's okay we came by," Kim said quietly. Without the hard hat, I got a much better look at the bandage above her eye. It looked like it was covering stitches. "Nate is a nurse. I thought you might want him to look at your arm."

Her thoughtfulness meant so much to me. To think we'd only just met, and she, with a bandaged head, was now looking after *me*. "It's fine—great, really. It's just, Mom is finally asleep and I don't want to wake her. Why don't we go around to the back?"

After checking the gate, I led them around the house to the loungers on the back deck. It looked pretty much the same except for a clay pot that had tipped over, spilling some dried-up bulbs onto the deck. I righted the pot and dropped the bulbs back in it, leaving the dirt to deal with later.

"Lucy, my roommate, Nate. Nate, Lucy."

Nate was adorable: round, exuberant, and sporting a riot of colorful woven Guatemalan wristbands. I liked him immediately. "Girl," he said, gesticulating with his chubby hands. "What you've been through! You must have been terrified!"

Kim shrugged a green backpack from her arm. "I brought you some food. A baguette, some cheese, a few apples, a bottle of wine. I hope you like Zinfandel." She set a cloth bag on the large spool that served as a table.

I mentally added the Zinfandel to the two bottles of Cab I'd brought with me from Portland and felt positively rich. "That's so kind." The bravado I'd felt earlier, when I'd told myself I would make her mine, suddenly felt brash and premature. "Um..." I believe I said next.

"How's Alice?"

"Not good. Her bottles—"

"Oh no! Did she lose them? All of them?"

"Pretty much." I didn't tell her about the four she'd destroyed. The vision of Alice's cold stare as she smashed one, then the next, then the next, was enough to make me want to grab that bottle of Zinfandel, bite off the cork, and start guzzling.

"I'm sure she took that hard."

I could hear Alice bumping around in the garage. Sweeping and bumping. Who knew how badly her workshop had been hit? I gestured to the food they'd brought. "You guys hungry?"

"Nope. That's for you. Nate had the foresight to hit the grocery store before the lines started forming. We should be good until sometime next year."

He opened his palms to the heavens. "Gotta have food."

Alice strode out of the garage, broom in hand, and stopped dead when she saw Kim and Nate.

"Alice," Kim said, standing. "I'm so sorry to hear…"

Alice, who thus far hadn't said more than ten words to me, pivoted in her boots to face Kim, leaned the broom against the outside wall of the garage, adjusted her Clark Kents, and attempted to straighten her skewed ponytail. "Oh, hi, Kim."

Glad as I was that she'd stepped up, had been *able* to step up, it made me sad to see her have to. She wasn't used to having people in her house, and the circumstances made it all the more difficult. Like an exotic nocturnal animal caught in the beam of a flashlight, she stood before us looking exposed and confused.

"It's okay, Alice," I said. "They've just brought us some food."

Nate wiggled his fingers. "Hey, Alice."

She switched her off-center focus to Nate. "Hello, Nate."

At least, she knew him; that helped.

She attempted to brush the filth from her torn kilt, then aimed herself toward Kim. "You understand," she said, in her most professional voice, "that this natural disaster has robbed us of our ability to employ you. I apologize for not having a set of unemployment papers for you at the moment, but I hope, considering the current state of affairs, you will forgive me."

It wasn't until this moment, hearing Alice talk business, that it occurred to me what the destruction of the bakery meant to my future, to our future. If there was no bakery, there was no potential for upping its productivity. If there was no upping its productivity, there was no amassing the funds needed for getting Alice the help she needed to care for Mom—rather, getting *us* the help we needed.

I glanced at the bottle of Zinfandel, wishing like hell I had the nerve to crack it. Under the circumstances, Kim and Nate would understand, wouldn't they? Even if it *was* just a tad after eleven? I'd survived an earthquake. Didn't I deserve a glass of wine? Two? Of course, I didn't touch the bottle, not yet. I wanted too much to impress. In retrospect, perhaps I should have poured myself a glass, thus spreading out my consumption of the contents of the bottle rather than guzzling it, as I did later in the day. Perhaps then, things would have turned out differently.

Aftershock

They're saying the epicenter is in Aptos, up in Nicene Marks Park, apparently, there's a huge gash in the earth."

"Ouch!"

Nate checked my range of motion, while Kim filled me in on what was known about the earthquake. This to the backdrop of Alice trekking back and forth from house to garage, carrying what appeared to be hankies filled with miniatures. I worried she'd wake Mom, but I sure wasn't going to say anything.

"And phones are out. I guess you know that. Actually, it's just local. The lines are flooded, but out-of-towners are randomly getting through. Oh, and the Cooper House. It got hit bad."

"Here's what I'm thinking," Nate said. "And mind, I'm no doctor..."

I rubbed the place where my shoulder met my neck. "Is it dislocated?"

"More like a torn rotator cuff."

I didn't even know I had a rotator cuff, let alone that it could tear.

"It's a group of muscles that allows you to do this." He rolled a shoulder seductively.

"So much for my belly dancing career."

"I've heard those hurt," Kim said. "One of the guys I work with in the union tore his when we were building platforms for Elton John. He was out of work for a month. Had to have surgery."

"I still can't believe you refused to sneak me backstage to meet him," Nate said and pursed his lips.

Kim laughed. "Hell, *I* never even got to meet him. I was just starting out, remember? All those boys would let me do was follow them around with the compressor."

"She's the only woman in the stagehands union," Nate confided to me. "Did you know that? We're all very proud her. Our little butch prodigy."

She mock-slapped his cheek Three Stooges style. "You are such a bitch."

Much as I enjoyed their bantering—such a relief to be talking about things that weren't life and death!—I was anxious about my recovery. "How should I care for it?"

"Ice, if you can find any. Rest. In a few days you should get in to see a doc, get some x-rays to corroborate my diagnosis, but right now the emergency room is a complete clusterfuck. They might recommend surgery, or a steroid shot. In the meantime..." He dug around in his pocket and came out with an amber prescription bottle. "Take these."

"Valium," Kim said. "His personal stash."

Nate gave her a withering look. "Now who's being a bitch?" He turned to me. "For your information, *Lu*-cy, I keep a few around for my back. Stagehands aren't the only ones doing heavy lifting."

I tried not to look desperate as I snatched the bottle from him.

"But don't say where you got them, and no more than four a day. Space them out. They should give you some relief. The sling is a good idea too. It'll keep you from overusing it."

"Someone gave it to me at the bakery."

"The Good Samaritans were out on the mall in droves today," Kim said. "One gal, I swear to God, was offering free back rubs."

"That is *too* Santa Cruz," Nate said. "Speaking of, we should probably head back."

Kim took a deep breath and got to her feet. She looked exhausted. "Yeah. A couple of our friends had to move in with us."

"Their house fell off its foundation," Nate added. "They are fer-eakin'."

"Are they okay?"

"Physically, yes. But every time there's an aftershock, Janna has a," he used air quotes, "panic attack." Then he switched to a baby voice. "And she needs her Kimmie Wimmie to care for her."

Kim whapped his arm with the back of her hand. "It's not like that. She's traumatized."

Nate milked the hit, rubbing his arm. "Who wouldn't be? When she was trying to get out of her house, the deck pulled away and she fell into the space between steps and house." He shivered. "But the girl also knows how to use it, if you know what I mean."

I remember thinking: *That's nothing compared to what I've been through! And you're going back to her?* The difference, of course, was that this Janna and Kim were friends, while I was only someone Kim had just met—her sort-of boss, no less. Who was I to think she'd go for me? Women clearly threw themselves at her all the time. I stood, mentally preparing myself to never see her again, to be just one more in a long line of needy women.

She took my hand—my good one—and held it gently in hers. "Is there someone nearby who can help you if you need it?"

I nodded. I had one Zin, two Cabs. What better friends?

"Okay then, we should go. I want to check on the animal shelter too. Make sure they're doing okay."

I'm not kidding. She said that, about checking on the poor little animals at the animal shelter. She would deny it until the day she died—"I would never have put the animal shelter above you!"—but Kim was the real deal, a born Girl Scout. If there was a treed cat in a ten-mile radius, she would find it and save it; an orphaned raccoon yowling for its mama, she'd bottle-feed it until it was ready to fend for itself.

"What about you? Your injuries? Shouldn't you be resting too?" I loved the feel of my hand in hers. It fit so perfectly. If only—

Nate laughed. "Good luck trying to get her to take her own advice!"

"I'll see if I can find you some ice," Kim said, giving my hand a squeeze then letting go. "I'll bring it by if I do."

We hugged good-bye. I walked them to the gate. Kim and I hugged again, lingering in each other's arms longer than was necessary. I told myself not to read too much into it as I watched them drive off. Then I just stood there looking at that empty road, fighting the urge to call out after them. When there was nothing left to do but return to the house, I made my way slowly back to the yard, where I popped a Valium and stretched out on the deck lounger. I'd barely swallowed it when the earth, once again, began moving beneath me. I gripped the edge of the lounger mat as if it were a life raft and rode out all five seconds of those tectonic plates shifting, eyes squeezed shut, jaws clenched tooth-cracking tight. Then I took another Valium and began to cry. And cry. And cry. Life as I knew it was over! Even if I could find a way to stay in Portland, I'd have to come down all the time. I was furious at Mom. Of all the ways to go, hers *would* be one that was most high-maintenance, drawn out, and demanding everything from everyone, especially me and Alice. I cried so long that I cried right through to gratitude: I was alive! I'd almost died, but I didn't. I was alive! And it was a beautiful day! All this family stuff was just a silly little mess that could be worked out. I could do it! And then I cried more, right into as deep a sleep as I have ever experienced.

I woke to my leg being jabbed with the handle of a screwdriver. "Earth to Lucy. Earth to Lucy. I'm going to check on my bottles down at the bar. You need to look after Mom."

"Wha…?"

"You need to look after Mom. I'm going down to the bar to check on my bottles."

"Okay, okay, give me a second."

According to the sun, it was late afternoon. I'd slept for quite a while. Five hours? Six? Alice was all cleaned up, her knees and calves a collage of Band-Aids, and had her bike ready and raring to go in the yard. I felt remarkably refreshed. It was great to see Alice out of her funk. I sat up and rolled my neck a few times. My shoulder still hurt like hell, but I wasn't as upset by it. The sleep had done me good, and the Valium, or more accurately, the Valium*s*. My adrenal glands were no longer banging: *SOS! SOS! SOS!*

I yawned. "Is she still sleeping?"

"Nope."

"Is there electricity yet?"

"Nope"

"Okay." I rubbed the sleep from my eyes. "We should be fine."

"Make sure Mom drinks water. It's hot. She gets dehydrated. And she still hasn't had her BM. Keep an eye on that."

"O-*kay*. Is there any protocol for…?"

"Watch. She'll wander around like she's looking for something. Herd her toward the bathroom." And with that sage advice, Alice took off on her bike.

I wasn't worried. I was glad for a turn at Mom duty, glad that Alice was going to check on her bottles. I'd survived an earthquake; taking care of Mom was going to be cake. Belatedly, it occurred to me I should have asked Alice about flashlights and candles. But as there were no cell phones back then, I resigned myself to waiting until she got back, which I assumed would be shortly. Downtown wasn't very far.

I found Mom standing in the hallway leading to the bedrooms, and miracle of miracles, she was using her walker. I wondered if this was the "wandering" Alice mentioned.

"Hey, Mom, can I help you with something? Do you need to go to the bathroom?"

She frowned. "What happened to your arm?"

"There was an earthquake. I fell."

A horrified expression swept across her face. "Earthquake! Is everyone all right?"

"Fine. Everyone's fine."

She took a few steps toward the living room, her walker thumping in front of her, then stopped.

"Do you have to go to the bathroom?" I repeated.

She thought for a moment, then continued thumping purposefully toward me, steamrolling me out of the way.

I chased after her. "Are you hungry? Do you want me to fix something?"

Plopping down on her recliner, she picked up the remote and pressed it. "It won't turn on."

"It's the earthquake. We lost all power."

The same horrified expression lighted on her face. "Earthquake! Was anyone hurt?"

"Fine. They're all fine."

"What happened to your arm?"

"I fell."

"Is it broken?"

"Nope. They think it's a torn rotator cuff."

She noticed the remote in her hand and tried using it. "TV's not working."

"There's no electricity."

"What a nuisance. What happened to your arm?"

We might have lingered on any of these topics—my arm, the TV, no electricity, the earthquake—longer than I've indicated, but what I remember of that evening, of that endless conversational loop, was that it felt like being on a Ferris wheel where the motor never turned off; we went round and round and round—my arm, the TV, no electricity, the earthquake, my arm, the TV, no electricity, the earthquake—until my post-nap euphoria was worn to a dull headache. I uncorked the bottle of Zinfandel. Took another Valium. Tried to get Mom to eat canned tuna fish on crackers to which she said, "Put some mayonnaise on it." Which, of course, I couldn't do without risking salmonella poisoning. So, of course, she asked why there was no refrigeration, and we were back on the loop again. I did manage to distract her a few times. We took a stroll in the backyard, talked about "her daughters" (one of whom was "difficult," though she never said which one), but she was tired and wanted her TV and I couldn't provide it. She made endless trips to and from the kitchen. I chaperoned most of these junkets. Pulled the lounger cushion back into the living room, the floor getting farther and farther away each time I had to get up or down. Ultimately, I dragged a whole lounger into the living room and stretched out on it with my bottle of wine.

The third Valium was a bad idea. Especially on top of the wine. I got sluggish, maudlin, drifting in and out of a restless sleep. During my waking moments, I got it in my head that I could talk Mom out of her dementia, that I could dig down inside the addled old woman staring at the blank TV to find my real mom, the witty woman of my childhood, the one whose acerbic observations had always thrilled my friends: *That man could start an argument in an empty house. Did you see her slacks? They were so tight you could see her religion. That fella couldn't find his ass with both hands in his pockets.* The mom who let me drink my first beer on the Fourth of July when I was fourteen because it was better I learned to drink with her than with *those little inbreds down the street*; the mom who, when I came out as a lesbian said, *Well, just don't tell anybody and we should be fine.* Even that Mom would have been better than this one, who didn't know me; at least I could fight with her. But the more I tried to excavate her, the more agitated she got. She called me Evokia so many times, I actually began responding to it.

By the time Alice returned, two and a half hours later, Mom was back in her recliner and I was a mess: fucked up and sprawled out on the lounger in the living room, responding to Mom's endless questions about the out-of-order TV with nonsensical answers, my empty wine bottle on the floor next to me. *It's not actually a TV, Mom, it's a toaster. I've never even heard of electricity, how does it work?* It sounds cruel. Maybe it was. If so, Mom didn't remember it from moment to moment. Sometimes, it even made her laugh. Other times it sent her to the kitchen cussing me out. I didn't care. It felt so good lying on that lounger. And what damage could she do? The food that could spoil already had.

Suddenly, there was Alice. Breathing heavily, cheeks flushed from her evening ride home, arms akimbo, she looked as happy as I'd ever seen her—and superhero strong. "You'll be happy to know my bottles at the bar are hunky dory. All six. The straps held! The owner was amazed, he was! Gave me a slice of cold veggie pizza and Dr Pepper. Drew was there too. His car got crushed under a tree, but he was ready for a new car anyway. The transmission was going out. So no big deal. That's what he said."

She prattled on about her social afternoon at the bar, about people's earthquake experiences, how they said she should make a bottle to commemorate the earthquake. All the while the dusk crept in the house and the shadows grew. I adjusted the back of the lounger to make myself appear more alert, blinked a few times. "That's great, Alice," I slurred. "I'm happy for you." I was having trouble focusing through the thick fog wrapped around my brain. The ceiling blurred into the wall, the wall into the floor. Alice herself was disappearing into the evening's gloom. Still, I could feel what was brewing: Mom didn't like someone else getting the attention; she wanted it for herself.

Finally, when she couldn't put up with one more second of Alice's enthusiasm, she slapped the arm of her recliner and spat, "For heaven's sake! Enough already! You're giving me a headache! All your talk about this and that! As if anyone here gives a good goddamn!"

Poor Alice was caught completely off guard. She stepped backward.

I tried to speak up in her defense, to say something about her being deserving of respect, that she was, in my mind, solely responsible for saving my life, but my sluggish tongue wouldn't cooperate. Nor would my mind, which purred: *Do you really want to step into this? You've been through so much already. Relax. Everything will work out for the best.* This left the field wide open for Mom to zero in on Alice. Which she did. Like a smart bomb. She funneled all her frustrations of the last few hours into a single nasty bolt of rage. "Stupid little goat! Always talking, talking, talking. I. Am. So. Sick. Of. You!" She punctuated this last bit by slapping the arm of the recliner on each word.

Her venom struck like a poison dart. Alice looked down at her feet, fiddled awkwardly with her Clark Kents.

That's it! I said to myself. *I don't care how addled Mom is, she's gone too far! Time for me to step in.* I tried to swing my legs off the lounger; they looked back and me and said, *What? You want us to move?*

"Hover, hover, hover," Mom went on, slapping her knees now. "It's all you do! Chasing after me like I can't care for myself! And now something's wrong with the TV!" Mom snatched up the remote and brandished it at Alice. "It won't work!"

Alice let her satchel drop to the floor *Clunk!* then glared at me.

"What?" I said.

She sniffed the air. "Has she had her BM?"

If I'd had any control over my motor skills, I would have kicked myself in the head. I'd forgotten all about Mom's BM. "Not sure," I said, only then noticing the stink. "Kim brought over some cheese and bread. You hungry?"

"I just *told* you, I had pizza." She began to storm off, then stopped in her tracks and swiped a wine bottle from the table by Mom. "You let her have *wine*?"

I squinted at the bottle, trying to make sense of her meaning. Of course I hadn't given Mom any wine! But then, what to make of what looked to be a half-empty bottle of Cab? Had Mom found it and figured out how to open it? Or had I, and then forgotten about it? I had no idea.

"This is not good, sisteroo, not good at all." The room was quite dark now, but there was no mistaking Alice's rising anger. I had summoned Mama Hyde, and that was bad news. Alice shifted from one boot to the other, gripped the pleats of her kilt.

"She must have found it," I said defensively. "I never would have given her wine!" I managed to stand. The room began to spin. I steadied myself on the back of the lounger. "I probably drifted off and she found it." I tried to think of a way to get the attention off of my shortcomings. "Any chance there's a flashlight around?"

Alice strode off, banging the bottle of wine down onto the kitchen counter before slamming out the sliding glass door to the backyard. I wasn't sure if she was coming back.

"She sure has a bee in her bonnet!" Mom said.

"When did you get the wine?"

"What wine?"

"Never mind. Stand up. We need to get you to the bathroom."

"It's dark."

"The electricity's out."

"When did that happen?"

"Just now, okay? Now stand up!"

Needless to say, Mom didn't. The alcohol was making her obstinate. I stepped toward her, hoping to appear in control of the situation, but stubbed my toe on the back of her chair. "Shit!"

"For God's sake, turn on some light."

"I can't!"

"Why?"

I swallowed back what I wanted to say: *Because the goddamned electricity is out! Because there was a goddamned earthquake! That almost killed me! Almost killed Alice! Both your daughters almost died! Did you hear that? Died!* I was so angry at her, at myself, while at the same time oddly removed from the scene, as if I had stepped into a part in a play I didn't know but whose lines were somehow being spoken through me.

Alice returned with a flashlight. "Here."

I thought she was going to storm back to the garage, leaving me alone to deal with Mom's poop. I think *she* thought she was going to too. We both knew I hadn't a clue how to go about it, especially in the dark. Fortunately, she took pity on me, leaned down, and took Mom's arm. "Upsy-daisy, Euvonda. It's potty time."

"Hands off!" Mom said.

"Come on, Mom, Alice is right. You've had an accident."

"No!"

We tried a number of strategies to coax her out of the chair, including luring her with the Chanel No. 5. None of them worked. She was having too much fun defying us. Finally, Alice simply lifted her up and out of the chair by her armpits. "Come on, Euvonda. You stink."

"Careful!" I said.

"How dare you?" Mom said.

Ignoring both of us, Alice set Mom briefly on her feet so she could adjust her hold on her, then lifted her like a bag of groceries and toted her all the way to the bathroom, Mom beating a weak fist into her back, me trotting along behind, arcing the flashlight above their heads so Alice could see where she was going.

Once in the bathroom, Alice set Mom down in front of the toilet, reached behind her, yanked up her float, and tugged down her shit-filled panties. The menstrual pads, also covered in shit, came with them.

Mom said, "This is ridiculous!"

Alice was so angry I don't think she even heard her. "Hold her up," she barked. "I need to get her feet out." So I did. I set the flashlight down on the sink and held our writhing mother while Alice lifted one foot, then the other, out of the shit-filled panties. The stink made me nauseous. Still, I did my best to reassure Mom.

"It's okay, Mom. It's okay."

"Oh," Mom said, slipping into sarcasm. "I can see it's okay. Everything is just fine."

"It's not okay!" Alice yelled. "She's drunk! She BMed her pants!" Her hands were covered in shit.

"Stupid little goat! Of course it's not okay! See what you did? You made a mess!"

Alice tossed the panties into the trash, ran her hands under the sink, grabbed a washrag, and began roughly wiping Mom's butt. It was a tight fit, Mom backed up to the toilet, Alice reaching around her. The smell was overpowering. I stepped out of the way. Alice rinsed Mom's butt by scooping water from the toilet using a small handled measuring cup, apparently kept there for that very purpose.

Mom twisted and turned. "Stop it! Stop it! Keep your dirty hands off me!"

"Blame me," I said. "I should have gotten you to the bathroom." But my words hung in the room with nowhere to land. The brutal, tightly choreographed dance was under way. Alice sloshed water everywhere, Mom thrashed this way and that, but they both knew their parts. It was the perfect storm: Alcohol, Autism, Alzheimer's, all of them swirling out of control to create this horrific scene.

But I stayed. I picked up the flashlight and aimed it toward them to feel as if I were helping. My stomach would not settle. The lack of sleep, the PTSD, the mourning of my mom, the Valium, the wine, the pain, the shit, all of it got the better of me, all of it at once. Only the toilet was in use. So I set the flashlight on the sink, swallowed back my puke, and charged through the dark hall, the dark kitchen, and out to the dark yard where I finally let loose, right next to Mr. Scratch. I puked again, and again, until there was nothing left but bile. By the time I finished, I was trembling and weak-kneed, and dropped onto the big spool on the deck, elbows on knees, head hanging, shoulder throbbing.

I stayed that way for some time, forehead clammy and dripping sweat, focusing on my breath, trying to calm my queasy gut. I was dying of thirst but couldn't imagine swallowing anything. I breathed some more, snorting my exhales like a bull. While nowhere near as pitch-black as the tunnels, the darkness pressed against me, pushing me toward a panic attack, so with each deep breath I took, I drew on whatever reserve of courage I had left. Finally, when I felt like I could stand without puking, without hyperventilating, I turned on the old garden hose and drank and drank, praying the water was potable, washing off my face and bare feet. Then I tried to clean off Mr. Scratch's grave. The water just made the puke soak further into it.

I cranked off the hose. Coiling it back onto its hanger seemed impossibly difficult, but I did it. I didn't want Alice yelling at me. Also, I suppose I was avoiding going back in to help. I knew I should. Stood by the back door listening to see if I could hear anything. But it had grown quiet. Very quiet. Did I take note of how quiet? Only in retrospect. At the time, I assumed Alice had some trick to settle Mom. I pictured her putting Mom in a fresh nightdress. Pictured her helping Mom slip into her soft bed. A part of me wanted to join them, to be the good daughter helping her ailing mother and put-upon sister. And I longed for the flashlight. I was so tired of the dark. But I didn't go to them. I told myself it was best for everyone if I didn't, told myself that my joining them would just stir Mom up.

I felt my way back into the kitchen, shaky and unsure of my footing, wishing I'd thought to ask Alice about candles. Surely she had some stashed away somewhere. The baguette and cheese were where I'd left them on the counter. I could just make them out by the breadbox. I ripped off a piece of sourdough baguette, then ripped a smaller piece from that and placed it on my tongue. The bread was crusty, hard on the outside, soft and fluffy on the inside. I swallowed it down. I needed something in my stomach besides the sloshing hose water. The act of chewing calmed me. The sound of talking and laughing from a few houses down did too. It drifted through the sliding screen door. But still there was nothing from Alice and Mom, which seemed odd. I checked my sling. It was skewed from my bout of retching. I fixed it. Took another bite of bread, this time letting it sit on my tongue until it grew moist and chewy. The neighbors' conversation became my world. "No kidding? The whole foundation?" "Yeah. And who has earthquake insurance?" It occurred to me that maybe it was a little too quiet. Or maybe it didn't occur to me, maybe I was that out of touch. I've revisited this scene so many times, wanted to believe so many things—wished I'd done this or that—that all that's left of the truth is a muddy soup.

I remember the neighbor's conversation ending. "Come by if you need anything!" "How about a little electricity?" "Yeah, yeah. Night!" "Night." I remember sea lions barking, a breeze rattling the window shade above the sink. I remember listening and finally feeling my way down the dark hallway. "Alice? Is everything okay?" I remember padding my way toward the sliver of light illuminating Mom's closed bedroom door. I remember standing outside the door and whispering, "Alice? Alice?" afraid to wake Mom if she was sleeping.

Here is a possibility: I knew what was going on.

Here is another: I didn't.

But this is what I did: I walked away.

I decided Alice knew what she was doing, that she had it taken care of, and I walked away, returning to the kitchen, to my stale bread. I felt I deserved it. What I didn't do was kill that second bottle of Cab, and that wasn't my style, not back then, not when I was in that kind of pain. A bit of puking and a headache wasn't enough to scare me straight. But I didn't reach for that bottle. That's something. I comforted myself with the thought that Mom would forget the horrible BM scene.

I didn't think about the fact that Alice wouldn't, that this was just one more in a long string of potty episodes for her. Alice probably figured she'd be doing this for more years to come, seeing as her mother was so physically healthy, and her older sister, while well intentioned, was clearly going to be no help. I'm sure that's what she thought. But then, who knows what she thought? All I know is that some time later, I heard Mom's door creak open, saw the beam of Alice's flashlight angling down the hallway, lighting up the portraits: the Yam Queen in the dime-store frame; six-year-old me, my arm thrown casually, protectively, around little Alice's neck; Dad with a full head of hair and a new Chrysler. I swallowed the glob of bread in my mouth and listened to Alice's footsteps as they approached.

They paused just before entering the living room.

"Alice?" I said quietly. "Is everything okay?"

Her footsteps resumed.

When at last she entered the kitchen, I could tell she was shaken. I felt it more than saw it. She held the flashlight at her side in a loose grip, illuminating her boots, as if it were too heavy to hold up. Her breathing was shallow, irregular, staccato; it seemed to barely reach her lungs.

"You okay?" I said.

Her response came in a lifeless monotone. "You bet, old sport. I'm off to the garage. Got some stuff to do, I do."

"How's Mom?"

Apparently forgetting that she'd just said she was going to the garage, she pulled back a chair and dropped, straight-backed, into it. She let me take the flashlight from her, barely even noticed me doing it. I set it on the counter where it caught her in its beam. She looked completely emptied out.

"Alice?"

When she still didn't respond, I swiped up that flashlight and tiptoed briskly down the hall to Mom's bedroom. The door was shut. I quietly nudged it open. But there was no need to be quiet. There would be no waking Mom. She lay on top of the bedspread, one of her hands gripping the white polyester of it, the other rested on her chest twisted at an odd angle as if she were trying to push something off her. Her head was arched backward, her mouth open, as if she were gasping for air. The pillow was on the floor.

THE FINAL MAKEOVER

I held the flashlight beam centered on Mom's chest. I couldn't bear to light her face directly. As it was, the harsh light was casting macabre shadows, turning Mom's terrified expression into some horrible Halloween mask. Clearly, she was dead. Still, I had to be sure. If she weren't, if she suddenly gasped for breath, she'd remember what Alice had done. Or would she? My own heart, alive and well, slammed in my chest as I tried to muster the courage to make the short walk from the doorway where I stood to where she lay twisted and tortured looking on the bed. Alice had killed her. Alice had killed our mother.

Then, with no forewarning from my dazed limbs, I was walking to her side, placing a hand in front of her mouth. Of course, I felt nothing. Not even a whisper of life. When Alice did something, she did it well. Mom was dead. Dead dead. Alice had fulfilled her promise to Mom and solved our problems in one fell swoop.

I was horrified. Terrified. My body trembling spasmodically. My voice stuck somewhere between crying and screaming, but nothing coming out. I pressed my hand against my own mouth. Bit it to keep from howling in pain. Paced the bedroom. Closed the window. Drew the shade, even though it looked out onto the backyard, and it was too dark to see anything. I paced some more. Sat on the side of the bed. Talked to Mom. Apologized. Sobbed. Gripped her hands in mine. Kissed her forehead. I could not believe she was gone, and at the same time was kind of relieved that she was. And not relieved at all. I felt raw. Gutted. Wretched. I remember thinking about her last moments. How frightened she must have been. And about Alice. How frightened she must have been. Or was she? What had she been thinking? *Had* she been thinking? All this and much more in just those few minutes. Seconds, maybe, because there was no time. We had to figure out what to do! Anyone seeing Mom like this would know what had happened, and I couldn't do that to Alice, couldn't have them lock her up for doing what she'd thought was right.

Had she thought it was right?

Maybe she'd been angry. Maybe she'd been trying to shut her up, hadn't meant to kill her. But at the time, this didn't seem nearly as important as: What if someone came over? What would we say? I had to make it look like Mom had died of natural causes, had slipped peacefully off in her sleep. I hadn't a clue how long it took for rigor mortis to set in.

I set the flashlight on the dresser and went to work, lifting her hand, tugging the bedspread from her frail grip, carefully, as though I might hurt her, then arranging the hand and arm on her chest to look as if it were just resting there. I was trembling horribly, panting breaths. Blinking back tears, I lifted her other arm, the one that had tried to push Alice away, positioned the wrist and arm at a more natural angle across her belly, making sure to arrange the fingers to look peaceful.

Reshaping her face was the hard part. I took the pillow from the floor and propped her head into a more comfortable angle. I had to wipe my tears from her face, I remember that. And how, when I tried to close her mouth, it wouldn't stay shut. I had to adjust the pillow just right. Then I moved to her eyes, the windows of the soul, closing one, then the other. It was hard to do, my hands shook so much. Oddly enough, I was afraid I was hurting her. But I managed.

Finally, when I'd done all that I could, I stepped back to assess. Something was wrong; she looked too perfect. I tilted her head to the side, it helped but something was still off. Then I realized what it was: she was on top of the bedspread! If we were going to tell people she died in her sleep she needed to be under the covers.

I considered getting Alice to help me lift her but, and I know this sounds odd, involving Alice would have made the whole thing too real. I also wanted to prove to myself that this last act, this last gift to my mother, I could do myself. Because I saw what I was doing as a gift. Mom would want her corpse to look good.

I took off my sling. I would need both arms to maneuver her under the bedspread and sheet. Put the sling on the dresser by the flashlight. Then slid my good arm under the pillow to lift her head and torso. She was so light! With my bad arm, I slid the bedspread and top sheet down past her shoulders. The pain was excruciating. I reveled in it. Her head rolled into my breasts. I kissed the fine hair of her skull and set her back down, then moved to the other side of the giant rococo bed to slide the rest of the bedding from beneath her. At one point I almost rolled her off the bed entirely, one of the truly horrible moments of my life. Ultimately, I had to climb up on the bed and straddle her with my knees. I was grateful she'd shit earlier so I didn't have to deal with that.

When at last I had the blanket out from under her, I bunched the bedspread and sheet at the bottom of the bed so I could once again arrange her body. I kept her on her back, putting one leg straight out and one slightly bent. Too perfect, and she'd look posed. She was growing cool, which threw me into another panic. I picked up my pace. Pulled the sheet and bedspread up to her chest. Left one arm under it and resting on her belly, the other on top of the bedspread. Her mouth had gaped open again. I decided it looked natural. Rumpled the blankets so the scene didn't look so neat.

Then came her hair. I was of two minds about it: Keep it as it was, rumpled from Alice's and my manhandling of her, which, ironically, made it look slept in, or to poof it out a bit, the way I knew she'd want me to. *Don't you dare let people see me like this!* I could hear her say. So I went with poofing.

As I did some final adjusting to her float to make it look more slept in, I said a few tear-soaked words to her. "I know you didn't mean to become such a burden. But it's okay now. We can all rest. I love you. Always will. So does Alice. You were a great mom. And you should be proud of Alice. She's taken good care of you." I kissed her on the forehead. "Go on now. Go wherever it is people go." I was sobbing at this point. And so confused. Was what I was doing right? Part of me thought it was. She would hate what she'd turned into. But taking her life, her breath, against her will…Everything about it seemed so wrong.

I remember sitting there sobbing. Sobbing because I missed her, my real mom, Euvonda Mae Lipscomb, the Yam Queen, who would be laughing at me for being so sentimental. *For God sake, Missy!* I could imagine her saying. *Pull yourself together. The real show is just about to begin!* Sobbing because I hadn't seen this coming, and should have. Sobbing because I hadn't been around enough, back when she was still herself. Sobbing because there were still so many things I didn't know about her life. So many things I wanted to ask her, and now never could.

But mostly, I sobbed because I wasn't sure we'd get away with it.

Sept. 10, 1970

Dear Euvie,

Santa Cruz sounds wonderful! Perfect for you two. Personally, I don't know how you do it. I never even rearrange the furniture, and here you two are changing businesses again. And moving! It exhausts me to even think about. Oh, and I can't believe you sold your oil rights! I'm sure Mama is rolling over in her grave. How many times did we hear "Never sell the mineral rights!" But if it's setting you up in Santa Cruz, I say, good for you! Hugh's vending machine business sounds like a perfect fit. Fingers crossed it works out good for you.

How's Alice doing with the adjustment? Any talk of her ever moving out? What is she now, thirty-two? Three? I can just picture her and Hugh driving around to the different vending machines, filling them up and collecting the cash. He is good with her. Always was.

Any word from Lucy up in Portland? She returns my letters but never says much besides basics, doing well, working at the sandwich shop. I guess she's doing some baking there. Says all their sandwiches are served on fresh baked bread. Can you imagine? When it's so easy to buy! She's got a roommate she seems to like, I know that. Some woman who's a carpenter? You don't hear about that every day. Do you know if she's got someone special in her life? I all but came out and asked her in my last letter, but she didn't take the bait. She's such a pretty one, you'd think the boys would be clamoring to take her out.

News on Daddy, he's not doing too well. Had another small stroke and is having trouble walking, so we moved him to our place. You can imagine how happy that makes him, but it's just not safe for him to live alone, and I sure wasn't gonna move over there like he wanted me to. If you can swing a trip home, it would mean the world to him. Ever since Mama died he's been as lost as last year's Easter egg. Not that he'd ever admit it. I keep offering to drive him down to the Sit and Sip to hang with the rest of the old-timers, but he's got it in his head that they still hold a grudge about him closing down the packing plant.

And now for some good news. I put up so many pickles and cream peas this year I'm going to have to bring some down to the Salvation Army! Frank says, Don't you dare! Course he could eat cream peas and cornbread every day of the year. Anyhow, we won't be starving anytime soon. That's about all there is to say here, except I'm ready for it to cool off. I'm sweating like a sinner in church sitting here writing you this letter, and I've still got the laundry to put up and a casserole to make for the church potluck. I've half a mind to just bring watermelon!

Love, your overworked and under-appreciated sister,
Evokia

PS. My know-it-all husband says to tell you to make sure you stock plenty of Three Musketeers bars in your machines. He's sure because they're his favorites, they're everybody's.

LYING

Alice was right where I'd left her in the kitchen. Sitting in her waiting-to-be-punished pose, ramrod straight in the chair, boots firmly planted on the ground, hazel eyes staring at the wall in front of her like she had x-ray vision. It broke my heart. For all that Mom had put her through over the years, good and bad, she was the center of Alice's universe, making this last expression of their relationship so painful. I couldn't imagine what she was going through, what it had been like for her holding that pillow over Mom's face, watching Mom writhe, as she must have, because, in the end, no matter how ready we think we are to go—and I'm not saying Mom was; she was too busy getting ready for the company that never showed—these bags of bones we live in don't want to give up. My friend Toi's heart thudded in her cancer-ridden chest long past her desire to live. "Am I still alive?" she'd croak, so weakly you could barely hear. I'll never forget how crushed she looked when I had to nod yes, she was still alive.

I stood in the doorway of the kitchen—this kitchen, where I am sitting this morning—afraid to say a word. Surely, speaking would set the reel in motion. Whatever I said—would *choose* to say—held such portent, would shape what was to follow. Yet all I could think was: *How are we going to survive the next few minutes? seconds? night? What can I say that will make acceptable the unacceptable?*

Then it came to me, clearly, in a single thought.

I wiped the tears from my eyes. Cleared my throat to let Alice know I was there.

She huffed a short exhale. Lifted one boot off the ground as if to take off running, then set it back down on the floor.

"Mom's asleep," I said.

Her eyebrows furrowed, tilting her Clark Kents toward her

forehead. She rubbed her palms down her kilted thighs, left them there, on her knees. Cocked her head. She was trying to make sense of what I was saying. She appeared to be panting lightly, as if she were afraid to let her breath go too deep, lest it pull up whatever she was feeling. That's my guess.

"You should come see," I said. "She's out cold."

She rotated her focus from the wall to just past my right shoulder. She was clearly puzzled.

"Come on," I said, and began walking back to the bedroom with the flashlight. I was acting much more confident than I felt. I had no idea if my "plan" would work. Plan is the wrong word. I had no plan, just a sense of putting one foot in front of the other.

Alice didn't follow immediately. I stood by Mom's closed door, hand on the doorknob, listening for her footsteps. Why wasn't she coming? Finally, I heard the creak of the chair, the tentative steps through the living room. *Step step. Pause. Step. Pause.* When she rounded the corner into the hall, I cracked Mom's door open.

Alice halted.

"Come on," I said. "She looks so sweet all sacked out." I admit, I, too, was afraid to look. I was afraid of what I'd done, what we'd done, or that Mom might indeed still be alive, and that she'd know.

Alice resumed her funeral march down the hallway, running a resistant hand along the wall behind her.

When she reached the doorway, I said, "It's okay, look." Which meant I had to look too. I shone the flashlight into the room. I'd done a good job. Mom looked like she was sleeping, mouth slightly agape, head tilted into the pillow. Alice took this in, her fingers gripping the doorframe so tightly her knuckles whitened. "You—"

"Helped her get to sleep. She was so tired. You put her to bed. I helped her get to sleep." I spoke deliberately, hoping Alice would understand what I was doing, though I barely did. Noticing my sling on the dresser, I had a moment of panic. What other clues had I left behind? I shone the flashlight around the room and didn't see any, other than the sling. I grabbed it from the dresser, slipped it on, then tiptoed to the edge of Mom's bed, as if there were a possibility of waking her. "Sleep tight," I whispered.

Then the real acting began. I had no overall strategy. The next move just appeared. "Oh my God," I looked up at Alice. "She's not breathing!"

"Sh-she's not?" Alice said.

I placed my hand under Mom's nose, the close proximity to her soft skin calling up more tears. "Come see for yourself." My voice cracked.

Alice wouldn't get any closer, but that was okay, I could see on her face that she was buying into the story we were creating, of how we came in to check on Mom and found her dead in her bed.

"What should we do?" she said, looking off down the hallway. She was getting nervous. She wanted out of the room. I let her go, following her into the dark hallway. What *were* we going to do? The phones were out, so there was no calling the police. I wasn't even sure they were who to call. But we had to tell someone, had to act out the charade, to cement it into truth.

"I don't know," I said, "but I think someone needs to pronounce her dead, someone official." I thought about Kim's roommate, Nate the nurse, who lived across town. Thought about driving to the hospital, but I didn't want to leave Alice alone with Mom, nor did I want to leave Mom alone in the house. Which doesn't make sense, I know. What more could happen to her? She was dead. I wasn't thinking clearly. Besides, the hospital would be packed with earthquake casualties.

"Emma," Alice said.

We were in the kitchen now, having drifted down the hallway and through the living room.

"Emma?"

"We can show her that she died in her sleep." She headed toward the front door.

Suddenly, I was the one feeling unsure. "Which one of us found her?"

"Both," she said over her shoulder. As mentioned earlier, Alice knew how to lie.

I raced to catch up.

That was the closest we ever got to admitting our deception— even to ourselves. "Which one of us found her?" "Both." As if our story were something to be figured out instead of merely reported.

What followed was an Academy Award–winning moment for Alice.

"Mom's dead!" she said as soon as Emma opened the door. "She was sleeping and then she was dead."

Emma glanced at me to corroborate. I nodded. I was standing behind Alice, who continued. "She pooped her pants and I had to clean her up. Then we put her to bed and she died, she did."

"We…just wanted to…tell someone," I stammered. I didn't have to fake the tears. "I'm—we're—not quite sure what to do next."

Emma threw her arms around Alice. "You poor things!"

Alice grimaced.

"You've been through so much, and now this."

I was next. I prepped myself for the big hug, hoping that I appeared appropriately bereft, which, of course, I was. But guilt was making me paranoid. I prayed Emma couldn't sense it as she held me, tried not to scream in pain as she crushed my bad arm to my chest. "I'm so sorry, so sorry. Your mother was a wonderful woman, a real class act."

"She was," I said into her neck.

"But in some ways it's a blessing." She held me at arm's length, looked me right in the eye. "You know that, right? Your mom would have hated—"

I nodded, saving her from what would have been an awkward sentiment: that our captivating, charismatic, gorgeous mom would have hated to know she'd turned into an old, confused lady who shit her pants. More tears. I took a deep, shuddering breath. Still, I couldn't meet Emma's eyes. "With the phones out—"

"We can't call nine-one-one," Alice blurted. "That's what you're supposed to do. So they can pronounce her dead."

"Of course." Emma held up a finger. "Just a sec. I'm going to tell the troops what's going on. My sister and her kids are spending the night. They live up in Aptos and got hit hard. Wait. What am I thinking? My sister is a hospice nurse. She can do the pronouncement for you. That's probably all you need tonight. The mortuary can wait till morning. That is, if that works for you." She waved away the question, her silver bracelets clinking. "But we can figure all this out. There's time. Let me go get my sister."

I nodded dumbly. A hospice nurse! Would she be able to tell that Mom had been suffocated? Were there ways to tell? On the other hand, better it be someone who knew us, or so I prayed, and I was praying that night, a foreign activity for me in those days. Still is.

It was close to eight o'clock and the night had grown cool. I was numb to it, save for the goose bumps sprouting from my arms. I remember looking down, seeing them there and thinking, *hmmm goose bumps; it must be cold out.* I was so out of my body. My sling tugged at my neck. I adjusted it. Alice walked out into the empty street and stared up at the gibbous moon. It cast ghostly shadows across people's yards and houses. I strolled out to join her. A siren wailed in the distance. I remember that. I remember thinking I should go check on Mom, then realizing I didn't have to. It felt...spacious, and not in a good way. That's the only way I can describe it. It was as if there was suddenly too much room in the world.

"It's going to be okay," I said.

"Mom died in her sleep," she said.

The night was quiet enough that we could hear waves crashing at the beach a few blocks away. Some of the windows on the street glowed with candlelight, others were dark.

Emma and her sister bustled out of the house, Emma shining the flashlight down the short, lavender-lined walkway from the house to the sidewalk. "Your poor girls!" she said. "The earthquake and now this!" Her sister was tall and stocky, but from where we were standing, I couldn't make out the details of her face. I hoped she was as nice as Emma, hoped she wasn't too detail oriented, or naturally suspicious.

They met up with us in the street. Introductions were made. Condolences given. That provided a sigh of relief, the condolences, I mean. To be cast in the role of mourners instead of...well...There really is no good word for it, is there? For regular people like Alice and myself who assist in a loved one's death? That is, if that was even Alice's motive, which I have to believe—*had* to believe. If only it hadn't followed that awful BM scene, I could have been sure. But I wasn't. I'm still not. Will never be. Alice did what she did. I did what I did. That's about all there is to it. Just the act. *Plain as cream*, as Mom would say.

The walk to the house was full of small talk—and by that I mean, the earthquake. There wasn't much to say about an old woman dying in her sleep, and Emma's sister had lots to say about the earthquake. Her grand piano had slid into her china cabinet. Her beloved grandmother's china was gone save for one teacup, which had fallen onto the cat's pillow. Once inside, she barely looked at Mom. Actually, that's not true. Blatantly not true. She looked, we all did, filed into Mom's room as if viewing the body at a flashlight-lit funeral, but she didn't look close enough. I remember thinking that, and feeling both grateful and troubled by it. I also remember not really understanding what we'd done until that moment. I think this must have been true for Alice too, because she hooked the hem of my T-shirt with her finger. I don't think either one of us was breathing.

Emma blew her nose and said, "She looks so peaceful. As if she just drifted off." I think that's when I started breathing again, but kept a close watch on her sister, who stayed very professional, checking Mom's pulse and such. I was glad for the lack of light. She apologized for not having her stethoscope, said something about a discharge packet she was going to have to fill out, asked if we were comfortable calling the funeral home, which we both said we were.

"Can do," I remember Alice saying. Emma's sister spoke in soft tones, caring tones, but to her, Mom was just another old woman who had died peacefully in her sleep. She suited our purpose, sure, but it made me not like her. The awful woman didn't have the mindfulness to realize that our mother had taken with her a little of the world's light.

Once we were done with that horrible ordeal, and Mom was "officially" dead, Emma took my hand. "You two okay spending the night with her?" I nodded, Alice saluted, and they were gone. We probably said a few words, but I have no memory of it. All I could think was, *They didn't notice!*

I wanted to say as much, once they were well out of earshot, but knew I couldn't, shouldn't. We'd rewritten the last hour, which meant no referring to what we'd done. Ever.

"You really don't have any candles stashed away?" I asked. "It's just the one flashlight?"

Alice held up a finger. "But I do."

My mind swirling, I followed Alice into the kitchen, studying her every move, wanting to ask her what had happened, warning myself not to. I watched her climb up on a chair and pull a box of plain white household candles from the small cabinet above the fridge. Watched her take our dad's Zippo lighter from a drawer, hold its flame to the bottom of the candle to soften it and stick it on a saucer. Watched as she raised the flame to the wick. Watched it take. That first flare of light.

And here we were again, twenty-eight hours later, counting the seconds, minutes, and hours by the light of a single flame. Only now we had a lighter, my dad's special engraved one, three whole candles, and a flashlight with four extra batteries. And we were grateful for these things. Or I was; I don't know if Alice ever felt grateful for anything. She took things as they came. But for me, there was so much to be grateful for, so many people: Emma, Richard, Tillie, but most of all, Kim. The very presence of her in the world, and the possibility of us meeting up again, gave me a future to hang on to. That was something I really needed on that night that seemed to be circling back in on itself, my mother lying dead in the next room, dead by Alice's hand, a future worth living.

Alice opened some applesauce and we ate it out of the jar. That and the stale bread and cheese. The idea of sleeping seemed wrong. The desire to stay together, strong. Two sisters sitting and talking: about Alice's bottles, my life in Portland, the earthquake. All the while, waiting for the sun to rise. In fact, we did drop off to sleep, later. Alice in her room; me on the lounger in the living room. We were too exhausted not to. But in those precious, candlelit moments, the two of us dipping our spoons into the jar of applesauce like when we were girls, all I could think about was what the next day would bring.

So there it is, Alice and I killed our mother. Not just Alice, both of us. For surely, that's the conclusion you have come to. It's certainly the one I've come to. I quit drinking, cold turkey, the day after, if that eases your mind. It doesn't mine. I've forgiven Alice. I did that a long time ago. Forgiving myself hasn't been as easy. I'm haunted by a vision of Mom from that last day, when I was babysitting her, Alice out checking on her bottles at the bar. I see her sitting in the kitchen, the sun pouring in through the sliding-glass doors. She's wearing her pale pink float with lavender flowers. The food she's just emptied from the refrigerator litters the counters—eggs, butter, cheese, ketchup. For the moment, she's done, ready for whatever guests her addled mind thinks are coming. Like a cat, she tips her head toward the sun. She looks so happy.

Who knows what was going on in her mind? Nothing to do with reality, or the current reality. But did that make her happiness any less valid? Her life? I weigh this against the cruelty she inflicted on Alice. Against her own wishes, made early in her life, sure, but still *made*: that we spare her the indignities of losing her mind. Of course, when we're young, we cannot imagine what it is to be old. We see old people tottering down the street, leaning into their walkers, their steps tiny and frightened, their mind scrambled like eggs and think: *God! May I never turn into that!* But now that *I'm* the one tottering around, *I'm* the one having to ask a second and third time what the pretty young cashier said, I'm a little less sure. Each and every day I get to walk the beach, make myself a cup of coffee, brush out my thinning hair, feels like a gift worth fighting for.

But I am not a danger to myself, or don't think I am. There's the rub. Who's to say my thoughts can be trusted? Who's to say any of what I'm putting down here is true? Talk about a loop! I hope what I have put down is accurate, that it isn't a bunch of gobbledygook, or that I haven't made myself out to be too…I don't know…blameless?

Anyway, you see what a knot this is. The point is, for better or worse, we took our mother's life. But I ask you, in all your opinion making about what we did, that you consider Alice. There is a reason on that Christmas night so many years ago, when we were cresting the hilly roads of East Texas, the rain pouring down around us, that Mom asked *her* to be the one to find an iceberg, not me. I am far too slow to take action. Always have been. I've a tendency to ponder.

On another note, the crematorium called to inform me that Alice's ashes are ready. The synchronicity of my finishing our story and the phone call is, I'm sure, significant. Maybe Alice is glad I told all. I hope so. I hope Mom is too. The house seems quieter. Maybe it's just my conscience. Whatever it is, so be it.

I walked to Lighthouse Field this morning to see the monarch butterflies. They winter here, hundreds of them hanging like grapes off the eucalyptus and pine trees. They're easy to miss when it's chilly. They keep their wings shut. But oh, when the sun shines and those clumps of brown warm up and begin to flash orange! Soon the sky is filled with butterflies. It is a wonder to behold.

I returned to the house to find Dita cutting back the bamboo. I'd barely mentioned it yesterday and there she was, hacking away at the hedge like a beaver. She was dressed in overalls, no less, and one pink and one green Converse sneaker. "Hey, Ms. Lucy!" she said, holding up a gloved hand. "My friend who works at the Bagelry gave me some day-olds. I have a bag for you too, if you want them. Cinnamon raisin."

I'm considering letting her move in. I know she's unhappy where she is. I would let her work off her rent. We'd start with Alice's bottles: finding them a home, clearing out her workshop. There's probably some money to be made there. If that works out, we'll start on clearing out the house. After years of accumulating stuff to make my life more *comfortable*, our home cozier, I'm coming around to Alice's way of thinking: the less the better. I'll have Dita help me sort through my piles of clothes, the drawers of papers, the shelves of books, all the artwork in exchange for free room and board. And if *that* works out, I'll leave the house to her. God knows, the girl could use it. Her parents want nothing to do with her, and she has such potential! Smart, clear about what she wants from life. And she's been such a help to me. I feel I can trust her. I know, I know. They say a person should wait one year to make changes after a significant loss. But who's got that kind of time?

Anyway, I've started a list of wishes to be carried out at my death. Not that I'm eager to die, not even close. Alice's death has simply brought home how quickly it can happen. And at that point, decisions will have to be made. And who will make them? Not the state, thank you very much. I'd rather put my faith in earnest little Dita. She's young but so full of integrity.

This manuscript will be one of the things I pass along to her at my death. I'll stipulate in my will that she read it, and pass it on, or bury it in the backyard, in an as yet-to-be-acquired watertight container, whichever suits her fancy, leaving it up to Karma whether it ever gets read or not. (I can just see some unsuspecting person coming across it when planting bulbs!) I will also ask that she cast my ashes in the bay so that I, too, can *swim with the fishies*, as Alice would say. I'll take out these side notes, leave her just the chapters. Poor girl, she has no idea what she's gotten herself into by being nice to me. Ah, well.

Lastly, I got Alice's obituary written. That's a load off. I'll drive it over to the parlor later today. They said I could email it, but that seems disrespectful somehow. I hope I've done her justice. As my dear Kim said to me from her hospice bed four short years ago, the late afternoon light casting long shadows across her frail body, "We are, all of us, dying, all of us, living, all of us, doing the best we can." Amen to that, I say.

Alice Ann Mustin
August 17, 1938–October 23, 2015

Alice Ann Mustin of Santa Cruz, CA, died as she lived, doing what had to be done. She leaves behind one older sister, Lucy Louise Mustin, and a collection of Perfect Little Worlds, each one encased within a bottle. Her work can be viewed at various locations around Santa Cruz including the Catalyst and the Museum of Art and History. She never drove unless she had to, preferring to ride her old green three-speed cruiser. Viewed by some as eccentric, she came to be known around town as the Kilt Lady, which, for the most part, pleased her. She was an avid recycler. Any kind acts of charity may be sent to *savethefrogs.com*, whose cause Alice was passionate about.

NOTE TO THE READER

This is a work of fiction. But the Loma Prieta Earthquake really did happen. People really did die. The tunnels under Santa Cruz's downtown really did exist. And the Plaza Bakery at the top of the Pacific Garden Mall, where I worked before the earthquake shut it down, really was a fixture of downtown Santa Cruz. The rest, though, I made up. Any resemblance to actually living persons, living or dead, is entirely coincidental. However, if you walk the streets of Santa Cruz, California, you might just spot a leftover daylight brick or two.

About the Author

Clifford Mae Henderson (http://www.cliffordmaehenderson.net), also writing under the name Clifford Henderson, was named after her grandmother Clifford who once wore a nightgown to a formal event because she liked it better than any of the dresses she could find. Clifford Mae has attempted to follow in her renegade grandmother's footsteps, spending as much time as possible trying to shake things up. Her novels have garnered a variety of awards, including a Foreword Review Book of the Year Award, an Independent Publisher Book Award, a Rainbow Award, and a Golden Crown Literary Award. When not writing, Clifford Mae and her life partner of over a quarter century run an improv school in Northern California, the Fun Institute, where they teach the art of collective pretending.

Books Available From Bold Strokes Books

Alias by Cari Hunter. A car crash leaves a woman with no memory and no identity. Together with Detective Bronwen Pryce, she fights to uncover a truth that might just kill them both. (978-1-63555-221-8)

Death in Time by Robyn Nyx. Working in the past is hell on your future. (978-1-63555-053-5)

Hers to Protect by Nicole Disney. Ex–high school sweethearts Kaia and Adrienne will have to see past their differences and survive the vengeance of a brutal gang if they want to be together. (978-1-63555-229-4)

Perfect Little Worlds by Clifford Mae Henderson. Lucy can't hold the secret any longer. Twenty-six years ago, her sister did the unthinkable. (978-1-63555-164-8)

Room Service by Fiona Riley. Interior designer Olivia likes stability, but when work brings footloose Savannah into her world and into a new city every month, Olivia must decide if what makes her comfortable is what makes her happy. (978-1-63555-120-4)

Sparks Like Ours by Melissa Brayden. Professional surfers Gia Malone and Elle Britton can't deny their chemistry on and off the beach. But only one can win... (978-1-63555-016-0)

Take My Hand by Missouri Vaun. River Hemsworth arrives in Georgia intent on escaping quickly, but when she crashes her Mercedes into the Clip 'n Curl, sexy Clay Cahill ends up rescuing more than her car. (978-1-63555-104-4)

The Last Time I Saw Her by Kathleen Knowles. Lane Hudson only has twelve days to win back Alison's heart. That is, if she can gather the courage to try. (978-1-63555-067-2)

Wayworn Lovers by Gun Brooke. Will agoraphobic composer Giselle Bonnaire and Tierney Edwards, a wandering soul who can't remain in one place for long, trust in the passionate love destiny hands them? (978-1-62639-995-2)

Breakthrough by Kris Bryant. Falling for a sexy ranger is one thing, but is the possibility of love worth giving up the career Kennedy Wells has always dreamed of? (978-1-63555-179-2)

Certain Requirements by Elinor Zimmerman. Phoenix has always kept her love of kinky submission strictly behind the bedroom door and inside the bounds of romantic relationships, until she meets Kris Andersen. (978-1-63555-195-2)

Dark Euphoria by Ronica Black. When a high-profile case drops in Detective Maria Diaz's lap, she forges ahead only to discover this case, and her main suspect, aren't like any other. (978-1-63555-141-9)

Fore Play by Julie Cannon. Executive Leigh Marshall falls hard for Peyton Broader, her golf pro...and an ex-con. Will she risk sabotaging her career for love? (978-1-63555-102-0)

Love Came Calling by C. A. Popovich. Can a romantic looking for a long-term, committed relationship and a jaded cynic too busy for love conquer life's struggles and find their way to what matters most? (978-1-63555-205-8)

Outside the Law by Carsen Taite. Former sweethearts Tanner Cohen and Sydney Braswell must work together on a federal task force to see justice served, but will they choose to embrace their second chance at love? (978-1-63555-039-9)

The Princess Deception by Nell Stark. When journalist Missy Duke realizes Prince Sebastian is really his twin sister Viola in disguise, she plays along, but when sparks flare between them, will the double deception doom their fairy-tale romance? (978-1-62639-979-2)

The Smell of Rain by Cameron MacElvee. Reyha Arslan, a wise and elegant woman with a tragic past, shows Chrys that there's still beauty to embrace and reason to hope despite the world's cruelty. (978-1-63555-166-2)

The Talebearer by Sheri Lewis Wohl. Liz's visions show her the faces of the lost and the killers who took their lives. As one by one, the murdered are found, a stranger works to stop Liz before the serial killer is brought to justice. (978-1-63555-126-6)

White Wings Weeping by Lesley Davis. The world is full of discord and hatred, but how much of it is just human nature when an evil with sinister intent is invading people's hearts? (978-1-63555-191-4)

A Call Away by KC Richardson. Can a businesswoman from a big city find the answers she's looking for, and possibly love, on a small-town farm? (978-1-63555-025-2)

Berlin Hungers by Justine Saracen. Can the love between an RAF woman and the wife of a Luftwaffe pilot, former enemies, survive in besieged Berlin during the aftermath of World War II? (978-1-63555-116-7)

Blend by Georgia Beers. Lindsay and Piper are like night and day. Working together won't be easy, but not falling in love might prove the hardest job of all. (978-1-63555-189-1)

Hunger for You by Jenny Frame. Principe of an ancient vampire clan Byron Debrek must save her one true love from falling into the hands of her enemies and into the middle of a vampire war. (978-1-63555-168-6)

Mercy by Michelle Larkin. FBI Special Agent Mercy Parker and psychic ex-profiler Piper Vasey learn to love again as they race to stop a man with supernatural gifts who's bent on annihilating humankind. (978-1-63555-202-7)

Pride and Porters by Charlotte Greene. Will pride and prejudice prevent these modern-day lovers from living happily ever after? (978-1-63555-158-7)

Rocks and Stars by Sam Ledel. Kyle's struggle to own who she is and what she really wants may end up landing her on the bench and without the woman of her dreams. (978-1-63555-156-3)

The Boss of Her: Office Romance Novellas by Julie Cannon, Aurora Rey, and M. Ullrich. Going to work never felt so good. Three office romance novellas from talented writers Julie Cannon, Aurora Rey, and M. Ullrich. (978-1-63555-145-7)

The Deep End by Ellie Hart. When family ties become entangled in murder and deception, it's time to find a way out... (978-1-63555-288-1)

A Country Girl's Heart by Dena Blake. When Kat Jackson gets a second chance at love, following her heart will prove the hardest decision of all. (978-1-63555-134-1)

Dangerous Waters by Radclyffe. Life, death, and war on the home front. Two women join forces against a powerful opponent, nature itself. (978-1-63555-233-1)

Fury's Death by Brey Willows. When all we hold sacred fails, who will be there to save us? (978-1-63555-063-4)

It's Not a Date by Heather Blackmore. Kade's desire to keep things with Jen on a professional level is in Jen's best interest. Yet what's in Kade's best interest…is Jen. (978-1-63555-149-5)

Killer Winter by Kay Bigelow. Just when she thought things could get no worse, homicide Lieutenant Leah Samuels learns the woman she loves has betrayed her in devastating ways. (978-1-63555-177-8)

Score by MJ Williamz. Will an addiction to pain pills destroy Ronda's chance with the woman she loves, or will she come out on top and score a happily ever after? (978-1-62639-807-8)

Spring's Wake by Aurora Rey. When wanderer Willa Lange falls for Provincetown B&B owner Nora Calhoun, will past hurts and a fifteen-year age gap keep them from finding love? (978-1-63555-035-1)

The Northwoods by Jane Hoppen. When Evelyn Bauer, disguised as her dead husband, George, travels to a Northwoods logging camp to work, she and the camp cook Sarah Bell forge a friendship fraught with both tenderness and turmoil. (978-1-63555-143-3)

Truth or Dare by C. Spencer. For a group of six lesbian friends, life changes course after one long snow-filled weekend. (978-1-63555-148-8)

Children of the Healer by Barbara Ann Wright. Life becomes desperate for ex-soldier Cordelia Ross when the indigenous aliens of her planet are drawn into a civil war and old enemies linger in the shadows. Book Three of the Godfall Series. (978-1-63555-031-3)